Staying Afloat

Greta Beekhuis

Andrew Benzie Books
Walnut Creek, California

Published by Andrew Benzie Books
www.andrewbenziebooks.com

Copyright © 2018 Greta Beekhuis

This book is a work of fiction. Names, characters, places
and incidences are the product of the author's imagination or are
used fictitiously. Any resemblance to actual events, locales or
persons, living or dead is coincidental.

Printed in the United States of America
First Edition: April 2018

10 9 8 7 6 5 4 3 2 1

Beekhuis, Greta
Staying Afloat

ISBN: 978-1-941713-73-0

Cover and book design by Andrew Benzie

This book is dedicated to the Morning Star.
Long may she sail!

ACKNOWLEDGEMENTS

During the course of writing this book, I rekindled my long dormant relationship with sailing. It was just research at first, because I like to get things rightly accurate, but I truly felt healed being near, and then ON the water again.

The quest began with a visit to a marina in Redwood City, to witness a group of spinal cord injury athletes rowing their adaptive crew boats with a freedom denied to them on land. Their joyous competitive spirits lifted mine, and I was inspired.

Along the way, I made many new friends, including Linda and Michael Duffy, Hank Easom, MaryLou Miller and I fell deeply in love with a sailboat, the Morning Star.

She's a Danish built fractional rigged sloop, designed for ocean racing.

This book would not have been possible without Rachael Herron, Amy Norris, and David Hiscoe. I am deeply appreciative of your support and encouraging words.

Special thanks to Adele Ray and Lori Cope, as always, for being sisters of my heart.

Thanks to my circle of friends who ask good questions and make delicious meals to keep me on track. In particular, Jane and Harry Edelstein sustained and cheered me on during a particularly difficult time.

It has been a delight to work again with Andrew Benzie to bring this book to print.

I was diagnosed with Breast Cancer during the second draft of this book. I'm happy to say that, like the athletes who first inspired this book, sailing into Survivorship is my long term plan!

Thanks to Kalle Kanerva, Keith Roberts, and Kenny Murray for bringing the Morning Star safely down the coast when I was in the middle of radiation treatment. I am forever grateful.

CHAPTER ONE

The young woman pounded on her baby's back and screamed. "Please, can you get us to the nearest emergency room? He isn't breathing!"

"I thought you wanted to go to the hotel." The taxi driver looked at her in his rear view mirror and tried to stay calm. He'd only had his taxi license a few months, and he'd never had an emergency before. He called in to the dispatcher. "How do I get to the hospital from the marina? I have an emergency in the cab."

The radio crackled and the dispatcher calmly gave him directions. He gripped the wheel and prayed under his breath, "Please let the baby breathe. Please." He was terrified of losing his chance for the dream to drive a cab in America, to send money back to his family so that someday they might come here as well. He thought about his wife and their young child. What if it was his son that was in the back of this cab, how would he ever...

The radio crackled again. "One more left turn and you'll see the Emergency entrance sign."

He nodded and shouted to his passenger "We're almost there, we'll make it!"

She continued to pound on the baby's back and a small whistle of air seemed to be getting through, but he was struggling, and turning blue.

He felt the sweat running down his back, his hands slippery on the wheel, and his own throat constricting, as if in solidarity with the baby.

He pulled his cab into the Emergency hospital entrance with a screech of tires and she pushed open the door and ran with her baby into the reception area before he was completely stopped. Peering in after her, he saw a group of people surrounding the young mother and her son. He looked in the back seat and saw that she had left her purse and her baby's bag on the seat.

"Did you get the fare?" the dispatcher came on again.

He did not answer. For just a moment he allowed himself to remember the feeling of watching his own wife and child running through an opening to safety. He pulled the cab into the space marked Visitor Parking, picked up the purse and the baby bag and walked purposefully into the reception area. He could see the young mother sitting in a chair in the corner, her head in her hands. He approached her slowly and tapped her on the shoulder. "Is he going to be all right?" he asked with tears in his eyes.

She threw her arms around him, and he recoiled at the embrace from a stranger. "Oh, I hope so. I'm visiting from out of town and my husband is out on the ocean in a boat race. He has our van keys in his pocket, which is why I had to flag you down for a ride. Thank you for getting us here."

He tried to return her hug awkwardly and then held out her purse and baby bag.

She stood there for just a moment and he realized she didn't know what was happening.

"You left these in my cab." He said it very quietly. "I wanted to return them to you."

Then she took the purse, pulled out her wallet and handed him a twenty-dollar bill. "Is this enough? It is all I have."

"Yes, it is enough. I hope your baby will be all right.

What is his name?"

"Jason. His name is Jason, and mine is Paula." She began to weep, shaking involuntarily, her teeth chattering, now.

He backed away from her slowly and walked out to his cab. He had named it The Magic Carpet Cab and painted the slogan on it himself. "On time, every time, Radio Dispatched." It was his chance for the American dream. He pushed the button on the radio and replied to the dispatcher. "I've got it. Where to next?"

The doctor on duty called Paula in to the area behind the curtain. Jason was in a small metal crib and there were tubes and wires attached to beeping monitors and machines. Paula choked back her tears, still trembling. "Is he breathing? Will he make it?"

"Yes, and I think so. You did a great job getting him here in time; it looks like you knew just what to do. Are you a nurse?"

"No, I'm a photographer and a race reporter. My husband is here sailing in the big race. My parents didn't want me to bring Jason, but I wanted him to see the start of the race..."

"Well, you must have the magic touch, Mama. Tell me what happened." The young doctor seemed kind, and Paula felt like she could trust him.

"He gets these terrible colds, and it seems like the mucus is so thick, and it just chokes him. He's had the croup twice already, and I take him in the shower and let the hot water steam up the bathroom. We use a humidifier at home. The nurses in the hospital showed me how to thump his back to clear his lungs, and sometimes I have to suction out his nose, but we were in the back of a cab on the way to the hotel and I was afraid..."

The doctor was taking notes. "So the nurses showed you

when he was born, or later on?" Paula felt like he was evaluating her critically. She felt so young and inexperienced, and he was scaring her more than Jason's breathing episode already had.

"When we left the hospital and again at his first follow up appointment I think it was both times. We didn't have a regular pediatrician yet, so we went back to the clinic at the hospital for his checkup. They recommended that we find a pediatrician who is a specialist, but we can't afford..."

"Well, you came to the right place. This is a research hospital, connected to the University, so we can run some additional tests. Did they give him a diagnosis?"

"No, they said sometimes babies' respiratory systems take some time to mature, so they would run some tests when he is a year old if he is still having problems."

"How old is he now?"

"Eleven months. His birthday is..." Paula broke down sobbing and started to shake uncontrollably again.

The young doctor put down the clipboard and she thought he sounded a little more upbeat. "Well then, we'll just do some extra tests a month early." He handed Paula a box of tissues and wrapped a blanket around her shoulders before he said quietly, "I'll get a chair rolled in here for you so you can stay with him. I don't want you to worry."

"Thank you, doctor."

Paula leaned on the crib and tried to calm herself down, but her limbs seemed to be moving on their own, and her stomach felt like it was cramping. Jason looked like an angel to her now that he was asleep and breathing more regularly with the nebulizer mask. His color was returning to normal, and he was twitching slightly. Paula thought maybe he was just dreaming, and hoped that he might not remember any of the scary cab ride or her screaming or the rushing around in the hospital when they first arrived.

She was so grateful for the kindness of the cab driver, and his return of her purse and especially of her camera bag. She had padded her father's precious camera with Jason's diapers and extra baby clothes in the quilted bag she had found at the thrift store. He could have very easily driven away with everything, how would she ever have explained that to her parents, or to Michael?

The pictures of Jason waving to the fleet as they left the start of the race were in that camera, and Paula hoped she would be able to share them with Jason's grandparents at his party next month.

Her face flushed with shame as she remembered rushing Jason in his pajamas out to his car seat in the van over her mother's protests.

"He's not feeling well, Paula. Let us keep him here for you during the race. It is no trouble, he's such a good baby."

"I want him to be with us, this is Michael's first really big race." She had defiantly buckled the straps on the car seat and turned back to hug her mother. "You worry too much, Ma, we'll be fine."

What if she hadn't been so stubborn? What if Jason had choked in his playpen at her parents' apartment and she had been miles away cheering on Michael in his first big race?

She reached over the rail of the crib and held Jason's little hand. "Please be all right, Jason. Please."

An orderly rolled a recliner into the narrow space next to Jason's crib. "You probably won't get much sleep with all of the beeping machines, but do try and get some rest if you can."

Paula nodded gratefully and tried to take her mind off of

her surroundings by imagining how the race might be going for Michael. The race was scheduled for them to be gone for two days, and hopefully she and Jason would be there to see him cross the finish line. It would be quite a coup if he could keep up with the more experienced sailors who had been doing this race for years.

Michael and Paula had whispered about the race the night before, too excited to sleep and not wanting to disturb Jason who was sleeping fitfully in the bed between them

Their original plan had been for Paula to stay in the small hotel by the marina and take Jason out to see the sights while Michael and his crew were out on the ocean. She had been especially looking forward to visiting the Aquarium. They had paid for the room when they arrived and then gone over to the marina for the start of the race.

Paula had planned to check in with the race organizers this evening to see if there was any news of the fleet, but now she just hoped that they wouldn't have to spend more than one night here in the hospital. She had the key in her pocket for the room; it seemed like ages ago when the desk clerk had handed it to her.

The nurses came and checked on Jason every half an hour, and Paula looked away when they did the blood draw for the tests. What was it that the young doctor had said, that she might be a nurse? Paula smiled. Not likely, it was probably just the adrenaline rush of thinking something might happen to Jason. She'd never been very good around blood, but having a baby she'd gotten used to all kinds of bodily fluids that would have made her gag before.

Paula thought she might lie down in the recliner, just for a few minutes. She pulled the blanket around her and fell almost immediately asleep.

When the nurse shook her gently to wake her up, Paula sat up with a start, not remembering right away where she was.

"We're ready to release you and the baby, dear. The doctor will be in to talk with you in just a few minutes. Can I get you some water or anything?"

"Is there a restroom I can use? I guess I fell asleep."

"Certainly dear, there is one right across the hall."

Paula sprinted across to the restroom holding her arms under her chest. She hadn't weaned Jason yet, and her breasts were heavy with milk. She peed quickly and splashed some water on her face. How long had she been asleep? The tears started to come again and she wiped her eyes on a paper towel before going back across to Jason's crib. "I need to feed him," she whispered to the nurse who was unhooking the monitors, "is he awake?"

"He will be when I take this tape off of the IV, nobody sleeps through that!"

She handed the now crying Jason to Paula and wheeled the crib out, pulling the curtain around them before she left.

Paula unbuttoned her blouse and held Jason close to her. He suckled greedily and choked, spitting milk and vomit all over Paula. She tried again, and he settled in to his usual routine of drinking and gulping in air. Paula held him up over her shoulder and patted his back. He belched, and she switched him over to the other breast.

A doctor pulled back the curtain and stepped in to the small space. "I'll get you some towels to clean up, Mrs. Visser. It looks like you and Jason have this breastfeeding and breathing thing mostly figured out. There were some elevated enzyme numbers in his blood work, I'd like you to follow up on those with your regular pediatrician, but I think he's just got a bad cold. It says here that he is sick like this a lot?"

Paula nodded and burped Jason again. "Yes, it seems like as soon as he is over one cold, he gets another one. None of us around him are sick, and we don't seem to catch it from him."

"Well, please take these reports to his pediatrician when you get home. How long will you be in town?"

"Just two days, for the sailboat race. My husband is competing in the…"

The doctor cut her off. "Well, get him home as soon as possible and see his regular doctor."

He signed the forms and handed them to the nurse, who rolled her eyes as the doctor swept out of the space, not bothering to close the curtain behind him. "He's not got much of a bedside manner, that one. I'm glad he wasn't on duty when you first got here. Now let's get you ready to check out. I'll get you two cleaned up first. Would you like to take a quick shower?"

Paula nodded gratefully and went back across the hall to the bathroom with the towel that the nurse had given her. She rinsed off quickly, wiped off her clothes as best she could, and dried off with the towel. At least she wouldn't smell so much like milky baby spit up at the finish line.

The nurse wheeled them out to the front desk and Paula handed over the insurance card. Her hand shook with dread as she tried to fill out the paperwork while the nurse rocked Jason, who was happily snoozing and making milk bubbles. What if the insurance wouldn't cover the hospital visit, what then? Paula's hands were damp with sweat and she felt her mouth suddenly go dry with fear.

When they got out to the front of the hospital, Paula whispered shakily to the nurse, "I haven't got any money for a cab ride back to the hotel, I gave it all to the cab driver who brought us here. Is it very far to walk?"

The nurse looked around quickly. "I'll call you a hospital shuttle. Where are you staying, dear?"

"The Seaside Inn. Four blocks from the Marina."

"Oh, that's not far, they'll drop you off, no problem. He's a beautiful baby. I'm glad he's all right."

Paula gave her a quick hug. "Thank you. I feel so blessed. I hope this is a good omen for the race."

The shuttle pulled up before the nurse could ask any other questions. Paula settled into the front seat with her bags, and pulled the small pack that she carried Jason in out of the camera bag while the other passengers boarded. She strapped him in against her chest as the shuttle lurched forward.

"Employee parking garage, first stop!" The bus driver called out and opened the door for most of the passengers to get off.

"Visitor and long term parking, next stop!" All of the other passengers except for Paula and Jason stood up to get off the shuttle.

"And where might you two be going?" he asked cheerfully.

"The Seaside Inn, please. The nurse said you could..."

"Yes, ma'am. I love to look at all of the boats, I'll get you there in a jiffy."

"Oh, thank you. Everyone has been so kind, and I gave my last bit of cash to the cab driver that brought us in. He saved Jason's life, I think."

"Well, that's a new one, usually people are complaining about the thieving taxi drivers. I'm glad to know there is a good one out there. Me, I got a good job with a regular salary, and I like driving the bus. Don't you worry about a thing, Miss."

Paula sat back against the seat and counted her blessings. Jason seemed to be back to his regular cheerful squirmy baby self, and she would be back at the hotel before Michael and the rest of the fleet came in.

"Here you are, Miss. Hope you and your baby have a good day, now." He opened the door and Paula stepped carefully down the stairs, a bag on each arm, and Jason sleeping contentedly against her chest.

"Bless you. Thanks again."

She went up to the desk clerk and handed the key from her pocket over the counter. "I had to take the baby to the hospital, and so we never even opened the room. Do you think we could..."

The desk clerk glared at Paula. "No refunds. It's the policy. Sign here. You paid cash, right?"

"Yes, cash. I understand, I just thought..."

"No refunds, no exceptions. Sign here."

Paula sighed and did as she was told.

"Has the fleet come back in yet from the race?"

"What do I look like, the news channel? I just work the front desk, and in fifteen minutes my shift will be over, thank God for small favors."

Paula took the receipt, went out the front door and walked the four long blocks down to the Marina. She hurried down the dock to the tent where the Race officials were looking out over the water with binoculars. "Excuse me," she said "Can you tell me if..."

"First two boats are rounding the mark, heading for the finish. Here come our winners, ladies and gentlemen."

Paula pulled the camera out of the bag, trying not to disturb Jason. She walked to an open space on the dock and put the camera up to her eye after removing the lens cap. Her heart leapt at the sight in the viewfinder. Michael was in first place by half a boat length over the next competitor! There were no other boats in sight.

She started snapping photos, and adjusting the focal length until she could see Michael at the tiller, his jaw set in his typical determined manner. The crew whooped and hollered as they sat with their legs over the side, their arms raised in victory along the rail.

"Your Daddy is going to win it, Jason, he's coming across the line, first! What a day for the Vissers!"

Paula couldn't wait to get all of the details so she could post her race report, but wondered how she was going to explain what her last two days had been like to Michael. They could decide together what to tell her parents, if anything.

Jason belched a mouthful of milky bubbles and smiled.

CHAPTER TWO

As Jason got older, the family traveled together to boat shows and regattas the way other folks commuted to work. Paula and Michael kept an apartment as their home base, but they were always on the go. In the off-season, Michael tried to keep up with the never-ending quest for sponsorship and funding. Paula managed to squeeze in her freelance writing after Jason was asleep and before Michael woke up so they could pay their rent and buy groceries. She sometimes felt like the apartment was a burden, something that ate every spare dollar that came their way. She wished they could just live on a boat. Paula had grown up with stories about the canal boats in her parents' native city of Amsterdam.

Most of the other competitors in Michael's races had what seemed like a bottomless supply of money and time. They were the beautiful people, with trust funds and family memberships in the yacht clubs that stretched back generations. Their children had nannies and monogrammed outfits to match the color scheme of their latest boats. They had summerhouses, and winter ski lodges, and private jets to whisk them off to their next adventure.

Jason and Michael never seemed to let it bother them. They were just happy to be near the water, on the water, surrounded by beautiful boats and the thrill of racing. Paula tried not to mind when the other families left them out of the after race parties or treated her like the hired help. She had grown up on the outside looking in, and had developed a pretty thick skin when it came to entitlement and privilege. She was well respected by the publications that published her race reports and her photographs sold well on race weekends. Paula and Michael met at a yacht club in the 1970s. Paula was waiting tables to save up for college, and Michael gave sailing lessons to the junior club sailors. Paula often shared her lunch with him on her break as he regaled her with tales of the lessons. He told amazing stories about his dreams of racing at the highest levels of sailing and the places he'd like to take her. It was hard not to get caught up in his excitement and think about what the future might hold for them.

Paula hoped to get a business degree at the local community college and planned to go into event management so she could move up from her waitressing and catering gigs, but she loved working at the yacht club, surrounded by the enchanted world of the best that money could buy. She especially loved watching Michael charm his way onto the various racing boats, and cheered him on when the Wednesday night races were held. She usually took the camera her father had given her and developed the black and white photos in the lab at school. Truth be told, Paula loved the photography and art classes far more than math and science classes, but she knew it would be a struggle to make a living as an artist like her parents.

Her father earned most of his income from wedding and portrait photography. He often did three or four weddings a season at the yacht club, and had encouraged Paula to apply for a job there. "Those people tip well, Paula. You'll make twice as much as you would in a restaurant downtown." He introduced her to the wedding planner he worked with and Paula started working at the club as soon as she got her driver's license. She didn't have a car yet, and still rode her bike to school and to work everyday, hiding it under the back stairs of the restaurant and locking it to the railings of the support structure.

Many of Michael's students arrived driven by the family chauffeur or, once they turned sixteen, in all manner of exotic and classic cars. The parking lot was a great place to take photographs, and Paula loved focusing in on the details of the wire wheels and the insignia badges of the various chariots. She learned all of the names of the vehicles and the years they were built and who owned them. She'd ask about the cars while inquiring after the health and welfare of the children and grandchildren, and found that her tips increased substantially when she wondered aloud about what kind of wire wheels or convertible tops she noticed had been added recently. Giving her regular patrons a chance to brag about their latest acquisitions seemed to endear her to them.

Her father encouraged her to enter the car photos in the annual photography contest being held for the yacht club's newsletter. Paula was surprised when she won not only a fancy blue ribbon with the name of the club in gold letters, but that the newsletter editor also offered to pay her to use the photographs in their quarterly publication. When the first glossy magazine appeared with her name in the Contributors section, Paula asked for a copy to show her parents. The editor gave her two copies and said he'd be happy to see any and all of her car photos, but perhaps she'd like to try and get a feature spot by taking photos of the social races on Wednesday nights and the regattas on the weekends. Paula's parents weren't too keen on the idea of her riding her bike home after dark, but Paula argued that she'd buy a light for the bike once the editor bought some more of the photographs.

Her father loaned her the additional camera equipment she'd need. She spent more and more time in the darkroom at the high school, and her photography teacher gave her tips about developing photos that would appeal to the editor.

"Make it as easy for him as possible, Paula. Think about the space he has available in the magazine for these photos. You aren't going to be producing art gallery work." Paula quickly figured out that the editor snapped up the photos of the wealthiest patrons' boats. The photos she took of Michael crossing the finish line ahead of everybody else ended up on her bulletin board at home.

Her mother asked her about Michael one day. "Who is that, Paula? You certainly have a lot of photos of him!"

Paula blushed and answered quickly "He wins most of the races, Ma. He teaches the junior sailors and races their parents' boats on the weekends."

Her mother smiled and put an arm around Paula. "He's very handsome, dear. Why don't you invite him around for supper?"

Paula panicked. "Oh no, Ma. I don't even know his last name or anything." Her mother was already halfway down the hall.

"Well find out, for heaven's sake. Keep me posted."

Paula put her head in her hands. She couldn't imagine bringing the handsome sailor back here to their small apartment for dinner. The walls were covered from floor to ceiling with her parents' artwork. Her mother's paintings were wild, brightly colored abstractions of decaying flower gardens and hallucinogenic sunsets. Her father's photographs were mostly close ups of architectural details and manhole covers in stark black and white. Paula preferred to take photos with people in them. Not as the main subjects necessarily, but to give the photo a sense of scale, and to place characters in the story. The automobile photos were mostly to catalog the details so she could remember them and get better tips.

Her family ate standing up in the kitchen, because the table was always covered with some sort of work in progress. Usually they discussed the latest news as they twirled spaghetti on their forks or sopped up soup with crusty bread from the handcrafted pottery bowls that her mother had made. Compared to the glittering crystal and porcelain place settings at the yacht club, Paula much preferred their humble pottery, but she wasn't sure anybody else would feel that way.

The next Wednesday night, Paula's father stood next to her on the dock as she photographed the race. He gave her some tips about the dwindling light, and waited with her until all of the boats were in. He went straight up to Michael and extended his hand. "Good racing out there, young man! My daughter has pictures of you all over her bedroom wall, so I thought I ought to at least know your name!" Paula wanted to throw herself off the dock and into the water, but she knew that would draw even more unwanted attention, so she turned around and went to get her bike out from under the stairwell. She heard her father's loud laugh and cringed.

He came running up behind her. "Put your bike in the back of my car, sweetie, no sense in us both going home separately." Paula loaded her bike into the back of the rusty station wagon, and prayed silently that they could make their getaway before anyone saw them.

"Papa, how could you embarrass me like that?"

Paula's father laughed again and kept his eyes on the road. "His name is Michael Visser, and he'll be at our place for dinner on Friday night, so you'd better get over being embarrassed by then. Seems like a nice enough young man. Very polite."

Paula changed her clothes three times after school on that Friday, and finally decided just to wear a nice pair of white jeans and a pink gingham shirt. She tried to get her mother to straighten up a little so they could actually eat at the table, but her mother just laughed.

"Paula, we are who we are. Why would you want to be friends with someone who doesn't like you just the way you are?"

Paula shook her head. Maybe that was why she didn't have many friends at school. She watched as her mother took the homemade bread out of the oven and placed it on the counter with a crock of fresh butter. "What are you making for dinner, Ma?" Paula asked nervously. The kitchen smelled strongly of fish, and onions. Paula wrinkled her nose.

"Fish stew, of course. What else would you feed a hungry sailor? It's your great-grandmother's recipe. The one she caught her husband with!"

Paula blushed and stamped her foot "Ma! I'm not trying to catch anybody. What are you and Papa up to, anyway?"

Her mother held the handle of the heavy pot with her apron and stirred the soup with a wooden spoon. "We just want you to be happy, dear, is that a crime these days?"

Paula sighed and leaned against the refrigerator. "No, I guess not I just..." Paula's father stepped into the kitchen and sniffed appreciatively.

"Ah," he said, "that bait smells delicious!" He kissed Paula's mother on the back of her neck, making her giggle.

"Thank you, Willem, the soup is almost ready for taste testing. Will you volunteer?" She lifted the heavy lid of the

Dutch oven with a crochet potholder, and scooped out a small serving with a wooden spoon.

Paula ran back to her bedroom to try and straighten up in there a little at least. She put her stuffed animals in the closet and smoothed the quilt on the bed. Then she went down the hall to the bathroom and made sure there was a clean towel without paint on it, and some of the fancy soap her father often brought home from his gigs at the big hotels. Paula brushed her hair again, and looked in the mirror. What would Michael think of her family? She tried to remember what her mother had said, but her stomach flipped over nervously when she heard a knock on the front door. She heard her mother greeting Michael and decided to make her way back out to the front room. She got there just in time to see Michael handing her mother a bouquet of tulips. The frilled, fancy parrot tulips that her mother loved. They appeared often in her paintings and now she was rushing in to the kitchen to put them in water and exclaiming to Paula's father.

"Look, Willem, my favorites, isn't that sweet?"

Paula's father shook Michael's hand and put his arm around his shoulders. "Come on in, Michael, let me show you around."

Michael slipped off his shoes on the small mat by the door where Paula's family's shoes were lined up. He didn't seem to think it was weird, like some of the girls that Paula had brought home after school.

Willem was waving his arm in large sweeping motions toward the walls of the apartment. "These are Sophie's paintings, and of course a few of my photos as well. Oh, and here is our most prized work of art, our daughter, Paula!"

Michael smiled broadly and extended his hand to Paula. She stepped forward and felt as though she might be sick.

She grasped his hand and shook it firmly. They stood there a little longer than necessary, until Willem cleared his throat. "It smells delicious in the kitchen, shall we go in and see what Sophie is up to in there?"

Michael stood his ground and said quietly, "I'd like to know more about that painting," he said, pointing to a small framed canvas in the corner "if you don't mind."

Willem patted Michael on the shoulder and laughed. "You have very good taste, young man. That is the most expensive piece of artwork in the place. One of Sophie's art teachers painted that, and gifted it to her when we moved out here to the West coast."

Michael took a step closer to look at the small painting. "It looks so familiar," he said, "is it Lake Michigan?"

Before Willem could answer him, Sophie called from the kitchen "Dinner is ready!"

Michael sniffed as he stepped into the kitchen "Oh, it smells like Waterzooi, my absolute favorite! I haven't had it since I've been out here, thank you Mrs…" he hesitated.

"Call me Sophie, Michael, we want you to feel at home here." She handed him a pottery bowl and ladled out the thick rich stew. "We usually eat standing up here in the kitchen, I hope you won't mind?"

Michael shook his head and reached for a thick slice of bread and buttered it. He slid the bread into the soup, letting the bread soak up the broth while the others filled their bowls. "I'm thrilled to have a home cooked meal," he said appreciatively "but I never expected Waterzooi!"

Willem leaned back against the refrigerator in his usual spot. "How in the world are you familiar with our traditional fish stew, Michael? Not many folks out here on the left coast even know what it is!"

Michael was eating quickly and efficiently, as if there might not be any more if he didn't hurry. "I've only been out here a year, sir. A Dutch family in Wisconsin, on Lake Michigan, adopted me when my parents died, and this was often our Sunday meal. After I managed to graduate from high school, they gave me a train ticket out here so I could follow my sailing dream. Sailing was the only thing that kept me in school, if I am honest. I had to keep up my grades to stay on the sailing team." Michael stopped and looked at the pot on the stove.

Sophie put her bowl down and motioned for him to hand her his empty bowl. "There's plenty of stew, would you like more bread?"

Michael nodded happily and said "It is all so delicious, Sophie. Thank you."

Willem finished chewing his bread and said quietly "You are welcome here anytime Michael."

Paula was taking in the scene in amazement. Every hair on her body seemed to be standing on end, tingling. A small shiver ran down her spine, and she felt like she might be running a fever. Michael had charmed her parents, just as she had seen him do with the wealthy boat owners. She was feeling a little bit charmed herself, if truth were told.

"Paula, any more for you?" her mother reached out for Paula's bowl.

Paula pulled it back. "Not yet, Ma. I haven't finished what I have here." They all ate in silence for a few minutes and Paula cleared her throat "Do you live near the marina, Michael?"

Michael threw back his head and laughed. "I live in the marina, Paula. I clean the boats and sometimes, when the owners are out of town, in Europe or wherever, I get to live on their boat and act as security while they are gone. I've had a good run of luck so far. People have been nice to me out here."

Paula shook her head in embarrassment and avoided looking at her mother. She had been so worried about what he might think of their small apartment, she hadn't stopped to think about his circumstances. Perhaps her mother was right after all. She saw Sophie look at Willem.

He nodded and then said, "If you ever need a place to bunk, Michael, you are always welcome here. We have plenty of room."

Michael put down his bowl and his bread and shook Willem's hand. "Thank you sir. You have no idea what that means to me. I hope I never have to take you up on the offer though."

Willem nodded again and went back to eating his soup. "Delicious, Sophie. Absolutely delicious."

After dinner, Michael helped Sophie do the dishes and then they had a tour of the apartment. Michael asked really good questions about the paintings and the photographs, and Paula could tell that he was genuinely interested in the process of the work, not just in the value of the end product.

When they got to her room, Paula hesitated for a moment. "Oh, I am sure Michael doesn't want to see my room, why don't we show him the roof?"

Michael looked straight at her and said, "The roof sounds interesting, but your father said the best photographs in the house are in your room. I'd like to see them, if you'll permit me."

Paula tried to keep her knees from buckling as she opened the door and followed him inside. She glanced over her shoulder at her Papa who winked at her mischievously. She sighed and stepped into her room.

Michael was holding a small book and turning the pages. "These are fantastic, Paula, you really have an eye for proportion and..." he was looking at her sketchbook.

Paula felt her face grow red and hot. "Those are just ideas, Michael. They aren't finished drawings."

Michael looked up from the book. "Well, I think they are great. Now tell me about the photos."

Paula stood next to him and described what she could remember of each of the scenes where the photographs had been taken.

He stood very still and nodded his head at each description. "You have a good way of telling the stories, Paula. Thank you for sharing these with me. It is kind of weird to see myself, you know, how I look to someone else."

Willem cleared his throat. "You look like a very skilled, competitive sailor, Michael, what do you say we go up and see the roof now?"

They all followed Willem out of the apartment and down the hall to the stairs. He took a large key out of his pocket and unlocked the door. They climbed the concrete stairs and at the last landing, Willem unlocked and opened a large, heavy door. They stepped out into the rosy light of the sunset.

"Oh, perfect timing!" exclaimed Sophie, "I'm so glad I have my paints up here." She uncovered a large easel and a toolbox full of paints and brushes that had been draped in a waterproof tarp. She started to sketch the sunset with a pencil she had tucked into her hair.

Paula and Michael walked to the edge of the roof and leaned on the railing. "Isn't it fantastic?" she said softly, "I just love it up here."

Michael stood right next to her, as close as he could possibly be without actually touching her. "Oh, this is amazing, Paula. What a luxury. It's like we are on top of the world!" Behind them, Willem was quietly taking pictures. Many years later he would say it was the moment he knew Michael would become his son.

When the sun had gone down completely and Sophie had finished painting in the shapes of the dark buildings against the glow of the sunset, she took the canvas off of the easel and they all went back downstairs to the apartment.

Michael shook everybody's hands and thanked them for the meal. "I'll see you around the club, Paula!" he said cheerfully as he slipped on his shoes and went out the door.

Sophie put her arm around Paula and kissed the top of her head. "What a charming young man, Paula. I hope we'll see him again. I remember the first time I met your father when we were even younger than you are now. It is good to be friends with the boys before you decide if you want to date them when you are old enough. When the right one comes along, you'll know it."

Paula nodded absently and asked to be excused to go to her room.

"Of course, dear. Do you have a lot of homework?"

Paula nodded again and walked back to her room. Her parents were talking quietly in the kitchen. She sat down at her desk and pulled a small notebook out from the drawer in the center of the desk. She tried to write down every detail from the evening so she wouldn't forget any of it. She wondered about the circumstances of Michael's parents' deaths and where in Wisconsin he had gone to school and been on the sailing team. She tried to remember in minute detail the feeling of standing so close to him as the sun went down, and how she wanted that feeling to last forever.

Dear Diary,

Michael, the sailor that I have been telling you about, came over for dinner this evening. I was so embarrassed when he came in to my room and saw my drawings, but it was thrilling, too. Like in the romance novels at the library.

Some days my parents treat me like I am still a baby and other days like I might be growing up. It is so confusing.

The whole house reeked of fish and we had to eat standing up in the kitchen, not at the table like a normal modern family, but Michael seemed okay with it. I was so nervous I could barely eat a thing. I was hoping Ma would try one of the recipes from Women's Day or Family Circle that I brought home from the library.

He is on his own and lives in the Marina! I could have died when he said that. I guess I am really self-centered, like Ma says. I just thought, since he brought expensive flowers and charms all of the fancy boat owners that he came from a rich family, and our old-fashioned one would embarrass him.

When we went up on the roof and watched the sunset and Ma was painting and Papa was taking pictures, it felt like I had known him forever, but that can't be true. I don't understand how life can change so quickly like that.

Ma told me she and Papa met when they were younger than I am now. I never knew that. It seems so weird to think of them as teenagers.

Papa always says I can't go on a date until I am at least eighteen. That seems like forever away, tonight.

She hoped nobody would ever read her silly journals, but she always felt so much better when she was able to write her feelings down on paper instead of having them rattle around in her brain and keep her from thinking clearly. She read over the paragraphs she had just written, and added the date to the end of the entry. Then she pulled out her school notebooks and started in on her homework. Her journal went back into the drawer and she tried to concentrate on balancing the chemical equations that were due on Monday.

Only a few more months of school and she'd be finished. She had already met with the career counselor and been accepted to a couple of colleges, but she and her parents had decided that a course of business classes at the local community college would be the best place to start.

The career counselor had sighed, as if he had failed in his mission and said carefully "Well, you can always transfer to a four year school after you get the Associate's degree!"

Paula couldn't imagine another four years in a school even larger than her high school, trying to fit in with people who could afford to be away from home and pay the outrageous tuition bills. Her parents both had degrees from Art Schools, but it certainly didn't seem to help them pay their bills. Paula thought she remembered that they had been accepted on some kind of scholarship program, but she was fuzzy on those details. It didn't really matter, did it? Her course had already been set.

She worked diligently on her homework, and yawned. Once she had finished the last of the reading assignments and all of the study questions, she stretched and piled the books in a neat stack. She pushed the chair away from the desk and went to get her pajamas out of the small dresser next to the closet. She retrieved the stuffed animals and placed them back on the bed. Maybe it was time to pack them away in a storage box, now that she was becoming the kind of young woman who had boys over to the house for dinner. Climbing into her pajamas, she tossed her clothes into the hamper and walked down the hall to the bathroom to brush her teeth.

On her way back to her room she called "Goodnight, sleep tight!" to her parents.

Her father's voice came back down the hall "Don't let the bedbugs bite! And if they do, take a shoe, and beat them till they're black and blue…"

Paula giggled as she always did, closed her bedroom door and climbed into her bed. Once the light was turned off, the glow in the dark universe that her parents had painted on her ceiling when she was a toddler began to shimmer. She sighed happily and fell into a deep sleep.

The next morning, she packed two sandwiches to take to work. Usually she just sliced off a couple of pieces of her Ma's homemade bread and made an egg salad with avocado sandwich for herself. Today she thought maybe Michael might like a sandwich as well. It was the beginning of a tradition, although she had no way of knowing that yet. She wrapped the sandwiches in waxed paper and put them carefully in her backpack along with her father's camera equipment, which was in a separate case that fit just perfectly in the bottom of the backpack. She ate a bowl of the granola her mother made every week and kept in a big glass jar on the counter of the small kitchen. She changed the water in the vase for the tulips, adding a pinch of sugar and a few drops of bleach to make them last longer. She knew her mother would paint them as they started to wilt and fade, but Paula hoped she'd have a few more days of their vibrant glory before they started to faint and drop their delicate fringed petals. After washing out the bowl and rinsing the spoon, she set them both carefully in the dish drainer off to the side of the sink.

She took a shower and got dressed in her yacht club uniform, which was really just a polo shirt with the club's logo and a pair of white cotton pants and a pair of Sperry Top-Sider shoes. She left her parents a note on the counter to let them know she had gone to work. There was a big regatta this weekend, the first of the season, and Paula had promised to come in early and help with the set up.

Her parents were not morning people and rarely got up before the middle of the morning on weekends. Paula preferred the early mornings, when it was quiet and still and she could watch the promise of a new day unfurl itself with the sunrise.

CHAPTER THREE

There was already a bustle of activity when Paula pedaled into the Yacht Club parking lot on her bike. Two large trucks from the party rental place were being unloaded, the tables and chairs placed neatly in a design that had been laid out with cardboard templates on a large easel.

The event coordinator was barking orders and checking things off her list. She waved to Paula and motioned for her to join her. "Here, Paula. I have all of the children's activities on your clipboard with the set up diagrams on the next page. All of the supplies are staged in my office. Thanks for being here early."

Paula took the clipboard. She stopped in the locker room to put away her backpack after taking the camera out and slinging it over her shoulder. Then she made her way to the coordinator's office. She checked her clipboard and found all of the supplies laid out in numbered, color coordinated Rubbermaid totes.

As the party rental crew transformed the simple plywood circles into elegant linen draped tablescapes, Paula set up the children's area. There were beanbag toss games, with nautical flags painted on the wooden targets. Each Rubbermaid tote had a laminated instruction sheet taped to the inside of the lid, so Paula could let her mind wander as she set up each of the games and laid out the name tags on the small table set up for the children. When she got to the last tote, it simply said "Hide the EGGS" and Paula unpacked carton after carton of brightly colored hardboiled eggs. She ran around the lawn area, tucking some of the eggs in higher, harder to reach areas, so that the older children might spy those first. She stepped back and squinted, then looked through the viewfinder of her camera and snapped a quick picture. It seemed like there would be enough eggs for each child to find at least a few. She went back to the staging area and carefully piled the empty totes, one inside of another, with all of the lids on top, and returned them to the coordinator's office. Then she took the straw baskets with the name tags already affixed to them and put them near the nametag table. Each of the baskets had been filled with a nest of green shredded plastic, which was somehow glued down just perfectly. Each and every one looked exactly the same except for the nametag on the top.

Paula sighed. These were so different from the baskets she had as a child. Her parents (who claimed it was the Easter Bunny) had made felt baskets and grew real grass from seed in a plastic container in the bottom. There were Dutch chocolate foil wrapped eggs and sugar covered chocolate filled eggs that looked exactly like robin's eggs. There was usually a stuffed animal and some other hand made toy in the basket. Paula's parents loved to create these little imaginary worlds for her, and she felt kind of sorry for the kids who were coming today to get these generic plastic baskets.

There was a large golden throne being assembled near her, with a sign that read "Photos with the Easter Bunny!" She was glad that she wouldn't have to do that photography job. The toddlers usually cried and screamed when they saw the giant stuffed bunny walking around and their parents grew exasperated trying to get them to keep their expensive

Easter outfits clean for the photographs. The servers knew they'd make good tips if they kept bringing more champagne and exclaiming over the adorable outfits. There were several assistants for the Easter bunny who straightened skirts and combed hair or tied ribbons. Most of the children looked miserable in their outfits, but as soon as they saw their candy filled place settings at the table they were in slightly better moods. By the end of the morning, their sugar consumption would have escalated far beyond reasonable limits, and there were sure to be many meltdowns and temper tantrums, by both parents and children. Paula just kept smiling, and took orders for brunch and whenever she could manage it, a photograph.

The coordinator stepped up onto the stage and took her place behind a large podium with the Yacht Club's insignia on it. She smoothed her skirt and patted her hair. "While you are waiting for brunch to be served, let's hear from our chairperson about today's regatta," she said cheerfully.

A large man wearing a white uniform took the microphone from her and addressed the crowd. "The competitor's meeting shall begin promptly at 0900 hours, in fifteen minutes time. I'd like to take this opportunity to thank our many volunteers who helped to set up this regatta." He named the chairpersons of the various committees and they rose to appreciative applause and acknowledged the crowd gathered in the dining room. "Our Race Committee chairperson is Dr. Reginald Smith. Reggie, why don't you come up and introduce your crew for today?"

Dr. Smith came up to the podium and called up his race committee members. They all stood at attention and then followed Dr. Smith off to the side of the podium. The Regatta Chairman spoke again briefly. "It is almost time for the meeting. We'll reconvene here at the close of the regatta for the awards ceremonies and pictures. Thank you for your attention."

The noise level rose again in the dining room, and brunch was served. Paula made sure her regular patrons were happy with their meals, and on her way back from the kitchen, looked out the window to see if she could see the starting line for the race. She knew Michael was out there, getting ready for the start. Once the meal was over, the servers cleared the brunch dishes and brought more champagne to the parents. The children were organized into groups for the games. Paula worked quickly to stack the plates and flatware efficiently for the crew that washed the dishes. By the time the children's prizes had been handed out and all of the eggs had been found, the tables had been packed away in the trucks and the chairs set up in neat rows for the regatta launch.

The coordinator checked things off of her list and waved her clipboard triumphantly as she smiled and made some announcements from a smaller podium out by the dock. "Have a Happy Easter, and enjoy the regatta!" she concluded.

At the end of the regatta, when the boats were all safely in their slips and the guests had departed, Paula went to her locker and retrieved her backpack. She sat on the grass near the dock and unwrapped one of the sandwiches. Michael was walking toward her from the dock. She waved and invited him to sit with her. "I brought you a sandwich," she said quietly "have a seat."

He sprawled out next to her and took the waxed paper wrapped sandwich. "Thanks, Paula. I haven't had anything to eat yet today." They ate silently, each lost in thought. Finally, Michael folded the waxed paper carefully into a neat collapsible box and handed it to Paula. "I need to get back to work," he said "please wish your parents a Happy Easter tomorrow."

Paula nodded, and before she lost her nerve said quickly, "Are you working tomorrow? You are welcome to come and eat with us in the afternoon if you want. I am working the Sunday brunch here in the morning."

Michael smiled. "There is a blessing of the boats after the brunch, so I'll be helping with that, but if you are sure it isn't any trouble, I'd be happy to have a place to be on Easter."

Paula crossed her fingers behind her back "No trouble at all, my parents always make more food than we can eat on holidays." It wasn't exactly the truth, but Paula didn't want to make it sound like it would be extra work to have him join them.

He jumped up from the grass and ran toward the locker rooms. "Okay, then. See you tomorrow!"

Paula packed up her things and went to get her bicycle from under the stairs. There was a small piece of paper folded into an intricate envelope shape tucked under the lock and chain. She removed it carefully and put it in her backpack. In fancy script letters it was addressed to "Paula and family."

When she got back to the apartment, she went straight to her room and wrote in her journal. She tried to remember exactly how Michael had looked as he ran toward her from the dock. How he had neatly folded the waxed paper into the beautiful little box she now had on her desk.

Dear Diary,

You'd be so proud of me; I didn't just hide behind the camera today. I asked Michael to join us for Easter tomorrow. I read in the etiquette book at the library that a proper young lady never asks a boy, but I don't care. Ma says it is good to be friends with boys as well as girls, and besides, he said YES!

He has such delicate hands. I don't know how he folded the paper like that, or where he learned it, but it makes me weak in the knees when I look at the box he gave me.

Also, his handwriting! I can't wait to show the note to Ma and Papa. I'm dying to know what it says.

She drew a small picture of the folded note in the margin and went to go find her parents. "Papa?" she called, "where are you?" No answer. She went into the kitchen, and on the refrigerator was a note, held in place by one of the magnetic letters Paula had played with as a young child. "On the roof!" the note said. Paula grabbed the extra set of keys from the top of the refrigerator and made her way to the roof. When she got there, her parents were both focused on an object sitting on a white pedestal. Her mother was painting, and her father was taking photos. They often worked together like this on the weekends. Paula stood very still for a few moments, not wanting to disturb them.

Finally her father let the camera swing back toward his chest and he put the lens cap back on. "Hi, Paula, what's up?"

Paula groaned. "We are!" she replied, and both of her parents laughed at the perennial joke.

"Yep, we are, up on the roof!" her father said loudly. Paula handed him the note. "Now what do we have here?" he said, turning the note over several times. "This is folded quite nicely. Shall I open it?"

Paula could barely stand it another second. Her heart felt like it was going to jump right out of her chest and she was breathing so rapidly it sounded like she had run a long way. "Open it, Papa, please."

Her mother was wiping the paint off of her hands onto her apron and came around the easel to see what they were looking at. Once the note was unfolded, by pulling on the pointed tab, they all leaned in to look. "My goodness, that is lovely!" said Sophie. "I've never seen calligraphy rendered in pencil before, have you, Willem?"

Paula's father shook his head. "No, I certainly have not. That is the most elegant thank you note I think I have ever seen." He handed it to Paula who held it carefully.

The words were simple, but the lettering was exquisite. "Thank you for the lovely meal," it said. Michael had signed it with his initials, in elaborately scrolled letters, MV. Paula tried to fold the note back into the envelope shape, but decided to keep it as it was. She'd put it on the refrigerator when they went back downstairs. She could hear her heart pounding in her ears. "I might have invited him for dinner tomorrow, for Easter. He doesn't have anyplace else to be."

Paula's mother put her arm around her. "That's wonderful Paula. What time do you think we should expect him?"

Paula thought for a moment. "He's working the blessing of the boats after brunch at the Club, so maybe the middle of the afternoon?"

Sophie nodded. "That will be fine dear, I'll have things ready around two. Nothing fancy, but I'd better get some bread started so there will be enough." She kissed Paula on the cheek. "I'm glad you invited him, dear. There's always plenty."

Paula went back down to the apartment. She put the note on the refrigerator door, and replaced the extra key.

At two in the afternoon, on Easter Sunday in 1975, Paula

ran to answer the door. Michael was standing there, with his hands behind his back. He was wearing a white dress shirt and a tie. Paula stood very still, afraid that he would be able to hear her heart pounding, and see the feverish blush rising in her cheeks.

He finally said, "May I come in, Paula?"

She nodded and then called to her parents "Michael is here!"

He stepped inside and removed his shoes, but kept his hands behind his back. "I brought something for each of you" he said, "but I'll wait until your parents are here to give them out."

Paula blushed fully now, but with embarrassment. She hadn't gotten him anything for Easter, or her parents either, for that matter. Every penny was going toward the start of college in the fall. She heard her parents coming down the hall. Her father had a suit on, and Sophie was dressed in a caftan of some sort, with brightly colored swirls bursting all over the fabric, like fireworks. Paula wished she had thought to change out of her yacht club uniform.

Willem reached out to shake Michael's hand, but Michael shook his head, keeping his hands behind his back.

"Ok, everybody, close your eyes!"

Paula stood in between her parents and shut her eyes and bowed her head. She thought maybe he was going to do the blessing of the boats for them.

"Ta-da!" he said, "You can open your eyes, now."

Paula looked at what Michael was holding in his out-stretched hands. Her mother clapped her hands and her father said "Oh, how clever!" There were three small rabbits, carefully folded out of delicate, colored papers. They looked as if they might hop right out of his hands.

"You choose first, Paula. Which one would you like?"

Paula reached out and picked the tiniest pink rabbit up by one ear. She placed it on her palm and looked more closely. The intricate folds were so complicated. How had he ever learned to do that?

Sophie and Willem chose their rabbits, and carried them into the kitchen. They put them on the kitchen windowsill next to the salt and peppershakers that were shaped like kissing Dutch children in wooden shoes.

Paula ran into her room and placed her tiny rabbit next to the waxed paper cup on her desk. She looked around frantically for something she could give him in return.

Her father appeared at the door. "Are you okay, Paula?"

"Yes, Papa, I'm just trying to think of what I can give him for Easter. I didn't know he was going to bring gifts!"

Willem laughed. "I think he is just being polite, bringing gifts for us since we are sharing our Easter with him Paula. The best gift you could have given him is an invitation to join us for dinner."

Paula stood up and her father gave her a quick hug.

"Besides, the Easter bunny might have already taken care of that." He winked slowly and Paula laughed.

"Okay, Papa." When they got back out to the kitchen, Michael was helping Sophie set the table.

Paula hadn't even noticed, but her parents had cleared off the table and replaced the clutter with a centerpiece. There was a large bowl of newly sprouted grass with brightly colored eggs scattered about and a few hyacinths in the center. There was a felt Easter basket at each place with a small nametag. Paula loved the delicate scent of hyacinths, and wondered when the fourth Easter basket had been created.

There were pussy willow branches in a vase on the kitchen counter, with the fragile egg decorations that Sophie's mother had made for them hanging from slender ribbons. It was a typical Dutch Pasen scene, and for once, Paula was happy about it. She guessed it was comforting for Michael to see the traditional decorations.

Paula felt a little ashamed, remembering her behavior on Easters past, when she had wanted a typical American Easter like in the Family Circle magazine she had brought home from the library to show her Ma. She had insisted it wouldn't be complete without plastic eggs covered in glitter and the fancy ham and pineapple dish in the food section. Perhaps her parents weren't as old-fashioned as she had accused them of being. It was so confusing, wanting to be independent and modern and on her own, and yet still loving the stuffed animals and glow in the dark ceiling in her bedroom. Her mother was pulling the salmon out of the oven. Paula started to offer to help, but she decided to go and get her camera to document the holiday instead.

CHAPTER FOUR

Jason loved to look at the old photos of his parents' first Easter together. As a toddler, he had pointed to the traditional rooster shaped breads and the smoked salmon on the cedar plank. "Chicken, fish!" he would exclaim happily.

Paula and Michael would smile and hold hands and tell the story again about how Sophie and Willem brought them together and how much they loved their grandbaby Jason.

Jason would turn the page of the photo album and look at his favorite pictures. "Sailboat!"

There were photos of Michael, at the helm, his hand shading his eyes "I am looking for the fastest way home to your mother," he would always say, and Jason would repeat, "Look for mother, Mama!" and clap his hands.

The plastic covering the pages was already getting a bit tattered by the time Jason went to kindergarten, and Paula was glad she had put all of those photos into archival albums during the scrapbooking craze. She and Jason still looked through the albums on holidays and special occasions, and repeated the old stories.

The next sets of photos were of Paula's high school graduation. Michael wore a navy blue suit and a tie. Paula was in her cap and gown, with the tassels that indicated she had graduated as an honor student. Her diploma was on the wall of their apartment, just as it had been in the apartment next door when Sophie and Willem lived there.

Jason turned the pages slowly, reciting the stories he knew by heart over many years of telling and retelling them. There was Paula getting her Associate's degree, Paula and Michael getting married at the yacht club. He suddenly closed the book and took his mother's hand, trying to squeeze it tightly to stop it from shaking. Jason sounded so much like her father, Paula thought wistfully, her heart lurching in her chest. She choked back a cry and cleared her throat.

Willem had doted on Jason when he was a small child, and they spent many happy hours together discussing art and photography and how the world worked. Sophie had loved and fussed over him as well, but Jason had been closest to his grandfather. He inherited his grandfather's wry sense of humor, and loved to wonder about how everything worked. Nothing was safe from his curiosity. He took apart the alarm clock to see how it worked, and miraculously, got it back together again. When his grandparents got him a bicycle with training wheels for his fifth birthday, he was far more interested in disassembling it than actually riding it. Once he was old enough to go to school, Jason spent a lot of time with his grandparents. He had nearly constant respiratory infections so Paula and Michael worried about taking him to the racing weekends when it was cold and rainy. Willem and Sophie loved having him with them and were very involved with his local Waldorf School. When school was out for the summer, Jason traveled with his parents as much as possible.

When Jason was six years old, he took his first sailing lessons. He'd been swimming for a few years already, and loved being on boats with Michael, but wanted to sail by himself.

One of the yacht club members had a small wooden sailboat that his children had used to learn to sail, and he generously offered to sponsor Jason for a series of lessons. "It seems like a fair exchange, Michael, for all of the trophies you've brought me. Please allow me to do this small thing for you and your family."

Michael did not want to take charity, but this argument won him over.

Paula shot a whole roll of film of that day, Jason looked so happy. Not surprisingly, he took to the sailing right away, and loved the little wooden boat. He drew pictures of boats in the margins of his schoolwork, and filled the notebooks his grandparents gave him with dreams of the boats he'd sail one day. By the end of that summer, he was winning match races against sailors twice his age.

His sponsor watched carefully. "There is a natural talent there, Paula. You've every reason to be very proud of him."

Paula was proud, but she insisted that the sailing not take preference over his schoolwork. "We can't afford to buy you a boat, Jason, you'll have to have a well-paying job that affords you that luxury."

Even at six, Jason was determined. "Don't worry, Mama, I'm going to go to a good school and be able to have my own boat. You and Pops can stop worrying."

They didn't stop worrying, though. Living next door to Willem and Sophie in the apartment building was a big help, but they still barely made it to the end of each month on their tight budget.

Paula had created a small garden on the roof of the apartment building, and Jason learned to start seeds in the small wooden boxes he built with his grandfather.

They made a protected frame from an old window Willem brought home from a photo shoot at a local historic remodeling project. In every season the family always had fresh lettuces and carrots and rows of zucchini squash.

Although he loved to grow them, Jason could not eat tomatoes, or anything with tomato sauce. When he was a toddler, they'd been identified as the source of his frequent rashes and the sores in his mouth. Once they'd figured it out with the help of a local pediatrician, Jason's parents and grandparents made sure that his meals were tomato free.

Jason learned to identify wildflowers and native plants. He collected seeds whenever he could. He kept a special notebook where he carefully drew the seeds he found and wrote their Latin names in neat script. Every week, Jason and Sophie went to the local library, and checked out books on horticulture and botanical illustration. He especially loved to grow flowers for Sophie, who did a whole series of paintings of them. By the time he was ten, he was helping at a local nursery, learning the arts of grafting and bonsai.

Jason had a small red wagon that he had found at a garage sale. During the height of the garden season, he loaded it up with tomatoes and squash and whatever else the family wasn't able to eat, and went door to door in the neighborhood. He kept careful notes in a ledger notebook, and Willem helped him open a savings account.

"I'm saving up to buy a boat," he'd tell all of his customers, "a beautiful wooden boat." Soon he discovered that the chefs at the yacht club were anxious to buy fresh ingredients and if he could deliver them before they headed out for their weekly shopping trips, he'd have an easy sale. He grew parsley, basil, cilantro and rosemary at first and then branched out into more exotic vegetables like endive, bok choy and tiny cucumbers for pickling.

He and Willem built ever more elaborate structures to do what they called "vertical gardening", getting the most out of the small footprint of soil in each raised bed. He made netting tents to cover his blueberry and raspberry plants; otherwise the birds would have stripped the bushes bare, as they did the first year. He rigged up a tow hitch for his bicycle so that he could pull his little red wagon and cover more territory. His savings account was growing, and he decided that perhaps it was time to have a chat with the owner of the little wooden boat he had learned to sail on.

He went down to the docks early one Saturday morning with Michael. The water was as smooth as glass that day, and Jason would never forget it. When his sponsor showed up, Jason took a deep breath and said boldly "I'd like to do some business with you, sir." Michael was already cleaning one of the other boats, getting it ready to take a party out for a lunch cruise.

"Come aboard, young man," said Captain Carter, as he was known around the club, "what can I do for you?"

Jason climbed aboard and stood as tall as he could, hoping the Captain couldn't see him shaking in his shoes. His mouth was so dry, and it was hard to swallow. He cleared his throat. The words came out in a rush before he could stop them or slow down. "I've been saving my money, sir, and I'd like to put a deposit down on the little wooden boat and someday make her mine."

Captain Carter looked at the serious young sailor in front of him. "Well now, I'll have to check with my boys, of course. I had planned to leave that boat to them, for their kids."

"But, sir, they never even come down here to sail, and they don't have kids yet!" Jason pleaded, wringing his hands and feeling his neck tense up. "I really want that boat, sir."

Captain Carter laughed. "I can see that you do, Jason. I'll

tell you what. We'll shake on a deal. I promise not to sell the boat to anybody else, and if my boys aren't interested, you can start making payments. If they do want it, I'll help you find another one of the Sid skiffs and broker the deal. How does that sound?"

Jason stuck out his hand, after wiping it on his pants. "That's the best offer I could imagine, sir. Thank you!"

They shook hands. Michael watched from the deck of the boat he was working on. He smiled to himself and thought what a good businessman Jason was becoming. Even he didn't have the courage to shake hands with Captain Carter. Shaking hands with a pirate could get you into some deep trouble.

Jason joined Michael and helped where he could. He told his father about the plans he had for buying the little wooden skiff and applying to the Sea Scouts to see if they would let him join at an earlier age.

"I think you have to be 14," said Michael "and you'll need a sponsor."

Jason nodded happily "Captain Carter already agreed to sponsor me, Pops. It was his idea to try for the early acceptance deal."

Michael shook his head "Sounds like you have it all figured out, Jason." He handed Jason a trash bag "Run this up to the dumpsters would you? I've almost got this boat ready for the lunch cruise."

"Aye Aye Pops," said Jason "see you later this afternoon!"

Michael watched Jason as he made his way off the boat and down the dock. There was something odd about the way Jason walked. To most people, it looked like Jason was stiff and slightly off balance, as if he were just about to trip over something. Michael knew that Jason wasn't clumsy, and that his fine motor skills were excellent. He couldn't quite place it, but there was a dark worry in the back of his mind from long ago. He went back to his duties and made a mental note to ask the doctor at Jason's next checkup.

That night at dinner, Jason happily chattered about his new boat. "She's a real beauty," he said as he reached for the salad bowl "worth working for, right Pops?"

Michael nodded, chewing thoughtfully on his mouthful of bread. "Just be sure to keep your grades up, son. That is your most important job. Don't forget that."

Jason piled steamed carrots and zucchini squash onto his plate. "Yes, sir. I won't forget. Please pass the cheese."

Michael looked at Paula and smiled "Are we all ready for tomorrow? I'd like to get an early start."

Paula nodded and pointed toward the front hallway. "Everything is already packed except for the cooler. Just remind me to get the food out of the fridge and pack it in the morning. The van has a full tank of gas and the maps are already in the glove box. Can you think of anything else?"

Michael shook his head. "Thanks Paula, other than bringing your magic touch for luck, I can't think of a thing."

CHAPTER FIVE

Jason filled pages of his notebook with drawings of the little wooden skiff.

I did it! I went to see Captain Carter and told him I wanted to buy the boat. It was terrifying of course, and I thought I would pass out when he said NO at first. I am never going to take NO for an answer. I felt like I could ride a hundred miles without stopping on my bike after I shook his hand. I'm going to join the Sea Scouts and be an even better sailor than my Pops someday.

He put the photos his mother had taken of his first match race win on the wall next to his bed. It was the first thing he saw every morning when he woke up, and the last thing before he drifted off to sleep at night. Every penny he earned at the nursery or from his door-to-door vegetable and flower sales route was logged in his ledger and deposited in the bank. He made sure to keep his grades up, as he had promised his parents, but school was easy for him and actually kind of boring, so he was often daydreaming about his boat when he was called on in class. "Could you repeat the question?" he'd usually say with the same charming smile his father used to talk his way onto a boat, "I want to be certain I understand your question."

The one class where he was very rarely daydreaming was his science class. On this particular day, the teacher was passing out the assignments for the science fair that was coming up at the end of the term. "There will be a $100 prize for the best science project this year, and a chance to win a trip to our nation's capital and the Smithsonian Institution."

Jason sat up straight in his chair. His heart was racing, just as it had when he shook Captain Carter's hand. One hundred dollars! That would certainly help his boat savings account. He read through the directions carefully, trying to slow his breathing down, and taking notes as his teacher drew an outline on the chalkboard. After class was over, he waited until the other students had left the room and approached his teacher. "Mr. Holden, I really want to win the science fair this year, sir. What kinds of projects usually have the best chance of winning?"

Mr. Holden was carefully wiping the chalkboard with the felt eraser. He turned around to focus on Jason. "Well, it should be a topic that captures the judges' imagination. You might want to start researching the projects that have won in the past. Let me know if you need any help with that, Jason. Good luck to you." He turned back to the board.

Jason picked up his notebook, put it into his backpack and headed out the door. "Thanks, Mr. Holden." He hurried to his next class, which was gym.

After school, he pestered his grandfather with questions while they were up on the roof tending the garden. "How do you capture a judge's imagination? How can I find out what projects have the best chance of winning? What should I focus on?"

Willem smiled and patted Jason's arm. "I think you might want to start at the library, Jason. Ask the reference librarian. I've never been very good at contests."

Jason thought about that. He knew somebody who was

very good at winning things. "Thanks Grandpa. You've just given me a really good idea." He decided to ask Captain Carter for advice about how to win the science contest.

In the meantime, he checked out all of the books that he could find about science. He badgered the reference librarian for clues about how to win a science fair. He rode his bicycle down to the dock every afternoon, and checked to see if Captain Carter was on his boat. Finally, one Saturday morning when the chefs had cleaned out his little red wagon that had been full of herbs and lettuces and vegetables, he saw the Rolls Royce pull in to the parking lot. He waited for Captain Carter to get out of the back seat and wave the driver off. He saw his opportunity and waved. "Ahoy, Captain!"

Captain Carter did not look like he was in the mood to discuss business. He was already looking out toward his boat. "What can I do for you Jason?"

"Well, sir, I have a chance to win one hundred dollars in the science fair, and I know you are an expert on winning, so I thought you might give me a few pointers."

Captain Carter laughed. "Okay, kid, but make it snappy. I want to get out on the water early today."

Jason walked along next to the Captain, trying to keep up with his long strides. He swallowed hard, his mouth dry as a desert. "I think there might be money to be made in hydroponics, sir. I'm thinking that would be a good science fair project."

Captain Carter stopped abruptly at the word 'money'. "Get me a proposal, kid, and I'll review it. I'll be in port until Tuesday."

Jason stuck out his hand "Yes, sir!" and they shook on the deal. After dinner that night, Jason wrote out his proposal to Captain Carter. His plan was to show that tomatoes could be grown much less expensively and with less waste, without using soil. His biggest challenge in the rooftop gardening was the soil itself, and he figured that there must be a solution to his problems that might win him the science fair prize as well. He would set up three stations of tomato plants. One conventionally grown, one grown only in water and fertilizer solution, and the third fed by the waste products of an aquarium.

Jason outlined the history of hydroponics, going back to the Hanging Gardens of Babylon, and then presented his economic impact statement. He knew that would be the most important part of his presentation to Captain Carter. For the science fair, he planned to present his tomatoes for taste testing and see whether his results were cheaper and more delicious. He practiced his presentation with his grandparents on the rooftop.

Willem and Sophie thought this was a very ambitious project. "Where are you going to get all of the supplies, Jason?"

"Good question, Grandma. My boss at the nursery is very interested in my project, and said he'd get me the supplies at wholesale cost. I plan to ask Captain Carter to invest in my project."

Sophie nodded and went back to her painting. Willem stood up and started clapping. "I think it is brilliant, Jason. I'll be happy to set up a tripod so you can take your progress photos. What else can I help with?"

Jason thought for a moment. "I think I have to do it all myself, Grandpa, or it won't be my project. I will need taste testers though, you can certainly help with that!"

Willem laughed. "You betcha. I'll be an official tomato taste tester, for science."

The next morning, after delivering his usual produce orders to the chefs at the yacht club, Jason walked purposefully to Captain Carter's boat. He was surprised to see him walking back and forth on the dock with his head down, leaning forward as if he was looking for something he might have dropped. Jason cleared his throat "Ahem, excuse me, sir. Is this a good time to look at my business proposal?"

Captain Carter straightened up slowly and focused on the young man in front of him. "Good morning, Jason, I do like an early riser. Shows ambition. Come aboard."

Jason followed him up onto the boat and then down below into the salon. He put his proposal in front of Captain Carter on the table and looked around him. The gorgeous wood of the interior of the boat was gleaming, as if it had just been polished a few minutes ago. Someday, he'd have a boat like this, he thought to himself.

The Captain picked up the proposal and began to read. He nodded his head several times and made notes on a small notepad he had taken from his jacket pocket. "Aha, Jason. I think this is a very sound proposal. I am willing to invest on one condition."

Jason leaned forward "Yes, sir. What would that condition be?"

"If the numbers work out the way you have outlined them here, I'd like to buy the rights to your project and put them into production."

Jason thought for a moment, his scalp tingling. "I'll give you the right to buy my idea if you will give me the right to buy your boat. We still haven't settled on a price for the skiff, sir." He looked straight at Captain Carter, who returned his gaze. They sat there for what seemed like an hour to Jason, and finally he blinked.

Captain Carter stood up and extended his hand. "You've got a deal, Jason. I'll keep this proposal, and you let me know when you need to buy the supplies. They can send me the bill."

Jason shook his hand. "I'd like to start right away, sir. I'll need to put a deposit down at the nursery. They won't extend me credit."

Captain Carter laughed. He reached into his back pocket and pulled out his wallet. He gave Jason two twenty-dollar bills and his business card. "Bring me the receipts, Jason. I'm not extending you credit, either."

Jason practically skipped back to his bike. He unlocked it from the rack and pedaled as fast as he could. He had his first investor! He rode straight to the bank and deposited the cash from his produce sales. That afternoon he sat down with his boss at the nursery and outlined his plan. He handed over the deposit from Captain Carter, along with the business card. His boss wrote him out a receipt, gave Jason two copies, and tacked the third copy with the business card to the bulletin board over his desk.

Jason typed his business proposal at school, in the classroom where he took his word processing class. He printed out an extra set of pages, so he had a copy for his records. He wrote the date on the bottom of the proposal, with a small note. "Deposit of $40 from first investor, Captain Carter." He pinned it to his own bulletin board along with the two copies of the receipt from the nursery over his desk in his room. He leaned back in his chair, his hands behind his head. He was well on his way to owning his first boat.

CHAPTER SIX

Jason worked diligently on his tomato-growing project. He got 12 identical seedlings from the nursery and divided them into 3 groups. He set up the camera on a tripod to be able to take a picture of the plants each day at the same time and carefully taped a square of duct tape on the floor so that the position of the tripod would not vary. He measured the water and recorded how often he had to water the control group in the soil. For the second group, he used a system he and his grandpa built from rain gutters and a plastic tub to store the water and the nutrient solution. He had purchased an aquarium pump from the nursery to regulate the delivery of the water and nutrient solution. The seedlings were grown in plastic drinking cups with holes punched in the bottom. The third group required a more elaborate set up, but virtually no maintenance or monitoring once the cycle between the aquarium and the plant cups had established itself. Jason was very pleased with his design.

The pet store had marked down a large reptile tank with a stand, and Jason had modified the cover to hold the four drinking cups with the holes punched in the bottom just like the second group. The hardest part of the whole project had been getting the stand up the stairs to the roof. Jason and Willem spent the better part of an afternoon getting it up and running and then carefully adding the small plastic bags of goldfish they had picked out at the five and dime.

Over the next few weeks, he was astonished to find how

quickly the seedlings grew in the second two groups compared to the control group. He lost one of the seedlings in the control group to a soil borne fungus or pest of some kind, and when he looked back over his gardening notebooks he realized that he had indeed lost about 25% of his young tomato seedlings to the same fate. He felt like he was on the verge of a breakthrough, but it wasn't until the third week when he realized how efficient the fish tank system was. The second system required careful monitoring of the water and nutrient levels. The solution had to be dumped out and replaced frequently so that harmful bacteria would not begin to grow and Jason made a note of the time it took to scrub the container completely clean and replace the water and add more of the expensive nutrients. The fish were doing that job in the third system, and they had nearly doubled in size. Jason thought about how to describe this in a way that would appeal to his investor, Captain Carter.

He titled the section "Savings in Labor Costs" and figured out the average cost over the growing season using his own earning potential at the nursery. He knew from the discussions with his boss that this was one of the highest costs of growing plants for sale.

Jason turned in his preliminary report to his science teacher, halfway through the experimental period. The next day, Mr. Holden sent a note home with Jason, requesting a meeting with his parents. He handed it over the table at dinner and his father frowned.

"Are you in trouble, Jason? You know how I feel about you keeping your grades up."

Jason shook his head. "No, Pops, I don't think I am in trouble. I've turned everything in on time."

Michael pushed his chair away from the table and went

into the kitchen to call the number on the bottom of the paper.

Jason could only hear a few words of the conversation.

"Ok, then. His mother and I will be right over." Michael put his shoes on in the front hallway and called to Paula. "Come on then, let's find out what our son is up to."

Paula looked at Jason and smiled. "I'm sure you aren't in trouble Jason. Can you do the dishes while we are at the meeting?" She kissed him on top of the head and squeezed his shoulders. "We won't be long."

Jason finished the dinner dishes and went up to the roof to take his daily photograph of the tomato plants. His skin prickled with astonishment to see that both the second and third systems already had well developed fruit on them, whereas the first one was just beginning to flower.

"Increased production!" he wrote jubilantly in his notes for Captain Carter, "More yield per growing season."

He weeded the control plants, and noted how much time it took him to complete the task. There weren't any weeds to speak of in the other two sets of plants. After this experiment was over, he'd have to try doing his lettuces this way as well.

The door from the stairwell opened and his parents came over to see his project.

Michael spoke first. "Mr. Holden thinks you have a good chance of winning the science fair, Jason, but he was very worried that we were doing the work for you. I assured him that we were very busy with our own work, and had no idea what you were working on up here."

Jason stood very still, waiting for his mother to speak.

She walked over to the tomato plants and looked at the goldfish in the tank. "I have to admit, Jason, this doesn't look like a sixth grade science experiment." Paula said softly.

"How did you think of this?"

Jason told his parents about the books he had taken out of the library and the research he had done. "Walt Disney tried hydroponics at Epcot Center, he introduced it the year I was born. I just thought there had to be a better way than all of the expensive chemical nutrients, and you know there is the koi pond at the nursery, and my boss grows expensive water lilies and stuff in that pond, and I thought it might work for the tomatoes." Jason shrugged his shoulders, trying to look nonchalant although his skin was crawling with excitement, "Besides, one hundred dollars would be a big help toward buying the boat from Captain Carter!"

His parents both laughed.

"Okay, Jason" said Michael, "you've convinced us. Be sure to tell that to Mr. Holden, or put it in your presentation somehow."

Paula hugged him tightly "I'm sorry we are always so busy, Jason. I had no idea what your science fair experiment was all about. This is brilliant."

Jason smiled with relief. "Thanks. I didn't want to bother you with it. I'm just growing tomatoes. Actually, when it comes time for the taste testing part, I will need your help. Grandpa already volunteered to be a taste tester."

Michael and Paula both nodded. They walked over to the railing and stood very close together.

Michael put his arm around Paula's shoulders. "Remember when we first stood here, Paula? Who knew we'd have a science pioneer on our hands?"

Paula leaned her head on his shoulder. "We're very lucky, Michael. So very lucky."

As it turned out, Jason didn't win first prize in the science fair. He came in second, and got his name in the local paper.

The judges were not convinced that Jason could have come up with the idea himself, and although they all agreed that the tomatoes grown with the fish nutrients were far superior in taste and size, they noted that there was an "ick" factor in eating something grown with fish waste. Jason was disappointed, and felt sick to his stomach, but not for long.

Captain Carter was thoroughly onboard with his idea, and drew up papers for Jason to sign. Jason refused to sign until they had settled on a fair price for the skiff, and then they shook hands.

Captain Carter signed below Jason's name on the intellectual property contract and looked at his watch. "I'm going to give you some business advice, young man."

Jason leaned forward, his scalp tingling again. "Yes, sir." There was a long pause.

Captain Carter put both hands on the table and pushed himself up to a standing position. "If you have any more ideas like this, come see me. But never tell people what's behind the curtain, Jason. Just feed them something delicious and charge extra for it. Even if it costs less to produce. People love to think they are getting the very best, something special. If you tell them it is cheaply grown with fish poop, you won't win the prize."

Jason nodded. "Yes, sir. I understand."

He never grew any more tomatoes for sale with his system. He felt like Captain Carter owned that idea now, and besides, his best sellers were really the specialty lettuces and culinary herbs. He tweaked his new system until he was able to nearly triple his yield of lettuces and the chefs all raved about the delicious taste and perfect shape. When they asked him how he was doing it, he said mysteriously,

"I have the magic touch for growing lettuce."

They happily paid a higher price for the produce, and Jason got closer to buying his first boat.

At the end of the summer, Jason went to the bank with Sophie and got a bank check made out to Captain Carter. He shook hands with his business mentor and together they launched and re-christened the little boat "The Magic Touch."

Paula and Michael stood on the dock with Sophie and Willem as Jason waved happily from his new boat. Paula and Willem took pictures, while Sophie sketched the scene on her drawing pad. Michael paced back and forth on the dock, his hands behind his back.

Captain Carter shook hands with the family, and said to each of them "That's quite a boy you have there. He really does have something special."

Michael grinned and hugged Paula. "He comes by it honestly, Captain, he gets it from his Mama. She's always had that Magic Touch."

CHAPTER SEVEN

Middle school was rough for Jason. He was bored in class, and didn't feel like he fit in with any of the established social groups. Some of the football players made fun of his odd gait and started calling him Gimpy. He was starting to have intense growing pains, and often woke up screaming in the early morning hours, his legs feeling like they were on fire.

Paula brought him ice packs and the pain medication that the doctor had prescribed, but Jason was miserable.

"I just want to be able to walk around like the other kids, or be invisible," he moaned "my legs are killing me."

Paula and Michael were worried that there might be something seriously wrong, so when it was time for his annual physical, they broached the subject with his new doctor. Jason had never had a regular doctor, they couldn't afford it.

Dr. Franks was a family physician they'd heard about who had been taking care of most of the families in the area for three decades. Apparently he was quite an art collector as he had both Sophie's paintings and Willem's photographs on the office walls. He was calm and reassuring, and often made house calls. He felt the musculature around Jason's knees, which were giving him more trouble than usual lately. "I'm hoping these are just growing pains, Jason, but I'd like to see you every six months instead of only once a year, just to make sure. Do you have any other symptoms, like numbness or tingling?"

Jason nodded. "Sometimes my hands and feet just sort of stop working. They feel like they are asleep or something. My scalp tingles sometimes, too."

Dr. Franks frowned and made some notes in Jason's chart. "How about the respiratory infections. Are they still a problem?"

Jason nodded again. "I get sick all the time, and it takes forever to get over it. The rescue inhaler helps some, but I wish I just didn't have to get sick so often."

Michael had been quiet for most of the visit, but now he spoke up. "Doctor, is it possible that this is an inherited condition? My parents died when I was very young, but I seem to remember my father having difficulty walking."

Dr. Franks made another note in the chart. "It is possible, Michael. I'd like to follow Jason more closely as he goes through his teenage years. If necessary we'll call in a specialist and do some more tests, but for now I think it might be wise to have him work with a physical therapist. I understand you are quite a sailor, young man."

Jason perked up. "Yes, sir. I love to sail. If the physical therapy will help me sail without pain, I'll go every day!"

Dr. Franks smiled and wrote out a prescription for the physical therapist. "You won't have to go every day Jason, but please go for the initial evaluation, and then do the exercises they recommend. We'll see if that helps with the pain."

He handed the prescription to Jason and then shook hands with Michael and Paula. "Give my best to Willem and Sophie," he said, "I trust they are well?"

Paula smiled. "Oh yes, I'll pass that along. Thanks again Dr. Franks." They walked out of the office together and Dr. Franks made some more notes in Jason's chart after seeing them walk down the hall.

On the way home in the car, Jason decided it might be a good time to tell his parents that he had been accepted into the Sea Scouts on a conditional early acceptance. "I'll pay my dues and buy the uniforms with my own money from the garden," Jason said, "but I need you to sign the forms."

Paula gripped the wheel a little tighter. "I wish we could help pay for the Sea Scouts, Jason, but right now…"

Michael jumped in "I think the Sea Scouts is a great idea Jason. We'll have a look at the forms when we get home. How did you get them to approve your early acceptance?"

Jason fidgeted in the back seat and began rubbing the sides of his knees. "Well, Captain Carter agreed to sponsor me, and told them they'd have a better chance of winning the regatta with me onboard."

Michael laughed. "Okay, son. Sounds like you are getting good practice for the competitive racing life. Always have to be on the lookout for sponsors."

Paula pulled the van into the space in front of the apartment building and turned off the engine. She looked in the rear view mirror. "Don't forget your most important job, though, Jason. Keep those grades up in school."

Jason swung his legs over the edge of the seat and used the doorjamb and the door itself to straighten himself up. "Yes, Ma. I'm doing fine in classes at school, except for gym. What's for dinner? I'm starving!"

Jason started going to the physical therapist two days a week after school. He did his stretching exercises every morning and right before going to bed. It reduced the growing pains, and helped him get a little more sleep.

After two months, the physical therapist asked Jason if his parents could come to the next session with him. Michael and

Paula took time off to accompany him to the clinic.

The physical therapist looked up from Jason's chart when they came in. He stood up and shook their hands and then sat back down on one of the massage tables in the treatment room. "I wanted to talk to all three of you today because the insurance will only pay for one more week of rehab therapy the way the prescription is written. I think there are some important decisions to be made so that Jason can continue to be active and healthy. I am not a doctor, so I am not giving you a diagnosis, but as a physical therapist I'd like to make some recommendations."

Jason fidgeted and rubbed his knees as he sat on one of the other massage tables. Michael and Paula remained standing.

"First of all, I think Jason should be excused from regular gym classes at school. There is too much emphasis on sports that compromise his situation, and if he wants to focus on sailing, he should be able to have that count as his physical activity toward graduation. Second, I think Jason should see a specialist. I've already spoken with Dr. Franks and he agrees. Your insurance should cover it if we act now, and we want to rule out ALS. I am going to give you a pamphlet to take home and read about it. If anybody else in the family has any of these symptoms listed in the paperwork, it is very important to note that in the family history section. Be sure to have it all filled out before you go see the specialist. Jason will need to continue to do his stretching exercises daily, regardless of whether he comes back to see me or not. Sailing is probably the best thing for him, so I would encourage you to consider petitioning to have that count in lieu of the regular physical education classes. Do you have any questions?"

Michael spoke first. "I have so many questions, I am not sure where to start, but I appreciate your professional opinion. We think the world of Dr. Franks and we're glad you are consulting with him." He held Paula's hand tightly.

She shook her head, wiping a tear away with her free hand.

Jason raised his hand. "What about riding my bike?"

The physical therapist smiled. "Good question, Jason. The bike is much better for your joints than walking or running. Continue to ride your bike whenever you can."

"Okay, what does ALS stand for?"

The physical therapist opened up another copy of the brochure and pointed out the definition to Jason. "It stands for amyotrophic lateral sclerosis. It is a progressive neurodegenerative disease that affects nerve cells in the brain and the spinal cord. We just want to be sure that isn't what is causing your symptoms Jason."

Jason nodded his head. "Well, if I do have it, can I still sail?"

Michael interrupted, his voice gruff. "We'll cross that bridge when we come to it, son. We've taken up the whole time of the appointment already." He turned to the physical therapist and shook his hand again. "Thank you for working with Jason and giving us this information. We'll hope for the best."

The three of them walked out of the office and got in the van.

Michael pounded his fists on the steering wheel before he started the engine. Paula and Jason had never seen him behave that way before. He backed out of the parking space and squealed the tires as they headed for home.

Jason looked back over his shoulder. There were black

tire tracks in the parking lot. "Hey, Pops. Pretty cool burnout there."

Michael stared at him in the rear view mirror. " Jason, I wish my parents hadn't left me so early. I feel like I don't have the answers for the doctors and it makes me really angry."

Paula reached over and patted Michael's arm in alarm, trying to calm him down. Her eyes were wide with fear, but she said slowly "Dr. Franks is very smart, Michael. He'll figure this out with whatever clues we do have. You can't control everything. Let's try to get home in one piece though, okay?"

After a mile or so, Michael relaxed his grip on the wheel and slowed to the speed limit. He mumbled, "Yeah, okay Paula. What should we tell Willem and Sophie? They've known Dr. Franks for a long time."

Paula was very quiet for a moment. "I think it is best to tell them the truth. We don't know what is going on, but we are going for more tests. What do you think, Jason?"

Jason was looking out the window at the passing scenery. "I think it is always best to tell the truth, despite what Captain Carter says."

They all laughed together and went in to the apartment for dinner. After they had eaten, mostly in silence, they went up to the roof to find Willem and Sophie.

Jason told his grandparents the news, feeling his stomach roll and churn. "You know, I've been working with the physical therapist, and he thinks maybe I am not really just clumsy, that maybe I have a disease." He tried to keep his hand steady as he handed over the brochure to Willem. "The best news is, I can get out of going to gym and stop getting bullied by the football players!"

Willem sighed as he was reading. "This sounds like an old person's disease, Jason. Why does the physical therapist think you might have it?"

Jason shook his head, still feeling nauseous. "I don't really know, Grandpa, but if there is something really wrong, I'd rather know, and figure out how to deal with it."

Sophie came over and threw her arms around Jason. "There's nothing wrong with you Jason, you are perfect, just the way you are. We love you."

Jason squirmed out of her grasp. "Thanks, Grandma. I do like to know what is behind things, though. I want to do more research at the library when we go this week."

Paula hadn't said anything since the ride home from the appointment. She reached for Michael and her parents' hands and drew them all into a circle around Jason. "We'll deal with this together, Jason. We are a very strong family. We can handle whatever comes our way."

CHAPTER EIGHT

Jason waited until his parents and grandparents had all started eating the Sunday fish stew. He cleared his throat carefully. "There is a new Math and Science magnet high school taking applications. I'd really like to go. If I can pass the entrance exam in the top ten percent, there would be no cost to attend, and I'd have a better chance of getting into a good Engineering school. What do you think?"

Sophie put down her spoon. "I think that sounds wonderful, Jason. Where is the school located?"

Jason pulled the paperwork out from under the table and passed it across the table to his grandmother. "Right down by the Marina, Grandma. I could ride my bike to and from school. Nobody would have to drive me!"

Sophie frowned. "We don't mind taking you to school, Jason. This looks like a very fancy place. How did you learn about it?"

Jason fidgeted in his chair. "One of the guys in the Sea Scouts, Grandma. His father is on the board of directors. They just opened up the application process this week for the fall semester."

Sophie passed the paperwork over to Willem and went back to eating her stew. Willem looked over the brochure at Jason. "There is a cost to take the tests, Jason."

"Yes sir, I know that. I have enough saved in my bank account and I think it is a good investment in my future."

Willem laughed. "You are sounding like an Engineer already, Jason, don't be in such a rush to grow up." He passed the papers over to Michael.

Jason's father had finished his stew. He leaned back in his chair and read the paperwork carefully. "Who are you planning to use as references, Jason? It says you need two references from the community."

Jason reached for the stew bowl in the center of the table. His hand shook as he spooned the stew into his bowl and he spilled half of it on the table. Paula jumped up to wipe off the table, nervous that this was happening more and more often. Jason sat back down. "My boss at the nursery already said he'd write a letter, and I'm hoping to ask Captain Carter this week if he is in port. If not, I'll ask the kitchen manager at the Club." He went back to eating his stew trying not to show how nervous he was.

Michael handed the papers over to Paula.

She put on her reading glasses and looked over the brochure and started to read the entrance requirements. "Jason, these tests look pretty rigorous. Have you started studying already?"

Jason nodded. "I checked out some of the books from the library, Mama. I think I can do it. I won't know unless I try, though."

Paula took off her reading glasses and smiled. "I think it sounds like a great idea, Jason. I know you are not happy at your school. I'll sign the papers after dinner. Fair enough?"

Jason grinned and felt his stomach relax. "Is it unanimous then? Have we reached a family consensus? All in favor say AYE."

They all held hands around the table and bowed their heads for a moment, and then said in unison. "AYE, AYE!"

Sophie stood up from the table. "Anybody want dessert?

I have something special, although I didn't realize we'd have a celebration this evening. Hands up if you want dessert."

They all raised their hands and Paula got up from the table as well. "Let me help you, Ma."

Michael cleared the dinner dishes and brought them into the kitchen. "What have you been up to, Sophie?"

She laughed and waved them out of the kitchen. "Shoo, you two. I'm not too old to bring the dessert to the table. Go and sit down."

Paula and Michael returned to their seats.

Sophie came out of the kitchen with a large platter. "I made gingerbread today. Jason grew this ginger in one of his garden science experiments, and it smelled wonderful while I was grating it. Here's to our future Engineer!" She sliced the gingerbread into thick pieces and everybody reached for the warm bread. Sophie went back into the kitchen. "Don't eat it all yet, there is ice cream for anybody who wants it!"

Willem pushed his chair back away from the table. "Let me help you with those bowls, Sophie."

Paula could hear her parents giggling in the kitchen. She reached for Michael's hand. "We are so lucky to have this family, Michael."

He leaned over and kissed her. "All because you invited me over for bait, Paula." They all laughed.

Jason fidgeted in his chair again and tried to rub the pain out of his knees. It felt like someone was stabbing him with a hot poker. "No ice cream for me, Grandma. The gingerbread is delicious, though. Was the ginger root easy to grate?"

Sophie brought the rest of them ice cream and big spoons from the kitchen. "Take a break from your business, Jason and just eat your dessert. It is a day of rest."

Jason excused himself from the table and went stumbling

into the kitchen, his knees screaming in pain. He opened the refrigerator and found the ginger root carefully wrapped in waxed paper. He unwrapped it and held it up to the light. It looked like he had been successful in this experiment. Now all he had to do was to try and figure out how to market it to the kitchen managers. Perhaps he would get his Grandma to make sample sized gingerbread cookies. He smiled, and tried to distract himself from the pain. Cookies, that should do the trick.

After dessert, the family went up to the roof to see Jason's latest experiments in horticulture, and Sophie's newest painting. It was Jason's favorite time of the week. He rarely saw his father on weekends during the racing season, but Michael was home for this one.

When Sophie held up her latest painting, Jason laughed out loud. "That's fantastic, Grandma. What do you call this one?"

Sophie put the painting on the easel and took a deep bow. "Thank you Jason, I call it Still Life with Lettuce."

Michael put his arm around Paula. "I'm so glad you lured me into this family with such a great sense of humor, Paula. I'm the luckiest guy."

Paula blushed. "It was Sophie and Willem who set the trap, Michael. I was too shy to even find out your last name, remember?"

"Oh yes, I remember, Paula. I also remember that you fed me every day down at the docks after you finished your shift. You know the way to my heart, you do." He grinned and kissed her on the top of the head.

Paula relaxed and leaned against him. "It certainly worked out for all of us that you took the bait, Michael." They turned to see the sun going down over the harbor.

Jason studied diligently for the Magnet School tests and got his reference letters from Captain Carter and his boss at the nursery. He did his stretching exercises and crossed off the days left until school was out for the summer. He hoped in the fall he'd be in the Math and Science School. Although his school had been a little more tolerable since he'd been excused from gym, he was well and truly bored in the rest of his classes. Even his science class had lost its appeal for him after Mr. Holden had been transferred to the high school.

The substitute teacher just read to them from the textbook and assigned the lessons at the end of the chapter. Jason spent a lot of time daydreaming and drawing pictures of boats in the margins of his notebooks. At least he had Sea Scouts to look forward to. Nobody made fun of him in Sea Scouts. He actually felt like he had friends there.

At the weekly meetings, the older boys treated Jason like an equal. They were all in agreement that he should have early admittance to their ship, and Jason loved everything about being a Sea Scout.

He loved the uniform and the teamwork and being out on the water. He had trouble with a few of the knot tying exercises, but learned to work with his shaky hands to tie them in his own fashion. The Scout leader could not tell his bowline on the bight from the others when he was finished. Jason especially liked the idea of the rescue knots and practiced them over and over again. He checked out the Ashley book of knots from the library so many times that he felt like it was his. The celestial navigation was fascinating, and he passed all of his First Aid classes with perfect scores. He stayed after every meeting to help clean up and ask questions of the leader about anything and everything. He just could not get enough of being around boats.

"It is an inherited condition," he told the leader, "my father is crazy about boats as well. We have the sailing disease."

The leader laughed. "Okay, Jason, I think we are wrapped up here for the day. See you next time! Don't forget your signed permission slips for the trip out to the islands at the end of the month."

Jason took the paperwork home to his parents. "We're going to sail to the islands! Here are the papers to sign, Pops."

Michael frowned. "We're going to be away that weekend at a race, Jason. I'm sorry we're going to miss the trip."

Jason stood a little taller, trying to look older and more responsible than he felt. "Don't worry Pops, only one set of parents is going along anyway. I'll be okay."

Michael signed the papers and handed them back to Jason. "I know you will, son. I just really like having you along on my race weekends. You bring me luck."

Jason smiled with relief. "Thanks, Pops."

Michael was doing very well that season, and Jason knew it had nothing to do with luck. There was talk around the Yacht Club that Michael would be tapped to join the crew for the big ocean race, and Jason was excited for him. He knew how hard he worked to get sponsorship and sometimes they got left out because someone with less talent would buy their way onboard.

"It is all part of the game, Jason. You can't ever take it personally. Always be gracious, whether you are selected or not. People remember that when they are choosing sides or teams. Be the gracious one." Paula always told him. She hoped that Jason wouldn't have to struggle the way Michael had, but the reality was that there were only a few spots for elite sailors, and it was a very expensive sport. Michael and Jason had a stubborn streak that Paula marveled at, but she was the one who managed the accounts and tried to figure out how to buy the groceries that they weren't growing on the roof.

Jason took his entrance exams for the Math and Science school on a Saturday. He rode his bike to the old bank building that was being converted into the school's main office, and handed his paperwork to the clerk at the window, along with his entrance fee. His legs felt like they were on fire. The money order represented almost six months of work for Jason. He hoped it really would be a good investment in his future. He took a deep breath and went into the testing room. There were rows and rows of desks and chairs and a large clock on the wall above a rolling blackboard. There was a binder on each of the desks, with two pencils and a calculator. Jason took another deep breath and sat in a chair by one of the tall windows. He put his backpack under the chair as instructed and read the directions on the board. Four hours to take the test. He looked around. Almost all of the desks were filled now, and everybody looked nervous. Jason didn't recognize any of the other students, except for one. The girl who had won the science fair prize, the one who had robbed him of the hundred dollars. Jason hadn't cared that much about the trip to the Smithsonian Institution. She waved to him. He waved back half-heartedly and gritted his teeth. He'd show her this time.

The proctor rang a small bell at the front of the room and began to read the directions from his printed sheet. "If you need to be excused to go to the rest room, raise your hand. You will not be permitted to take anything with you, and one of us will escort you. Any questions?" Nobody had any questions. The proctor raised his arm. "When my arm drops, you may open the binder and begin. When you are finished, stand up, and one of us will come by and pick up your exam binder. Results will be posted on Friday afternoon here in the main office. Best of luck to each of you. Ready? GO!" The proctor dropped his arm as if he was flagging a race, and Jason opened his binder.

The next four hours flew by. Jason worked quickly to solve the problems he knew the answers to, and saved the more complex problems for the end. He relaxed as he went through the exercises. So far, there wasn't anything he hadn't studied. When he had finished all of the questions, he raised his hand and took a rest room break. His legs were stiff and sore from sitting for so long without a break, and he stretched before returning to his seat. He went back over the questions again, changing only one answer along the way. His heart was pounding as he checked his answers with the calculator provided, and when he was satisfied, he stood up.

The only other person standing was his nemesis. She had finished just before he had. Jason tried to remember her name.

One of the proctors came and took his binder, shook his hand, and wished him luck. Jason walked out of the building, just behind what's-her-name. She got into a long, shiny black car that had been waiting for her at the curb and turned to wave to him. Jason waved back, trying to be gracious. He felt a deep sadness in the pit of his stomach that he didn't recognize. He got his bike from the rack and fiercely pedaled home, as fast as he could make his aching legs go.

Jason didn't sleep well at all that week. He woke up several nights in a row with nightmares and terrible leg cramps. He went and got the ice packs from the freezer and went back to bed, staring at the ceiling, trying to erase the dream about seeing his name with a big zero next to it on the wall. He did his stretching exercises and took the anti inflammatory medicine, but tossed and turned the rest of the night. By Friday, he had dark circles under his eyes and he felt nauseous.

Sophie was sketching the sunrise and frowned at him. "Are you coming down with something, Jason? You don't look well to me." She put the back of her hand on his forehead and shook her head. "No fever, though. What's going on?"

Jason tried to sound cheerful. "Today's the big day, Grandma. The scores of the test will be posted after school. I guess I am just nervous. I'll be okay." He hadn't slept more than an hour or so the night before. He had been up early and made himself breakfast before dawn.

Sophie had surprised him when he had gone up to the roof to tend his garden. She hadn't been able to sleep either. Every second of the day seemed to take an eternity. The clocks on the classroom walls ticked slowly.

Jason had an awful headache by the time he hopped on his bike to go and check his score. He pedaled as fast as he could to the old bank building, locked his bike and ran up the stairs. At the top of the list, with perfect scores, were two names. His and Mary Margaret C, there were no last names listed, just initials. So that was her name, his nemesis was Miss Mary Margaret.

She came up the stairs behind him and tapped him on the shoulder. "Congratulations, Jason. I guess we are in. Of course it would have been a terrible disappointment if I had not scored well, since my father is the Chairman of the Board of Directors of the new school." She leaned toward him and whispered, "I've been sick with fear all week, you?"

Jason nodded. He couldn't think of anything gracious to say, so he just stood there, staring at the list. There was a crowd of students coming up the stairs.

Mary Margaret turned to leave. "Well, good luck to you, Jason. I'll see you around."

Jason nodded again and waved in her direction, but could not tear himself away from the list. He'd done it; he'd passed with a perfect score!

Jason rode home slowly, savoring the moment, and practicing various ways to tell his family the good news. Perhaps he would keep it to himself until they asked about the test results, and just say casually "Oh, yeah, did I forget to tell you? I got a perfect score!" He knew that did not sound the least bit gracious, so he decided he would just play it by ear and see how it all unfolded. Jason locked his bike and went into the apartment. Nobody was home yet. He went next door to his grandparent's apartment, but they weren't in either. He got the key off of the top of their refrigerator and went up to the roof. Nobody was up there, either.

He went about his usual after school routine, whispering to his plants as he cared for them "I'm in, I passed the test and got in to the Math and Science school!" The lettuces didn't seem to appreciate the importance of what Jason was telling them. Once he had finished all of his chores and made his daily notes on the clipboard hanging on the hydroponics system, Jason went back down the stairs. He let himself in to his grandparent's apartment and replaced the key on the top of the refrigerator. He went back to his own apartment and opened the door.

"SURPRISE!" He almost jumped out of his skin. His parents and grandparents were wearing party hats and blowing noisemakers. There was a cake on the table, but it was nothing like the usual homemade gingerbread or carrot cakes they sometimes had for dessert. It had "Congratulations, Jason!" written on it in blue icing.

There was someone else there, too. Mary Margaret stood next to his mother, clapping her hands together and smiling. Jason felt sure he was going to wake up any moment from this crazy dream. What in the world was going on?

Before he could say anything, Sophie wrapped her arms around him and hugged him tightly. "We are SO proud of you, Jason. Mary Margaret came over this afternoon with the news, and offered to bring a cake to celebrate, wasn't that a sweet thing to do?" She turned Jason toward Mary Margaret and gave him a small push forward.

Jason felt like he was going to trip and fall and totally embarrass himself, but instead he managed to say "Yes, that was very nice. Thank you so much, Mary Margaret, but how did you know where we..." as he put out his hand to shake hers.

Mary Margaret shook his hand firmly and blushed a little. "I had my driver follow you home, Jason. I hope you don't think badly of me. I've been trying to get in touch with you ever since the science fair. You really deserved to win, and I thought maybe... well, anyway, you ran inside so fast I didn't have a chance to talk to you, and then your grandparents came over to the car to see if we were lost and needed directions. So we decided to have a party to celebrate. I went to the bakery and got a cake, and here we are." She looked down at her feet, and then back at Jason. "Will you show me your gardens after we have cake? I hope you like yellow cake with raspberry filling and chocolate frosting. It is my favorite."

Jason stood very still, trying to remember to close his mouth and be polite, to be gracious. He looked at his mother, who was smiling and had her arm around his father's waist. She nodded at him. "Um, thanks, Mary Margaret." Jason said slowly, "I'd be happy to show you my garden." He felt like all of the wind had gone out of his sails. He hadn't even gotten a chance to tell his family the good news. She had beaten him again, and he wanted to be furious at her, but how could he, really? She had gone out of her way to find him and then brought cake. His parents and grandparents seemed to think it was wonderful, but Jason was most thoroughly confused. He went in to the kitchen to help set the table.

Sophie waved him out of the kitchen. "Go and sit down with Mary Margaret, Jason. You two are the honored guests at the table today." Jason turned around and sat down heavily next to Mary Margaret.

She leaned towards him and said softly "Please don't be mad at me, Jason. I just wanted to have a chance to get to know you better. I didn't know it was going to turn out like this, honest."

Jason shook his head and shifted from side to side, rubbing his knees, not wanting her to see his weakness. "I guess I am still in shock, Mary Margaret."

She corrected him "You can call me Maggie, that's what my father calls me at home."

Jason was even more confused now, and his knees were killing him. "Oh, okay, Maggie. I still don't understand why you had to follow me home."

Maggie twisted her napkin in her lap. "Well, Jason, I have tried to get your attention at school every way I could think of, but you just ignored me, and rode off on your bike. It must be nice to just go and ride wherever you feel like it."

Jason tried to remember if he had even noticed Maggie in any of his classes. "I'm sorry, Maggie, I didn't mean to ignore you. I am just so bored in school, and I am usually thinking about how I can get out of there and go to work at the nursery or be out on my boat. Nothing personal."

Maggie nodded. "I can't wait for the Math and Science school to start. I don't really have any friends at school now, and my parents were going to send me to the Catholic girl's school, but we went on a tour and my mother was disappointed with the math and science curriculum. So she decided my father should start a school. My mother is a doctor, and wants me to be one, too. She generally gets whatever she wants."

Jason tried to absorb all of this new information. "What do you want to be, Maggie? Do you want to be a doctor?"

Maggie shook her head and shrugged her shoulders. "Nobody has ever asked me what I want to be, Jason. I'll have to think about that."

Sophie and Paula set the table around Jason and Maggie and then they all sat down.

Willem cleared his throat and raised his water glass toward Jason and Maggie. "We don't usually have dessert before dinner, but this is a special occasion. Here's to the newest class of the Math and Science school!"

They all raised their glasses and clinked them together. Jason took a long drink of water.

Sophie began to cut the cake into neat slices, and passed the first one to Maggie. "Join us here, anytime Mary Margaret. Thank you for the lovely cake."

Maggie sat up a little straighter. "Oh, please call me Maggie. I'm delighted to make your acquaintance."

Jason thought it might be a good time to tell everyone his

good news, even though they had already heard it from Maggie. "So did she tell you we both got the only perfect scores? All that studying was worth it!"

Maggie shook her head. "I didn't tell them that part, Jason. I knew you would ace it though. I almost fainted when I saw my name up there, too."

Willem raised his glass again "To the perfect scores!" and they all clinked their glasses together again. Jason took another long drink of water.

After everyone else had been served, Maggie took careful small bites of her cake and put her fork down between morsels. She smiled at Jason, and he suddenly forgot about wanting to dislike her. Perhaps it would be okay to show her the garden after all.

After they had finished the cake and cleared the table, Sophie offered the leftover cake to Maggie to take home. "To share with your family, dear."

Maggie shook her head. "Thank you, that is very kind of you, but my mother would not approve. Please, enjoy it here. Can we go see the gardens now, Jason?"

Jason pushed himself up wearily from the table. "Sure, Maggie. Let's go up to the roof."

Michael and Paula walked with them up the stairs and out onto the roof.

Maggie clapped her hands and said excitedly "Oh, it is like the Secret Garden! One of my favorite books!" She asked a lot of questions about the hydroponics set up and the different varieties of lettuce and why the famous magical tomatoes were not anywhere to be seen.

"I signed the rights away to that growing system, Maggie. It belongs to somebody else now," said Jason. "I'm mostly focused on lettuces and culinary herbs. Do you want to feed the fish?" He handed a small, measured amount of fish food to Maggie and showed her how to sprinkle it over the surface of the tank.

She watched carefully as the fish came to the surface and opened their mouths wide to suck in the food. "They are really beautiful, Jason. I'm not allowed to have any pets, but I love animals. Do they have names?"

Jason shook his head in confusion. "I don't think of them as pets, Maggie. They are part of the growing system. I guess they are beautiful. I hadn't really thought about it that way."

Paula came over and asked Maggie if she would like to stay and join them for dinner. "Oh, I'd love to, but maybe another time, Mrs. Visser. I'd better get home and practice my piano lessons before my mother gets back from the hospital."

They all went back down the stairs and Maggie shook hands with Willem and Sophie, thanking them for their hospitality.

Paula tried to give Maggie a hug, but she jumped back with a frightened look in her eyes and extended her hand to Paula instead. Paula and Michael and Jason walked Maggie out to the curb, where the long black car was still parked.

Maggie shook hands with Paula and Michael again and thanked them for having her. She shook Jason's hand too, and said quietly "I hope we can be friends, Jason."

The driver jumped out and ran around the car to open the back door for Maggie. He tipped his cap to Michael as she climbed in. "Good afternoon, sir." Michael nodded. The car sped away.

"Well," said Paula thoughtfully, "that was certainly a surprising afternoon. Congratulations on your perfect score, Jason. We are so proud of you!"

Jason smiled. "Thanks. I guess I am still in shock, but I am really looking forward to the new school!"

Two days later, a heavy envelope arrived addressed to the Visser family in beautiful script.

Paula opened it carefully and then handed it to Jason. "It is your official acceptance letter to the Math and Science Magnet School, Jason. Congratulations."

Jason read the letter several times. He wanted to remember exactly how he felt at this moment, so he excused himself from the table and wrote it all down in his journal.

I did it! I got into the school and now I won't be bored and bullied by the dolts on the football team.

I earned a scholarship. Unlike Miss Smarty pants Mary Margaret. She's rich I guess, like the Yacht Club people. I really want to hate her, but I am supposed to be gracious, and she wants to be friends.

It is all so confusing.

My legs are getting worse, and my hands barely have enough strength to lift a bowl at the table without shaking. I am so glad it doesn't take much strength to steer the Magic Touch, just a light touch on the tiller.

All I want to do is sail away from the pain.

When he came back, Willem and Sophie were leaning over the letter together. "This is a five year, free tuition grant, Jason. Good for you!"

Jason stood proudly behind his chair. "Thank you. I am very excited to be going to this new school."

The next two weeks flew by, and when school was dismissed for the summer, Jason could not have felt more relieved. He felt ten pounds lighter, the way he did when he was out on the water. When he cleared out his locker and waited on the curb for Willem and Sophie to pick him up, he saw the black car out of the corner of his eye. The driver got out and waked down the corridor. Jason decided to follow him. After all, they had followed him home, so it seemed only fair.

Jason tried to keep out of sight as the driver walked quickly to the end of the corridor and turned right. Jason peeked around the corner and saw the driver trying to take Maggie's books from her as she cleared out her locker.

She stamped her foot and put her hands on her hips. "Honestly, I don't know why everybody treats me like such a baby," she said impatiently. "I can carry my own books!"

The driver stepped back. "Yes, Miss. As you wish."

Maggie marched ahead of the driver and Jason could see that the books were really quite heavy for her.

He admired her determination, though. It didn't look like she wanted to take NO for an answer, either. He walked quickly down the other corridor to try and meet her by the curb.

When he came around the corner, one of the football players was standing there. He shoved Jason, knocking his books to the ground. Jason gasped in pain and reached for his knees. "I guess we won't be seeing you anymore, will we, Gimpy?" Before Jason had a chance to reach for his books, the football player was flat on his back next to him.

The driver had his foot just above the football player's chest and leaned forward menacingly, his arms outstretched. "Get up, punk. I'll be happy to show you how fighting is really done if you are interested."

The football player started to whimper. "No, no, it was an accident. He ran into me! I didn't mean to…"

The driver yanked him up off the ground with one quick movement. "Nothing I hate more than a bully, except one that lies. Come with me to the office, young man. We need to file an incident report."

Jason continued to pick up his books, keeping his head down. He wished he were invisible.

Maggie came over to help him. "Are you okay, Jason?"

"Yeah, I'm used to it. They pick on me all the time. Just one of the many reasons I won't miss this school one little bit."

"Oh, me either," said Maggie. "Not one little bit."

They sat down together on the curb to wait for their rides.

"What are you doing this summer, Jason? I am going to camp for two weeks, but other than that I will be around. I'd really like to see your boat sometime if you wouldn't mind showing it to me. Here is my phone number." Maggie handed him a small card.

"You have your own business cards?" Jason said in amazement, turning the card over in his hands.

"Oh no, Jason, it is a calling card. Something my mother wants me to carry. I guess it was all the fashion when she was growing up. It feels really old fashioned, doesn't it? I've hardly ever used them, but I'd like you to have my number. Call me any time."

Jason sighed. "I don't have a card or anything, but I'll write my number down for you."

Maggie shook her head quickly and blushed. "I'm not allowed to call boys, Jason. If my mother ever found out, I'd be grounded for the whole summer. Oh, that looks like Sophie and Willem!" Maggie stood up quickly and waved.

Jason struggled to his feet.

Maggie looked concerned. "Are you sure that bully didn't

hurt you, Jason?" She extended her hand.

Jason shook his head and allowed her to pull him up to standing. "No, Maggie, I just have growing pains and sometimes my knees hurt so badly, I..." he saw that Maggie looked like she was about to cry "but I always feel better when I am out on my boat. I can't wait to show her to you. Do you like to sail?"

Maggie wiped her eyes with her other hand and straightened up. "Yes, I'll look forward to it, Jason. Please do call me." They were still holding hands.

Willem and Sophie got out of the car and helped Jason with his books. They waited until Maggie's driver returned.

He gave Jason a big wink and said, "I gave that bully quite a scare, Master Jason. Dumb as a post, that one. He won't be bothering you again." He tipped his hat to Willem and Sophie and turned to Maggie. "Come along Miss Mary Margaret, we don't want you to be late for your piano lesson."

Maggie rolled her eyes. "Have a great summer, I'll see you soon!"

Willem looked in the rear view mirror at Jason after he got in the car. "Are you having trouble with bullies? All the better to get out of this school for the summer!"

Jason nodded. "Yes, Grandpa. I don't ever care to see this school again."

They had the leftover cake for dessert that night and raised their glasses in a family toast.

"To new adventures!" said Willem, and they all said "Aye, Aye" in unison.

At the next Sea Scouts meeting, Jason learned that they were expected to bring a guest with them on the annual sailing trip to the islands. He asked one of the older boys if it would be okay to invite a girl.

"Absolutely. Most of us are bringing dates. Just be sure to get the permission slips signed." He saluted Jason.

Jason stood very tall and saluted in return. He wondered if Maggie would be able to get permission to come on board for the trip. There was only one way to find out. He pedaled home as fast as he could go, and after locking his bike, ran into the kitchen. He pulled Maggie's card out of his wallet and dialed the number.

"Hello?" he heard Maggie's voice on the other end of the line.

"Hello, Maggie, this is Jason and my Sea Scout ship is going on a cruise out to the islands this weekend and we are supposed to bring a date and I wondered if you could go." There was a long pause. Jason could feel his heart beating in his ears.

"Oh, Jason, I'd love to go. My father will want to speak with your father about it, of course. What is your phone number?"

Jason repeated the number for her slowly, and she read it back to him. He could barely hear her as she whispered in to the phone.

"Let's not call it a date, though. My father says I cannot go on a date until I am sixteen. Can I be an invited guest?"

Jason laughed, relieved. "You can be whatever you want, Maggie. I hope you can go. The boat is a real beauty and the islands are great. My Pops gets home just after sunset, usually."

Maggie spoke a little louder this time. "Okay, thanks, Jason, I'll have my father call him tonight."

Jason couldn't think of anything else to say, so he just

said "Bye, Maggie."

"Bye, Jason, thanks again."

Jason put the phone back on the wall to charge and took a deep breath. Whether they were going to call it that or not, he was going out on his first date. With his former nemesis, Miss Mary Margaret. Life certainly was getting interesting these days. He went to go write it all down in his journal.

I am going on my first date! With someone I wanted to hate.

Why does life have to be so confusing?

The other guys are bringing dates, so I wanted to, just to fit in, but when I called Mary Margaret, I mean, Maggie, the pain in my knees went away, like it does when I am out on the water, so maybe it will be okay. I think she said she liked sailing, but I wasn't sure.

The garden is going great, and even though it feels awful every time I climb the stairs to go up there, and especially coming back down, no pain is too much to keep me from it.

Maggie is rich, for sure. She's going to camp this summer. She has business cards and everything. Her driver is pretty cool though, he stood up for me against one of the football bullies.

I'll never have to deal with that again.

He slowly closed the notebook and then went up to the roof to work on the garden. As soon as Michael and Paula got home to the apartment, Jason told them all about the plans he had made with Maggie.

Michael smiled as he washed his hands at the sink. "Ok, Jason, I think I've got it. It isn't really a date, even though it is. She'll be an invited guest of the Sea Scout ship for the cruise to the islands. Is that right?"

"Yes, sir. Thanks, Pops. I think she'll really like it, don't you?"

Michael dried his hands on the dishtowel. "Well, I know one thing, she really likes you!"

Jason turned red and started to say something, but the phone rang and saved him the embarrassment.

Michael picked up the receiver. "Visser residence, Michael speaking." He winked at Jason. "Yes sir, there will be adults on board and your daughter will be an invited guest of the Sea Scouts ship. She'll need to wear nonslip shoes and bring the signed permission slips." Michael listened intently. "Yes, sir. If you want to send your driver around for the paperwork this evening we'll be here." He gave the address and some general directions. "Yes, sir, thank you. Nice to meet you over the phone, sir."

Michael hung up the phone and hugged Jason, whose knees had stopped hurting again. "I think you are all set, Jason. Do you have the permission slips? We can meet the driver out by the curb. I'm sorry I'll be away at the race this weekend."

Jason nodded and ran to his room. He got the permission slips and slid his feet into his shoes at the front door. He and Michael went out to wait by the curb. "Thanks, Pops." Jason said quietly, his hands beginning to get damp with anxiety, "What did Maggie's father sound like on the phone?"

Michael thought for a moment. "He sounded like he was very worried about letting his daughter go out on a boat, Jason. I can't say I blame him. Sailors don't exactly have the best reputations." They laughed.

"I hadn't thought about it that way," said Jason, "I just really hope Maggie likes sailing."

Michael looked up at the evening sky and said in a faraway voice "Only one way to tell, son."

The driver pulled up to the curb and the window on the passenger side in the back slid down.

Maggie smiled up at them. "I convinced my father to let me come and pick up the paperwork," she said happily, "my mother is out of town at a medical conference. I'm not allowed to get out of the car, though." She giggled and reached out her hand for the papers. "Thanks, Jason, and thank you Mr. Visser. My father was delighted to meet you over the phone. He may be calling you back again if there is anything in the paperwork he is concerned about. There usually is something he is worried about, but don't take it personally, he..." she stopped and thought for a moment before continuing, "he just wants the best for me." She sighed and waved. "See you on Saturday, Jason, bright and early!" The window slid back up and the car sped away.

Jason and Michael walked back into the apartment and removed their shoes in the entranceway. Jason's heart was still racing as he looked around quickly. He wondered what Maggie's house looked like and whether they removed their shoes when they came in from outside.

Maggie's father called Michael several more times in the evenings that week. Michael assured him that there were Coast Guard approved safety measures on the boat, and that he would be happy to give him the phone numbers for the ship leader and Harbor Master if he would like to ask them directly.

"Apparently he already has the Harbor Master's number," Michael chuckled as he told Jason "and I guess he checked us out with Captain Carter. Seems they know each other from the club. We must have passed the test, because he says

Maggie will be allowed to go on the trip." Michael clapped Jason on the back. "Congratulations, son. Have fun on your first date!"

Jason smiled. "Thanks, Pops. Good luck in the race this weekend. I'll be there in spirit. I know this weekend is kind of a big deal, right? A qualifying race?"

Michael laughed. "Yep. We'll see if we can move up to the next level of ocean racing. The weather looks to be perfect for it. Nice and windy!"

On Saturday morning, Jason was at the dock extra early, dressed in his formal White Sea Scout uniform. He hoped he didn't look as nervous as he felt.

Willem had gotten up early and driven him to the club so he would not get bicycle grease on the crisply pressed trousers.

Jason paced back and forth, his stomach churning. He smelled cigar smoke and followed the scent. He saw Captain Carter walking on the dock, and hurried over to speak with him.

Captain Carter saluted him when he saw the uniform. "Looking sharp, there, Jason."

Jason saluted back. "Thank you, sir. I just wanted to thank you again for writing my recommendation letter and let you know that I got into the new Math and Science school on a full five year grant!"

"Well, good for you, Jason. Make the most of it, young man. I wish my boys had your gumption. They just want to have everything handed to them."

Jason saluted again. "Yes, sir, I will, make the most of it, I mean." He started to ask Captain Carter about Maggie's father, but thought better of it. "Good day for a sail out to the islands, sir. That is where we are headed with the Sea Scouts today."

Captain Carter looked out at the water and said gruffly, "Yes, indeed. A very good day for a sail." He turned and walked toward his boat.

Jason wanted to ask Captain Carter so many more questions about how he had made his fortune and all about the beautiful boat with the gleaming wooden salon, but it was time to go meet his fellow Sea Scouts and get ready to greet their guests. He hurried back to the meeting room.

The scouts were already milling about, chatting excitedly about the day's trip. Finally, the leader called them all to order and pointed to the chalkboard where the day's schedule was posted. He went over the agenda and reminded them all to be on their very best behavior.

They went outside and raised the flag and said the pledge of allegiance and recited the Sea Promise. "As a SEA SCOUT I promise to do my best;

To guard against water accidents.

To know the location and proper use of the life saving devices on every boat I board.

To be prepared to render aid to those in need.

To seek to preserve the motto of the sea; Women and Children First."

Then they went and stood in a line, straight and tall, ready to greet their guests.

Jason could see Maggie's car, but noticed that she waited until several other girls arrived and had been escorted on board before she got out and walked over to the group. Maybe she was nervous, too. Jason could see that she was wearing brand new Top-Sider shoes. He smiled and held out his arm to escort her on board after she had turned in her permission slips. He helped her on with her life jacket after putting on his own. "We call these personal flotation devices, Maggie. It isn't too tight, is it? You should still be able to breathe comfortably."

Maggie shook her head. "It is not too tight, thank you Jason. This is a beautiful boat. Tell me all about it, please."

They walked together around the boat and Jason pointed out all of the parts of the boat and explained what they were for. They stood on the bow of the boat and Jason pointed off toward Captain Carter's boat. "See that really big boat, there? Mine is in the slip right next to it. I don't think you can see her from here."

Maggie squinted. "I can't wait to see her, Jason. How do you know Captain Carter, anyway?"

Jason told her the story of getting him to sponsor the science fair experiment and Maggie listened carefully.

"Oh that explains a lot!" she said quietly. "Is that who bought the rights to your magic tomato growing system?"

Jason nodded and started to say something else, but Maggie was frowning.

She leaned forward and said quietly, "My father spends a lot of time with Captain Carter in court, Jason, and not in a good way. He says Captain Carter is the slipperiest weasel he's ever dealt with. He was very impressed that you were able to get a recommendation letter from him for the school. He said that showed great initiative on your part. My father is impressed by initiative, Jason."

Jason nodded. "What does your father do, Maggie? Why is he in court with Captain Carter?"

Maggie smiled. "He's a prosecuting attorney, Jason. Captain Carter likes to push the boundaries of the law. That's how my father describes it, anyway. Why are there different sized sails on the boat? Do they do different things?"

Jason admired Maggie's ability to change the subject and was glad she wanted to know about how the boat worked. He looked over his shoulder to see that many of the other guests were huddled in small groups, giggling and trying to keep their hair from blowing around.

Maggie had worn her hair in a sensible braid, straight down the middle of her back. She wore a navy blue jacket and had a hat and sunglasses on. She looked like one of the ads in the fancy sailing magazines that Michael sometimes brought home.

Jason was tongue tied for a moment, feeling like he was going to throw up. It was all so confusing. He tried to reorganize his thoughts and get back to explaining the sails and rigging to her.

She slid her arm into the crook of his, and they walked along the deck, leaning their heads together so they could hear over the wind, which was beginning to build. Jason suddenly felt very grown up. Like he was in someone else's body. Someone who didn't have weak knees or shaky hands.

When they stopped for a moment to look up at the mast, one of the other girls came over to them. "Oh hi, Mary Margaret! It is good to see you."

They pressed their cheeks together on one side and then the other, kissing the air. "Hello, Rosemary. Have you met Jason?"

Rosemary did a little curtsy and held out her hand. "I don't believe we've had the opportunity to meet, Jason."

Jason shook her hand as firmly as he could. "Nice to meet you, Miss."

Rosemary turned and went back to the giggling group.

Maggie sighed as she slid her arm back into Jason's.

"She's the town crier. Rosemary is very sweet, but she just cannot keep her mouth closed. You won't have to be introduced to any of the other girls, now. They'll all know your name. Now, tell me again about the mast and the sails and how they work."

After everyone was onboard, the leader called them all together and explained the safety procedures. He pointed out the lifeboats and the fire extinguishers and did a head count of all on board.

The Captain shouted orders as the boat was untied and the engine engaged to pull them slowly away from the dock where parents stood waving their goodbyes.

Once they were underway, most of the girls headed below deck to get out of the wind. Maggie wanted to stay on the deck, and leaned against Jason. She was smiling and laughing and Jason started to relax. He had been so worried that she wouldn't like being out on the boat, that she might get seasick, or be afraid to get her hair messed up like the other girls.

She's not like the other girls, he thought to himself. Not at all.

The islands came into view and Jason pointed out to Maggie where they were going to go ashore.

"Why don't we go straight there?" she asked. "We seem to be zigzagging. Is there a technical term for that?"

Jason smiled and took her to the pilothouse and showed her the charts and they watched the Captain steer the boat. "It is called tacking. It all depends on the wind, and the state of the sea, Maggie. Here is where the Captain gets a lot of that information."

Maggie's eyes widened when she saw the instrumentation in the navigation station. "It looks a lot like the cockpit of a plane. My father sometimes takes me up in his plane, but he says I'll never be allowed to learn to fly. He's afraid I'll fly away from him." Maggie sighed. "Being out on this boat is a lot like flying, Jason. I love it. What do those gauges tell you?"

Jason explained each of the gauges to her, and they watched from the Captain's side as he depowered the sails, dropped the foresail and guided the boat into the narrow channel where they were going to drop anchor and make land.

They went back up on the deck to watch several of the older scouts lash the sails to the foredeck.

Jason leaned over to Maggie. "I'm not really old enough to crew on this boat, even though I know how, Maggie, but I'll show you how it works on my boat, and you can learn too, if you want. It really is like flying!"

Maggie smiled at him again. "This is the best day I've had in a long time, Jason. Thanks so much for inviting me." She squeezed his arm tightly as they got ready to board the boat tender and motor out to the island.

Jason felt lightheaded, like he sometimes did when he stood up too fast.

The Sea Scouts made several trips, unloaded all of the picnic equipment and their guests and set up the tarp to act as a shade shelter.

Jason went back to find Maggie walking on the beach. "Excuse me, Maggie, I need to go help. You are a guest, so just look around, if you want. I'll see you in a few minutes." Jason joined the other scouts, and soon they had everything ashore.

Maggie looked out at the water, and walked a little way down the beach. She took a small camera out of the inside pocket of her jacket and began to take pictures.

She walked slowly back to the still giggling group of girls near the shade shelter. They spread out to let her in to the circle, and she made polite conversation with each of them. "It's SO windy, and the sand is going to get into everything," one of them wailed. "I'll never get my hair untangled!"

Maggie just smiled and turned to another one of the girls. "Isn't it wonderful," she said lightly "to be out on an island like in one of the adventure books? Do you think there will be pirates?"

The girls all gathered around her "What do you mean, Mary Margaret?"

Maggie told them a story about a shipwreck and pirates and buried treasure.

"To this day, they still haven't found the treasure! It might be right here under our feet. Can you imagine it, girls? A big trunk filled with jewels and gold coins..."

"Oh, I hope there aren't any pirates! I already feel a little sick. Does it have a happy ending, Mary Margaret?"

Maggie nodded and took the girl's hand, which was pale and trembling. "Yes, of course it does. Our brave Sea Scouts rescue us and take us back home safely and we all live happily ever after. I think we'd better get you a blanket and something to eat, Jennifer. Do you really think you are going to be sick?"

They had a lovely picnic on the island, and Maggie thought it was just about the best day she'd ever had. Most of the other girls were chatting about the upcoming events at the Club, and Maggie reached out for Jason's hand.

"Shall we go for a walk down the beach? I need to stretch my legs."

Jason wondered whether she had seen him trying to rub

the feeling back into his knees and nodded. He took her hand and she pulled him up. "That sounds great. Anybody else want to take a stroll?"

There was no response from the rest of the group, so Jason told the leader where they were going. "Just down the beach a bit, sir, to stretch our legs after lunch. We won't go far."

They walked slowly down to the harder sand by the edge of the water and turned toward the large rocks.

Maggie looked out toward the ocean again. "Thank you Jason. I just get so weary of all of the social chitchat. I've known these girls since we were all in preschool together, but they aren't really my friends, just acquaintances. Most of them go to the Catholic girls school I was telling you about. I see them at the stables or other functions at the Club."

Jason nodded, and said darkly "It is a world I don't belong to, Maggie."

She took his arm again. "I had more fun with you and your family at the surprise party than I've had at all the fancy Club parties put together. Really, you are so lucky."

Jason stopped and pointed out at the sea. "The wind is starting to pick up again. See how the waves are changing? I do feel like I am lucky, Maggie. I have to work hard for what I want, but I am going to go to a really good school and become an Engineer and design and invent things. I'm lucky because I get to choose." They looked at the ocean for a few long minutes.

Maggie said very softly, "Yes, Jason. That is exactly what I meant."

They walked back to the group and helped clean up and repack the ice chests for the trip back to the harbor.

One of the older scouts punched Jason on the shoulder.

"Did you kiss her, Jason?"

Jason turned bright red. "No, not yet. This is only our first date."

"Well don't wait too long. There are plenty of guys who would like to be walking arm in arm with Miss Mary Margaret. They are all afraid of her father of course, and for good reason." The older scout winked and carried the ice chest over to the small boat tender. He loaded it into the center of the boat and helped three of the girls into the boat before getting in himself.

Jason watched them motor back out to the ship and climb the steps of the ladder back onto the deck. The ship was rocking, as the wind was gusting now. Jason smiled. It would be an exciting trip back to the harbor. The scouts loaded everything and everybody as quickly as possible.

Most of the girls, and a few of the Sea Scouts were sick on the way back to the harbor. The sea was rough, and a storm was coming up from the South.

"Come on Maggie, stand next to me and let me show you how to roll with the waves. Are you scared?" Maggie stood like he showed her, with her feet firmly planted on the deck next to Jason. "No, I don't feel too scared, now. Oh this is exciting, isn't it Jason?"

He smiled. He hadn't been able to stop thinking about kissing Maggie once the older scout had put the idea into his mind. Right now, though, he needed to make sure she got back to the harbor safely. He knew from looking at the sky that they would make it back before the really heavy rain started, and he had great faith that the Captain had calculated all of that before they left this morning. Weather was nothing to make light of, and Jason kept an eye on the darkening sky. "Let's go below for awhile, Maggie. It is going to get pretty wet and wild out here, and I promised your father I'd get you back safely!"

Maggie frowned. "Okay. It really is exciting though Jason, I love stormy weather. My mother is absolutely terrified of it. One of the few things that she can't control."

Jason took her arm and steered her below deck. The other guests were all huddled up against each other or their Sea Scout dates, trying to make small talk. Every time a big wave would come, they all moaned a little. "Tell us one of your famous stories, Mary Margaret," said one of the girls, "Something light and sunny to keep our minds off of this roller coaster."

Maggie rolled her eyes at Jason and pulled him down to sit next to her. "Okay," she said, "I am going to tell you the story of an inventor who figures out how to travel through time and space." The girls all leaned forward. After a few minutes of the tale, Jason noticed that the Sea Scouts were all leaning forward as well. She had them all captivated.

Maggie told them a tale of a ship that could go fast enough to go forward or backward in time, so that it was always calm and beautiful weather to be out on the sea. "Just enough wind, to sail, of course, because otherwise he'd never get anywhere." The inventor wanted to go back in time to see whether Columbus had really sailed the ocean blue in 1492 and been the first to discover America. He hadn't quite perfected the timing though, and ended up in all kinds of different years until at last he met up with Christopher Columbus himself, a few years before the famous voyage. Maggie lowered her voice and they all leaned toward her. "He had to be really careful, not to alter the course of history, because none of us would have had a rhyme to remember if he got it wrong." She sat back on her bench and said "The End."

The Sea Scouts started to ask questions. "But we don't know how it turned out, Mary Margaret. What happened?" "What kind of ship was this?"

Maggie crossed her arms and shook her head. "That's all I'm going to tell you. Perhaps you can go to the library and figure it out for yourself."

Jason grinned. He hadn't seen any of this group in the library. Maybe there was a private one that he didn't know anything about.

They were just about back to the harbor, and nobody had gotten ill while Maggie was telling her story. She and Jason went back up on the deck when the other Scouts took their posts for their return to the harbor.

Jason shouted over the wind. "You are a great storyteller, Maggie. Next time I go to the library I am going to be sure to check out some books about Columbus!" Maggie smiled at him, and his thoughts went right back to kissing her. Instead, he put his arm around her shoulder and pointed toward the shore. "There's the harbor, Maggie, and the dock. I hope we'll be able to get a better view of the Magic Touch on our way back in." Maggie nodded and leaned against him. It had started to rain, and the deck was wet and slippery. "Be careful, Maggie. We should probably go below deck and watch from there. We don't want to get in anybody's way."

They pulled up to the dock just as the rain was beginning to get really heavy. The Scouts got umbrellas from the clubhouse and escorted their dates to safety. Once inside the warm, dry clubhouse, the girls went to the rest room and began to straighten their hair and reapply their makeup.

Maggie stayed behind and pulled Jason off to the side of the vestibule. "This was the best first date I could ever have imagined, Jason. Thank you so much!"

Jason straightened himself up and put the umbrella in the stand with all of the others. "Thank you Maggie. I hope your father will let me take you out again. It is only a year and a half until you are sixteen, right? I've got to go back and help." He turned and ran back out in the rain and back onto the boat.

Maggie stood there under the awning watching him until she began to shiver. She took a deep breath and went inside to join the other girls.

Willem arrived to pick up Jason, and waved to Maggie as her driver held an umbrella over her so she could get into the car. Jason finally appeared, and they headed home in the rusty old station wagon. "How was it, Jason? Maggie looked like she was soaked straight through."

Jason smiled. "It was great, Grandpa, just absolutely great. She seemed to be a little scared at first, but I think she liked the sailing. This rain will be good for the garden." They chatted on the way home about the garden and what Jason was planning on growing next. "I think I might want to branch out into some flowers, Grandpa. What would you think of that?"

Willem grinned. "Have you figured out which flowers are Maggie's favorites yet?"

Jason blushed. "No, sir. Not yet."

He took a hot shower and hung up his uniform to dry. The rain was really pounding down now, and the lights flickered several times before the power finally went out altogether. He got a flashlight and his rain slicker and went up to the roof. The hydroponic system needed to be shut down if the power was going to surge back on. As he moved quickly to turn everything off, he felt the hair on his arms tingle. He stepped back from the equipment and looked out toward the harbor. A huge bolt of lightning arced down from the sky, and nearly instantaneously; the crack of thunder shook the air.

Jason wondered whether Maggie was watching the storm from her house. He shut the system down and went quickly back to his grandparents' apartment, hung his rain slicker on the hook in the entranceway and slipped off his boots.

CHAPTER NINE

Michael and Paula did not get back home from the race until Wednesday. They called on Monday night and said there had been a problem with the race during the storm, and there were some repairs that had to be done before they could come home.

Jason didn't think too much about it until the front door of the apartment opened on Wednesday night.

Michael was on crutches, a cast on one leg all the way up to the top of his thigh. He was bruised and his face looked swollen.

Paula helped him into the apartment. "Please help me, Jason. I want to get him tucked into bed before Sophie and Willem…" she didn't have time to finish her sentence. Her parents were already there by her side, helping her with Michael.

Sophie clucked like a mother hen. "What happened to you Michael? What can I get you?"

Paula grimaced. "It was awful, Ma. The race got started even though the storm was already pounding the boats, and three of them capsized. Michael rescued one of the other sailors on his crew and we didn't realize how badly he was hurt until the Coast Guard brought them all in."

Michael tried to smile. "None of the boats sank, though, and everybody survived. That was some powerful lightning out there. I'm glad to be home."

Jason stood very still, watching his family. He'd never

thought about his father getting hurt like this. "What can I do for you, Pops?"

Michael tried to smile again, but winced in pain as he lowered himself into the bed. He patted the edge of the bed. "Come and tell me all about your Sea Scouts adventure. How did Maggie like it?"

Paula and Sophie and Willem were all out in the kitchen, talking quietly.

Jason cleared his throat. "She said it was the best first date she'd ever been on, Pops. You know, I was up on the roof turning off all of the garden equipment after the power went out. I saw the lightning. Did it strike your boat?"

Michael shook his head. "No. The winds just kicked up something fierce. The race organizers were going to call off the race, and then at the last minute decided to try and get it started. I guess because of the contracts with the sponsors. One of the boats slammed into another one, capsized us, and it all went downhill from there. I guess I am out for the rest of the season. I am not sure how we'll manage, Jason. Things are pretty tight around here as it is."

Jason sat up straight. "I can help with whatever needs to be done, Pops. You can count on me. I'm almost fifteen!"

Michael patted Jason's hand. "Thanks, son. I know I can always count on you. Will you go get me some water? I have to take my pain meds."

Jason ran in to the kitchen. He stopped suddenly when he saw his mother's face. He legs stopped moving and felt like they weighed two tons.

Paula was crying softly. She stopped and tried to put on a brave face for Jason, but pulled him close to her. "I was so afraid they weren't going to get your father to shore, Jason. I've never been so scared in all of my life. It was like that time in the taxi cab when you couldn't breathe."

Jason didn't know what to say. His whole body ached now and he was very tired. "I need to get Pops some water, Mama. He needs to take his pain meds."

Paula took a deep breath and released her hold on Jason. "Thanks, son. Did the storm cancel your trip with Maggie and the Sea Scouts?"

He got the water and took it to Michael. All of a sudden the best weekend he'd ever had didn't seem like it after all, and being more grown up didn't feel very good. Once Michael was asleep and Willem and Sophie had gone back to their apartment, Jason stood, switching his weight from one leg to the other, with his mother in the kitchen. "What can I do to help? Pops said it was going to be rough, that he would be out for the season."

Paula looked out the window over the kitchen sink. "I don't really know, Jason. Tell me about your weekend. It might help me feel a little better. Did Maggie have a good time? She is such a nice young lady, Jason."

He told her all about the trip, and how they had gotten back to the harbor just before the really heavy rain. "I wonder if it was the same storm. I saw the lightning from the roof, and I..."

Paula looked shocked. "What were you doing on the roof in a lightning storm, Jason? You know better than that!"

Jason clenched his jaw, stubbornly. "I had to shut down the system to the garden, Mama. It wasn't doing anything but raining when I went up there. I'm old enough to..."

Paula shook her head. "You are more important than the garden, Jason." She hugged him tightly again. "I'm sorry, son. I just don't know how we are going to manage."

Jason wriggled out of her grasp. "Well, the garden can

help with the bills. I am making some pretty good money on lettuce these days. We'll figure something out." Jason kissed his mother on the cheek and went to his room. He wrote everything down in his journal and drew a picture of a capsized boat.

I guess being grown up isn't all it is cracked up to be. Pops got hurt pretty badly and I'm pretty sure that means he didn't qualify.

I thought they were invincible. I've never seen Mama scared of anything. She yelled at me for being up on the roof, but I think it was because she was scared.

I don't ever want to need help with anything, from anyone.

Jason told Maggie all about the accident when he saw her at the library. She was checking out books on sailing, and Jason snuck up behind her at the counter. "Boo!" he said, making her jump.

"Oh, Jason, you scared me. I'm just checking out a few books. What are you doing here?"

Jason looked around and whispered to her "I'm trying to learn whether Columbus really discovered America. I heard some story about it..."

Maggie laughed out loud and the librarian shushed her. They walked out of the library together.

"My Pops got hurt pretty badly in his race this weekend, Maggie. He's going to be out for the season."

Maggie handed her books to her driver and started to get in the car. "Call me tonight, Jason. I want to hear all about it. I have to run to my piano lesson now. I am so glad we ran into each other."

The driver tipped his cap to Jason. "Afternoon, Master Jason. If your Pops needs a ride anywhere, you just let me know. I'm sure Miss Mary Margaret could spare me for an hour or so, and then the two of you could spend more time together." He grinned and winked at Jason after he closed Maggie's door.

"Thank you!" said Jason, "We may just have to take you up on that kind offer." He winked back.

Jason went back into the library and checked out some books on Christopher Columbus and the history of sail making. He asked the librarian if they had any books on ALS.

She looked at him over her glasses. "You mean Lou Gehrig's disease?"

Jason nodded. "Yes, ma'am. If there are any books about Jean Martin Charcot, I'd like those, too."

The librarian looked at her young patron again. "Are you thinking of becoming a doctor, Jason?"

Jason fidgeted and tried to stretch his painful legs. "No, I just want to understand a little more about ALS. I have to go see a specialist next week."

The librarian walked out from behind her desk and down one of the hallways. "I'll be right back, Jason, just wait there."

Jason reached down and rubbed the side of his knee. It wasn't helping.

Several minutes later, the librarian came back with a thick book. "This isn't available for general circulation, Jason, but I will let you check it out for one week. I know you'll take good care of it." She filled out the library card and stamped it with the date. Jason thanked her and waved to Sophie, who was coming in to pick him up.

They rode home in the old rusty station wagon. Jason tried stretched his legs and cleared his throat. "Grandma, do you think Pops would be offended if Maggie's driver offered to take him somewhere?"

Sophie looked at Jason in the rear view mirror. "Why would your father need him to do that, Jason? This car has plenty of room in the back for him to stretch out with the cast. We can manage."

Jason nodded. He hadn't thought about it that way. Nobody in his family seemed to want anybody to help them. He smiled.

Sophie changed the subject. "What kind of books did you get today, Jason?" They chatted the rest of the way home about Christopher Columbus and what it might have been like to sail in search of a new world, and how the sails were made back then.

Sophie pulled the car into the parking place in front of the small apartment building. "What's that big heavy book, Jason?" Before he could answer his grandmother, he looked up to see what the commotion was about.

Paula came out of the apartment and hurried toward them. "You are just in time, Jason. Can you come in and help me answer some questions?"

Jason struggled to keep up with his mother, balancing the books carefully. He put them on his desk and then came out to the kitchen. "What's going on Mama?"

Paula was leaning against the kitchen counter, a thick stack of paperwork in her hands. "I need to get this paper-work filled out for the neurologist appointment next week, and I can't remember when you started having problems with your legs. Are the pains worse now that they were when they first started?"

Jason shrugged his shoulders. "Some days are worse than others, I guess. It seems like as soon as I started getting taller, my legs just didn't stretch with me. Is that why you came running out to the car?"

Paula didn't look directly at Jason. "Well, no. Not exactly, but we have to get this paperwork filled out to take with us to the specialist next week."

Jason had never seen his mother get flustered like this. It scared him half out of his wits. Usually she was calm and matter-of-fact and handled all of the paperwork herself. "What's going on, Mama?" Jason slipped his arm around his mother and she held him tightly.

"I don't know, Jason, I just feel overwhelmed by all of this. I guess maybe it is a delayed reaction to the sailing accident. I haven't slept much, and I just don't know how we are going to manage."

Jason hugged his mother and tried to sound confident. "We'll handle it as a family, the way we always, do, Mama."

Paula kissed him on the top of the head. "Goodness Jason, you are going to be as tall as I am soon. You are growing so fast."

The phone rang, and Paula stepped away from Jason to reach for the receiver. "Hello, Visser residence, Paula speaking." She smiled at Jason and reached for the stack of paperwork and the pencil she had been using. "Yes, I'll relay that message to him, Thank you very much." She sighed as she hung up the phone. "That was the Club calling. They found a substitute sailing instructor to take over until Michael is able to teach again. That is a big relief." She headed down the hall to relay the news to Michael, and turned back to call down the hall, "Thanks for being such a great kid, Jason. We love you very much."

Jason nodded and went to his room. "Sure thing, Mama. Love you too." Jason took the small card with Maggie's phone number out of his desk drawer. He went back out to the kitchen and dialed the number.

Maggie answered on the first ring. "Thanks for calling, Jason. When my father gets home later, do you think it will be all right for him to call your parents?"

Jason wasn't sure what she was talking about. "I guess so, Maggie, why does he want to call them?"

Maggie started speaking very quickly. "I have to go to a lesson in a few minutes, Jason, but my father will be very interested in the sailing accident and how he can help your parents with the insurance companies. I wish I had more time to explain, but it was great to see you at the library today. What are you doing tomorrow? Could I see your boat tomorrow?"

Jason tried to remember what day of the week it was. "Sure Maggie. Any time you want to see her, is fine with me."

Maggie said something to someone else that Jason could not hear, and then came back on the line. "Okay, Jason. Ten o'clock tomorrow morning at Captain Carter's dock. I'll see you there." Before Jason could say anything, Maggie hung up the phone.

Jason walked back to his room and put the card back into his desk drawer. Then he went up to the roof to tend his garden. He completely forgot about Maggie's father. All he could think about was introducing his two favorite girls to each other. He smiled as he scrubbed out the containers for the hydroponic lettuce system. He hoped they'd get along, Maggie and the Magic Touch. He hummed to himself as he made his way through his chores on the roof. He'd have to figure out a way to double his production pretty soon, as the chefs at the club were clamoring for more lettuce.

Michael ate his dinner in the kitchen, standing up. He balanced with the crutches under his armpits and Jason thought the bruises looked even worse than when he had first seen him.

"You okay, Pops? Can I get you anything?"

Michael shook his head. "Thanks son, I guess I'll have to get used to this. The doctor said it might be two months before I can get rid of the crutches. That will be most of the best part of the racing season. I don't know how to not be on a boat, Jason. It will be really hard to not be racing." He took a few bites of his food and set the plate down on the counter. "Paula, would you mind getting me the pain meds? I am supposed to take them with food, right?"

Paula nodded and went to get the bottle from the bedroom.

As soon as she left, Michael whispered to Jason. "We need to be strong for your mother. She's not handling this very well."

Jason nodded, feeling a few inches taller, and said "Yes, sir, Pops."

When Paula came back into the kitchen they were eating their dinner as if they hadn't been talking about anything at all. Paula shook the capsules out into Michael's hand and he swallowed them with a large glass of water.

Jason helped his mother with the dishes and then asked to be excused. "I have some reading I need to do," he said "the librarian let me take out a book about the history of neurology, but only for a week. I want to get started on it." He hugged his mother and she kissed him on the top of his head.

"Thanks for helping with the dishes, son. Maybe we can

work on that paperwork, tomorrow, okay?"

"Sure thing, Mama. Tomorrow afternoon, maybe." Jason went to his room and closed the door behind him.

Jason was so engrossed in reading about Dr. Charcot, the father of modern neurology, that he completely lost track of time, and jumped when his mother knocked on his door.

"Can I come in, Jason?"

"Sure, Mama. I'm just reading."

Paula came in the room and sat down on Jason's bed. "That was Maggie's father on the phone, just now. He is going to send a driver around for Michael in the morning. They are going to have a meeting at the law offices while you and Maggie are down at the dock. What did you tell Maggie, son?"

Jason blushed. "I saw her at the library, and told her about the accident, that Pops broke his leg and was on crutches, and then when she said she wanted to see my boat tomorrow morning. I completely forgot to tell you, Mama, I'm sorry."

Paula shook her head. "That's okay, Jason. Even if you had told me, I might not have remembered. I don't know why I am so addled by all of this. I guess I just never thought anything like this would happen to your father. I've always thought of him as unbreakable. What are you reading?" She stood up and walked over to his desk.

"It is the history of neurology and neuromuscular diseases, Mama. I want to know as much as possible before I go to see the specialist."

Paula kissed him on the top of his head. "You'll probably come up with an idea that the doctors haven't even thought of yet, Jason. I am very proud of you."

Jason rocked back in his chair, balancing on the back legs, "I don't know exactly why, Mama, but I don't think I have

ALS. We'll see what the specialist says, though."

Paula was headed back out of the room. "Please don't tip the chair back like that. Do you want the door closed, again, Jason?"

"No thanks, Mama, you can leave it open." Jason went back to his reading and took notes in his new notebook. His grandparents had given it to him the day after the letter came admitting him to the new Math and Science school.

Jason was nervous about his appointment with the specialist. He had been reading about neuromuscular diseases and he knew his symptoms probably pointed to something in that group, but if he were diagnosed with ALS or MS he would only have a label, not anything he could do about it. Almost every description included the word incurable. He didn't tell his parents about his fears, but when Maggie met him at the dock to see the Magic Touch for the first time, he confided in her.

"Would you still be my friend if I had a neuromuscular disease, Maggie? I have to go see the specialist next week and I'm really nervous. I haven't told anybody else about this. My physical therapist thinks the cramps I have in my calves and the weakness in my hips might be ALS. Lou Gehrig's disease."

Maggie listened carefully and took his hand. "I will always be your friend, Jason. No matter what. I am so glad you are the person I went on my first date with, and introduced me to sailing. I think I might have the sailing disease. Do you think it is contagious?"

Jason blinked and swallowed with some difficulty before continuing. "No, Maggie, I don't think ALS is contagious."

Maggie punched him on the shoulder and giggled. "No, silly. The sailing disease. Do you think

THAT is contagious?"

Jason started to laugh and then couldn't stop. The two of them stood on the dock, doubled over in laughter.

Finally, Maggie stood up straight and wiped the tears from her eyes. "Okay, Jason, one of the things I love about you is how smart and funny you are. That won't change with a neuromuscular disease diagnosis."

Jason was still laughing, but he felt feverish as she praised him. "Well, Miss Smarty Pants, you already sound like a really good Doctor."

Maggie sighed. "It's hard sometimes, being smart, isn't it Jason? I hope the new school is more interesting than the last one. The only good thing about that place was meeting you. Now, before my father sends the car around to pick me up, let's get out on the water."

Jason saluted her. "Yes, ma'am. Welcome aboard the Magic Touch!" He took her hand and helped her on board, explaining in great detail everything on the little wooden boat. "She's a classic Sid skiff, Maggie. Hand built. I fell in love with her the first time I took her out for a lesson. Captain Carter let me use her as a favor to my Pops who won a bunch of races for him. I saved all of the money I made from my garden to buy her. That's why I wanted to win the Science Fair, you know. That hundred-dollar prize would have really helped me get her sooner. But I got beaten fair and square by a smarter scientist, so it just took me a little longer to get her."

Maggie frowned. "You really should have won, Jason. The judges just got all freaked out by the idea of fish poop, I think. Those tomatoes were delicious!"

Jason shrugged. "I wouldn't know. Can't eat them, my-self. They make me really sick. Always have."

Maggie took his hand again. "Be sure you mention that to the specialist, Jason. That might be important."

Jason squeezed her hand, not wanting to let go. "Thank you Maggie. It is on my long list of things to mention. Now, let's go through the steps of launching the boat and getting out on the water, shall we?"

Maggie nodded happily.

While Maggie and Jason were out on the water, Michael was sitting with Maggie's father in the law offices downtown. It took a few moments for them to get the chairs positioned so Michael could stretch out his leg with the cast.

Mr. Carlson opened his briefcase on the table, took out a large folder and began writing on a yellow lined pad. He looked at Michael carefully. "Have you taken pictures of the bruising since the accident, Mr. Visser?"

Michael shook his head. "My wife and my father in law are excellent photographers, but neither of them want to see me like this."

Mr. Carlson wrote some further notes on his legal pad. "Okay, Michael. Do you mind if I call you Michael? My daughter is a very persuasive young lady, and she insists that I should take your case. There will be no fee to you, just the usual percentage of the award from the insurance companies once the case is settled. I actually relish the chance to do battle with these particular insurers, so aside from the excellent recommendation from Maggie, I think we have a case here. I've gone through the medical reports briefly. How would I go about getting a report of the race conditions that day?"

Michael looked at the notes Mr. Carlson was making. "My wife Paula writes race reports for a sailing magazine and she has very detailed notes of the day's conditions, but I think you might need to have a conversation with the Committee boat. They had a fierce battle amongst themselves about cancelling the race at the last minute, but the sponsors insisted it be at least started. They got plenty of news coverage, but not the kind they wanted."

Mr. Carlson looked at him, steely eyed. Michael flinched. "That's the best piece of information you could have given me, Michael. Please call me Carl. My parents weren't very imaginative when it came to naming us as kids. I think we have a very good case here. Now, let's move on to the more important business at hand. How safe is it for Maggie to be out on a small boat with your son Jason for her first time on water?"

Michael smiled. "She did great on the Sea Scout boat, according to Jason, Carl. So this will be her second time on the water, and Jason is an excellent sailor. I'd never tell him this, but he has far more natural talent than I ever had."

Carl leaned back in his chair and put his hands behind his head. "Thank you, Michael. I appreciate your candor. Maggie is my only daughter, and I try not to be over protective, but you know how it is…"

Michael nodded. "I do. Jason is an only child, as well. We try to let him have as much independence as he can handle, but he's such a good kid, he's actually harder on himself than we ever could be. He is really excited about this new Math and Science program and plans to go to Engineering school. He gets his smarts from his mother." Michael grimaced as he tried to stand up.

Carl stood up and extended his hand. "Don't underestimate yourself, Michael. Please have your physician send all of the ongoing records here to my office, and do get some pictures taken. I'll be in touch."

Michael struggled to adjust the crutches, and knocked over one of the office chairs. He shook Carl's hand firmly. "Thank you for taking my case, Carl. I didn't even know I had one. I just, you know, I have to keep up appearances with the other sailors and I was hoping this race would qualify me for the next level. I'd hate for this case to screw that up. It is my life as well as my livelihood." He met Carl's gaze, and didn't flinch this time.

Carl walked around the table and righted the chair. He held the door open for Michael and watched him go down the hall on the crutches. Then he went back to the table and picked up the phone. "Send the car around for Mr. Visser, please."

Jason was amazed how quickly she picked up the names of the parts of the boat he showed her. "What's this?" he quizzed.

"The bow, and back there is the stern, and the left side is Port, right is Starboard?"

"Yep. You've got it."

As she quickly hoisted the sail under his direction, he realized she was quite graceful and much stronger than he had given her credit for.

He wanted to stay out on the water with her all afternoon. "We'd better head back to the dock, Maggie. I don't want this to be the only time you get to sail with me."

Maggie smiled. "Oh me either, Jason. This is so much fun! I'm so glad you have shared the Magic Touch with me. She's a great little boat!"

They took the skiff back into its berth and Jason helped her out of the boat. They walked together to the clubhouse and Jason saw the car pull up in front. "I guess I have to let you go," he said sadly, "but I hope we'll get to do this again."

Maggie laughed. "It all depends on my father, Jason. I'll do my best to convince him that I should spend this summer learning to sail." She squeezed his hand again. "Remember, we'll always be friends, no matter what."

Jason watched her walk to the car and slide into the seat after her door was opened for her. He was having that out of body sensation again, like he was much older and taller than he was now. His legs didn't seem to hurt a bit at the moment.

She waved to him, and her driver tipped his cap. Jason went and unlocked his bike from the rack and pedaled home, grinning wildly.

CHAPTER TEN

Paula and Michael went with Jason to the appointment with the specialist. Michael was still on crutches, but his bruising was now faded to a sort of yellowish green. When they checked in to the clinic, the front desk administrators all thought that Michael was the patient.

Once that was all straightened out, a nurse took Jason's vital signs and had him stand on the scale to record his height and weight. A few minutes later, she called all three of them back to an examining room and went over Jason's history.

She looked carefully at Michael. "How did you end up on those crutches, Mr. Visser? Were you in a car accident?"

"No, ma'am, a sailing accident, actually."

The nurse squinted and made a small note on Jason's chart. "All righty, then, the doctor will be in to see all of you shortly. I am going to leave you with some information to read about being in a study group for their latest clinical study. You don't have to decide today, but all of your medical care would be free if you decide to participate as a family." She handed them each a brochure and went out of the room, closing the door behind her.

Jason nervously opened his copy of the brochure. "Clinical study for the understanding of genetic neuromuscular diseases," he read out loud, hoping his voice sounded strong and confident "A newly discovered panel of genetic tests for ALS, MS and Spinal-bulbar muscular atrophy may help to avoid misdiagnosis." Jason put the brochure down and looked at his parents. "I really want to know what is going on. Do you think we can do these tests?"

Michael nodded. "I think it would be great to get to the bottom of all of this. It might even help me understand more about my biological parents, Jason. What do you think, Paula?"

Paula was still reading her brochure. "These tests sound very expensive. The only way we'll be able to afford to get this information is to participate in the study. We'll have to have a family conference and include Willem and Sophie before we decide."

The doctor knocked on the door, and then stepped into the room. He shook Michael's hand and then Paula's. "Thank you for coming in today, how can I help you?"

Jason stood up and shook the doctor's hand calmly. He liked him already. His throat began to relax, and he swallowed hard. "I really want to know what is going on. I don't think I have ALS. I have been reading about Dr. Charcot and he…"

The doctor put his arm around Jason and invited him to sit next to him on the examining table. "That's how I got started on my career path, young man. Dr. Charcot broke ground for many of us in the medical field. He also believed in some pretty strange ideas about hysteria and hypnosis. The whole field of psychiatry owes a lot to Dr. Charcot." He extended his right leg, and then his left. "Can you do this, Jason? Just extend one leg at a time for me." He hopped down off of the table and took a small triangular rubber hammer out of his coat pocket. He tapped the front of Jason's knees after Jason had extended each one and then let them hang down at a 90-degree angle. He felt Jason's calves and the sides of Jason's knees. "Any numbness or tingling in your hands or feet?"

Jason nodded.

"How about trouble swallowing?"

Jason nodded again. He thought he had been hiding that pretty well, but apparently not.

The doctor listened to Jason's breathing with a stethoscope. "I see from the records your neighborhood clinic sent over that you have had a history of chronic respiratory infections. Dr. Franks is a fine physician. Very well respected." The doctor looked directly at Jason. "I think you are correct, young man. I do not believe you have ALS either. In fact, I am pretty sure you have the very disease I have spent my career studying. Have you read the brochure about the study group?"

Jason felt a surge of relief at the news. "Yes, sir. We need to discuss it as a family."

Michael interrupted the conversation. "Would these tests help us understand more about my biological parents, Doctor? They died when I was only three, but I seem to remember my father had trouble walking."

The doctor made a note on Jason's chart. "Possibly, Mr. Visser. We'll certainly share all of the information with you. These tests are mostly to determine if Jason has an inherited form of neuromuscular disease, or what we call a sporadic form, which means he just drew the winning lottery number when he was developing. We are looking for a particular mutation in the gene for the androgen receptor. Jason is quite a bit younger than most of the patients I see, but it would help his prognosis greatly if we knew exactly what we were dealing with. Mrs. Visser, are your parents still with us?"

Paula laughed. "Oh, yes, Doctor, they are very much alive and well. They live right next door to us. "

The doctor made another note in Jason's chart. "Excellent.

I think I'd like to meet them at your next visit if that would be possible." He turned back to Jason. "Are you ready to donate some blood for science, Jason? We just want to do a more specialized panel than you usually get when Dr. Franks orders tests."

Jason confidently stuck out his arm. "Yes, sir. Anything for science!"

They all laughed.

The doctor called his nurse back in and then she wheeled in a cart with a row of tubes on the top. "Okay, Jason, think of something happy. This will take a few tubes of blood, and you'll just feel a little stick while I am getting this started..."

Jason knew exactly what to think about. "I'm going to be starting at the new Math and Science program in the fall," he told the doctor, "with my friend Maggie."

The nurse filled the tubes quickly. "Thank you Jason. I am going to put a Band-Aid on this, with a piece of cotton. Keep it on until you shower next. Let us know if you have any unusual bruising or swelling, or if it gets itchy, okay?" She wheeled the cart out of the room.

The doctor hopped back up on the examining table next to Jason. "Good luck in your new school, Jason. That's how I met my wife. We were lab partners in biology class. She is much smarter than I am. Perhaps you'll meet her at our next appointment." He shook Jason's hand. "Thank you for coming in today, and bringing your parents. Our front desk folks will set you up with your next appointment before you leave. Do you have any other questions?"

Jason swung his legs back and forth before standing up. "Yes, sir. I have about a million questions, but I guess the most important one is, can I still keep sailing?"

The doctor hopped back down off of the examining table.

"Yes, indeed Jason, in fact, that is probably the best medicine. Stay active doing something you love. Keep doing the stretching exercises that the physical therapist showed you. If you join our study group, you will have access to our clinic and we have a number of excellent physical and occupational therapists who will work with you on an ongoing basis." He turned to shake Michael and Paula's hands. "How about you two, any questions for me?"

Paula said quietly, "How soon do we have to decide?"

The doctor opened the door for them. "Take as much time as you need. We'll be here."

They were unusually quiet on the drive home from the clinic. Jason looked out of the window and tried to focus on what Maggie had said about being friends no matter what. When he looked back, he saw his mother clutching the wheel and trying to concentrate on the road. He knew she was worried about how to get the bills paid. With Michael's injury and his new clinic visits, they would be spending a lot more time in doctors' offices. Time that they weren't being paid to work. She glanced in the rear view mirror and met his eyes. He tried to smile bravely, for her. Michael was sound asleep in the back seat.

When they discussed the various options at dinner with Willem and Sophie, Paula hardly even touched her food. She twirled her spaghetti around her fork and set it down on the edge of the plate.

"You'd better eat something, dear." Sophie patted Paula on the shoulder on her way to the kitchen. "You'll need to keep up your strength."

Willem cleared his throat. "I think the most sensible thing to do is for me to take Jason to his appointments at the clinic and to his new school if he needs a ride. I miss the old days when I was involved with the school."

Paula took a bite of the pasta. "Oh, Ma. This is delicious. What did you put in the sauce?"

Sophie came back to the table with another plate full of food for Michael. "It is something new that Jason is growing. Green garlic. I really think it has a nice flavor. Do you want more pasta, Jason?"

Jason shook his head. "No thanks, Grandma. The green garlic is good with just the butter the way I like it, too. I think I'll take some to the chefs at the club on my next delivery date. Thanks for offering to take me to the clinic, Grandpa. Are we all in agreement that I should join the study group?" He looked carefully at his family around the table. His heart skipped a beat as he waited, full of hope.

Paula put her fork down again and said quietly. "I don't know how we can turn down an opportunity for you to get such good care for free, Jason. If your Grandpa is willing to drive you, that would be a big load off of my mind. What do you think, Michael?"

There was a long pause while Michael finished his mouthful of pasta. "I think we should go for it, if that is what Jason wants." He raised his water glass. "All in favor?"

They all clinked their glasses together "Aye, Aye."

The phone rang. Jason jumped up to get it, hoping it was Maggie. "Visser residence, Jason speaking. Oh yes, he is here. Hang on just a moment, please." He put his hand over the receiver. "Hey Pops, phone call for you."

Michael got up slowly from the table and reached for his crutches. He hobbled to the kitchen and took the phone from Jason and leaned against the refrigerator with his back turned toward the family. "Yes, sir. That would be a big help. I'll come in and fill out the paperwork first thing tomorrow morning. Thank you." Michael hung up the phone and came back to the table. He sat down and raised his glass again. "To good news!" he said firmly. "The club is going to pay me most of my sailing school salary as disability. I guess Maggie's father started the claim for me. It looks like they are going to start paying me to stay home and recuperate."

Paula clinked her glass together with Michael's. "What a relief, Michael. I know you want to get back to work, but this will be a big help."

Willem and Sophie and Jason raised their glasses as well, relief flooding through Jason's veins.

CHAPTER ELEVEN

Maggie and Jason went out on the Magic Touch every day the next week. They talked about Jason's clinic visit and the study group.

Maggie wanted to know all about the possibilities. "Will you still be able to come to school, Jason? How many times a week will you have to go? When will you have the results?"

Jason shook his head, overwhelmed with all of the choices. "I don't really know any of the answers to those questions Maggie. Let's just enjoy this week out on the water. When are you leaving for camp?"

Maggie frowned. "Friday evening. Usually I really look forward to camp, Jason, but I'd rather not go this year. I want to spend as much time with you as I can, learning to sail!"

Jason swallowed carefully. "Thank you Maggie. I know you will have fun at camp. We are going to be spending a lot of time together once school starts, but I will miss you." He cleared his throat again, trying to stay calm. "Will you write to me, and at least let me know what camp is like?"

Maggie nodded happily. "Of course I will, Jason. We have quiet time in the evenings when we are supposed to write to our families. Oh by the way, I have something for you when we get back to the dock. Don't let me forget. I got the pictures back from our Sea Scout trip. Our first date."

Jason grinned, and the dizzying feeling of blood rushing to his head again almost knocked him off balance. "You aren't calling it that at home, are you Maggie? I don't want you to get grounded!"

Maggie smiled back at him. "No, Jason, at home they are just known as pictures of the Sea Scout trip. Now, are we going to practice the intentional capsizing today? I didn't tell my parents about that, either."

Jason looked out at the water, which was fairly calm on that afternoon. "Yes, today would be a good day for that. Are you ready?"

Maggie sat up straight and saluted. "Ready, Captain!"

They worked on getting the boat back upright after intentionally capsizing it a couple of different ways that afternoon. Jason was happy to see that Maggie had paid attention to the instructions he had given her to study.

"Step One, when we know we are going to capsize, is to uncleat the main sheet and jib sheet, right Captain?" Maggie recited the steps for Jason as they went through them.

"Step Two is to clear the danger zone between the hull and the boom."

Jason nodded.

"Step Three is to check the status of the rest of the crew, make sure they're not trapped, hurt or in any danger."

They took turns being the Captain and the crew.

"Step Four is my favorite! Swim around to the underside through the back of your boat. Hold on to the dagger board to prevent the boat inverting further. Wait until the crew is also at the dagger board area."

"Step Five is to get the dagger board fully extended, push down on it and try to climb aboard."

"Step Six is to grab the side of the boat as it leans toward you, and Step Seven is to climb aboard and then assist others onto the boat."

Each time they successfully completed the steps, Maggie

would throw her arms in the air as if they had scored a touchdown. "We're a great team, Jason, don't you think?"

Once they got back to the dock, Maggie asked him whether she had passed the test.

"Oh yes, Maggie. You are learning really quickly. I'll bet you could pass your basic Seamanship certification by the end of the summer if we keep working together." Jason followed her proudly out to the car.

She reached in to a pocket behind the front seat and handed him a small book. "Don't look at it until you get home Jason, promise?"

He felt nervous, and his palms were starting to sweat. "Sure Maggie. Thanks. See you tomorrow? It will be our last sailing day before you go off to camp."

Maggie frowned. "Don't remind me. I'll see you bright and early tomorrow morning Jason."

Her driver came around to close her door for her. He looked at Jason. "Did she fall overboard, Master Jason?"

Jason laughed. "Nope. We practiced the intentional capsizing today. It is a really important skill to learn. You have to pass that test to get your Seamanship certificate. She did great."

The driver shut the door and shook Jason's hand. "It is all she can talk about. The sailing, I mean. I've never seen her so happy. By the way, you can call me Nikolas. I'll be driving your father for the next two weeks while Miss Mary Margaret is at camp. How is he feeling?"

Jason extended his hand again, feeling very grown up. "Thank you Nikolas. My Pops is not a very good patient. He is supposed to be resting, but he just wants to get back to work. Back to sailboat racing, especially. Thank you for driving him to the appointments."

Nikolas tipped his cap. "My pleasure, Master Jason. See you tomorrow morning." As he went around to the driver's side, Maggie rolled down her window.

"Bye Jason, see you tomorrow!"

Jason stood on the curb and watched the long black car pull away. He turned the small book over in his hands and then tucked it into his shirt for the ride home.

He waited until after dinner to look at the book. It was a small scrapbook, with photos and a story written in fancy handwriting. Jason turned the pages slowly, savoring each one. He hadn't even realized that Maggie had been taking pictures. The very last page was a picture of the two of them, sitting on the sand with the other Sea Scouts. Maggie was leaning her head on his shoulder, smiling for the camera. She must have given the camera to one of her friends. Underneath the photo she had written "our first date." Jason propped the book open to that page and leaned it up against the bulletin board. He placed a small rock against it to hold it open. He would look at it every day while she was away at camp, he decided. So he wouldn't forget that they would always be friends, no matter what.

Paula knocked on the door. "May I come in, Jason?"

"Sure, Ma." Jason stood up and went over to the door to let her in. "Come and see what Maggie made me. She's leaving for camp after our sailing lesson tomorrow." Jason hesitantly handed the scrapbook to Paula.

She turned the pages slowly, shaking her head. "Oh, Jason, these are terrific. She's a really good storyteller!"

Jason told her about the pirate adventure and how all of the scouts and their dates had been captivated by the tale.

Paula hugged Jason tightly. "We all really like Maggie, Jason. It is so generous of her father to take the case and provide a driver for your father the next two weeks. I wish I knew what we could do to thank them. Anyway, what I came in for was to tell you that the clinic called this afternoon. They want us all to come in tomorrow for the test results. What time will you be finished with sailing?"

Jason felt all of the blood rush out of his head at this news. Deflated, he thought for a minute. "Anytime after two would be okay, I guess."

Paula nodded. "The appointment is at four, so we should have plenty of time to get there. I will call them back and confirm the appointment. Thanks for sharing the book with me, Jason. It is lovely." She closed the door on her way back out to the kitchen.

Jason propped the book open again, ran his fingers over the picture of the two of them together, and felt a thrill run up his arm. He thought again about kissing her and then went to get the key for the rooftop. "I'll be up in the garden if anybody needs me," he called as he went out the front door.

The sun was just about to set when Jason finished checking on all of his plant systems and Sophie was humming as she worked on her latest painting. Jason wiped his hands on a small towel and walked over to see what she was working on. "Wow, Grandma, that is great!"

Sophie nodded and kept working. "Thanks, Jason, I am just trying to capture these last bits of light before the sun goes down. How are your sailing lessons going with Maggie?"

Jason grinned. "Fantastic, Grandma. She seems to really like the sailing."

"Well, she really likes you, Jason. She's a smart girl."

Jason flushed and felt his ears begin to burn. "Yes, Grandma, she is very smart. I'm glad we are friends."

He watched quietly as Sophie put the finishing touches on the painting.

She stepped back and looked out at the setting sun and then back at the painting. She put the brush into a cleaning solution and wiped her hands on her apron, opening her arms for a hug from Jason. "I'm looking forward to meeting your doctor tomorrow, Jason. It will be like a family field trip!"

Jason felt reassured and comforted by the hug. "I can always count on you to see the bright side, Grandma. Thanks."

Sophie took the canvas off of the easel and they went down the stairs together. At the bottom of the staircase they each turned a different way and went out onto the sidewalk and into their own apartments.

Jason thought of the small apartment building as a house. There were only the two units on this side of the building, mirror images of each other. On the other side, there were two more units, facing the other street. Jason hoped that someday he would have enough money to buy a property like this. A dream worth working for, just like his boat had been.

CHAPTER TWELVE

J ason and his family arrived early for his appointment. They sat together in the waiting room of the clinic, reading the available brochures and talking quietly about what questions they might want to ask. He wished he wasn't so nervous, but every chair felt like it was spiked and his legs were burning.

A tall redhead in a white lab coat came out to sit with them. "Hello, are you the Visser family? Why don't you come with me to the conference room?" She led the way down a long hallway and ushered them in to a room with a dozen chairs around a gleaming wooden table. "Would any of you like water to drink?"

They all shook their heads and sat down at the table.

Michael chose a chair at the far end of the table so he could stretch out his legs and leaned his crutches against the wall.

The tall redhead took her place at the head of the table.

"I'm so glad you came early today. It will give me a chance to meet each one of you and get to know you a little better. I run the clinical trial part of this practice and am always happy to answer any questions you might have. I'll give each of you my card. Please do not hesitate to call me." She passed around the cards, and Jason thought they looked similar to Maggie's calling card.

Maybe someday Maggie would be running clinical trials. He smiled to himself and tried to concentrate on the meeting.

He still had the brochure from the waiting room and he started to read the paragraph over again.

This condition is inherited in an X-linked pattern. A condition is considered X-linked if the mutated gene that causes the disorder is located on one of the two sex chromosomes. In males (who have only one X chromosome), a mutation in the only copy of the gene in each cell causes the disorder. In most cases, males experience more severe symptoms of the disorder than females (who have two X chromosomes). Females with a mutation in one copy of the Androgen Receptor gene in each cell are typically unaffected. A few females with mutations in both copies of the gene have had mild features related to the condition, including muscle cramps and occasional tremors. Researchers believe that the milder signs and symptoms in females may be related to lower androgen levels. One of the characteristics of X-linked inheritance is that fathers cannot pass X-linked traits to their sons.

Jason turned his attention back to the woman at the head of the table.

She was passing out notepads and pencils to each of them. "Sometimes it helps to take notes during these meetings," she said "and sometimes it helps to draw pictures to stay awake if we are giving you too much technical information." She passed out another sheet of paper to each of them. "Before we get started, please sign the form that allows us to share information with you as family members. If there is anyone else you would like to include, please let me know."

They all signed the forms and she collected them. "First of all, I want to thank you all for coming in today. My name is

Aileen, and my husband will join us in a few minutes and then we will get started. Do you have any questions for me about the clinical trial or study group?"

Sophie raised her hand "What is the difference between the two?"

Aileen stood up and went to the blackboard. She drew two boxes. Above the two boxes she wrote "Clinical Study".

She turned back toward the group. "A clinical study involves scientific research using human volunteers, also called participants, that is intended to add to our body of medical knowledge. There are two main types of clinical studies: clinical trials which are also called interventional studies, and observational studies." She labeled the first box "Clinical Trial". She continued, "In a clinical trial, participants receive specific interventions according to the research plan or protocol created by the investigators. For instance, I am the Principal Investigator of this study on Kennedy's disease, and if we had possible drugs to try, I would lead the pharmaceutical clinical trial as well. These interventions may be medical products, such as drugs or devices. They might be surgical procedures, or changes to participants' behavior, such as diet. Clinical trials may compare a new medical approach to a standard one that is already available, to a placebo that contains no active ingredients, or to no intervention at all.

We, as investigators, try to determine the safety and efficacy of the intervention by measuring certain outcomes in the participants. For example, investigators may give a drug or treatment to participants who have high blood pressure to see whether their blood pressure decreases." She labeled the second box "Observational Study". Jason drew the boxes on his notepad, and took a few notes, but mostly drew pictures of boats.

Aileen continued. "In an observational study, we as investigators assess health outcomes in groups of participants according to a research plan or protocol. We are studying Kennedy's disease, which is a rare condition. It is most helpful for us if we can follow a patient and their family from time of onset. In this case, Jason, you are not yet of the age where we normally see onset of symptoms, so it will be particularly valuable if we can follow your progress, and hopefully address any symptoms as soon as they come up."

The door opened and Dr. Fishback came in. He pulled up a small stool to sit next to Aileen. "Good afternoon. I see you've met my lovely wife, Aileen. Can we go around the table and make introductions? You'll have to forgive me, I have a particular difficulty remembering names."

They went around the table again, and Dr. Fishback made notes on his pad of paper. He drew a tree shaped diagram and looked at Michael. "So, I understand from our last conversation that your parents died when you were young. I think you may find the results of our tests helpful to understand more about them."

Michael sat up a little straighter and leaned forward.

The doctor continued. "We're here today because Jason's tests came back positive for Kennedy's disease. Most of the time, when genetic tests come back positive, we ask the immediate family members to be tested as well. This is so we can better understand the disease, but also so we can provide support and medical care for the whole family".

He smiled at Jason " I feel very fortunate to meet all of you. I have spent my career studying the neuromuscular diseases and have focused on Kennedy's disease as a particular area of specialty. Since it is a rare disease and symptoms often do not show up in patients until later adulthood, this is a wonderful opportunity to follow all of you as a family. Let's begin with you, Jason. How would you like us to focus on your disease management?"

Jason looked around the room, wanting to jump out of the chair and hug his mother, who looked terrified. "I just want to be able to keep sailing, sir. I don't want to take any medications that will keep me from being able to sail."

Dr. Fishback smiled again. "Actually Jason, as I mentioned last time, sailing may end up being the best medicine of all. Our goal here in the clinic, aside from studying the disease, is to provide you with the latest information and support so you can have the best quality of life possible. The good news is that Kennedy's disease does not impact the lifespan. You can expect to live as long as any of your classmates. The bad news is that it does affect the extremities, with progressive muscle weakness in the arms and legs. We hope with good physical therapy and some possible interventions that we are working on, that you will be able to sail as long as you like. I know you mentioned last time that you were about to start a Math and Science program, and that you hoped to go to a good engineering school. There is nothing in our understanding of the disease that will prevent you from any of those goals. As we get to know each other better, we will be able to tailor your physical therapy program to help you adapt to your changing muscles. How does that sound?"

Jason smiled and felt the stabbing pain subside a little bit. "It sounds great. Thank you." He drew more detailed pictures of sailboats on his pad of paper while the doctor went around the group and addressed specific concerns.

Paula was worried about Jason's frequent respiratory infections and the trouble he sometimes had swallowing or clearing his throat.

Sophie and Willem couldn't think of anything to ask at this meeting, but then it was Michael's turn.

"If this is an x-linked disease, Doctor, doesn't that mean I couldn't have passed along the gene mutation to Jason? I don't understand why would I learn more about my parents from participating in the genetic studies."

Aileen interrupted and directed her answer toward all of them. "We are just beginning to understand the patterns that exist in families, Michael. Someday maybe will have a map of the whole human genome, but for now, we can answer some basic questions about Jason's particular case, and often we find very interesting data along the way. We would be very grateful if each of you would consent to participate in a family study. We don't expect you to decide today, but I've included some information in the packet I'm going to give you now." She passed out a folder to each of them.

Michael didn't even open it before speaking. "Actually, I think we have already discussed it, and we are willing to donate blood today if you are ready to take it."

Aileen stood up. "We certainly are, Michael. It is a great honor for us to be able to work with you as a family. After we are finished here, we can go ahead and do the blood draws. Are you all sure you have discussed this thoroughly?"

Paula reached for Michael's hand. "We're all in this to-gether," she said carefully, "we are grateful that this clinic is so close to us, and we wouldn't be able to afford the care for Jason without this program."

Aileen nodded. "That is the beauty of this study. We are able to provide ongoing care in a specialized environment so that Jason gets the latest information and best quality of medical interventions when they become available. Speaking of which, I think it would be a good idea for you to wear a medical alert bracelet, Jason. We'll be happy to order one for you. That way, if you are ever in an accident or have an issue, the number of our clinic will be readily available to first responders or an ER doctor for consultation.

"There is an informational brochure in your packet that tells you more about that. Also, we'll write out a prescription for you to have regular physical and occupational therapy sessions with the provider you are already working with. Our clinic will pick up the bills, and all of the documentation from those sessions will be shared with us. You are welcome to come here to meet with our PT and OT staff at any time, but we want to make it as convenient for you as possible."

Jason just wanted to get home and see if he had another postcard from Maggie at camp. She had written to him nearly every day and the postcards were lined up along the wall of his desk. When they pulled up in front of the apartment, Jason hopped out of the car and went up to the front door. He opened the lid of the wall-mounted mailbox and reached inside. There were a number of pieces of mail for his parents, but no postcard. Instead, there was a thick envelope addressed to him in Maggie's elegant handwriting.

Paula opened the front door for him.

He put the rest of the mail in the basket on the kitchen counter and took the letter to his room. He laid it carefully on his desk. Maggie would be home from camp tomorrow, and he couldn't wait to tell her all about the clinic. He decided to save the letter for after dinner. All of a sudden he was starving.

Jason ate two helpings of pasta at dinner, and an extra

piece of Sophie's homemade sourdough bread slathered with butter. He felt really hopeful about the clinic. Maybe there wasn't a cure, but he could expect a normal lifetime. That was something to be positive about, wasn't it?

The family talked quietly during dinner, as if they were still trying to process all of the information from the clinic. They all agreed that they were very lucky to have found the clinic and that it was only an hour or so away.

Jason hopped up from the table. "Thanks for dinner! I want to go and read my letter from Maggie if you will excuse me." He didn't wait for an answer. After putting his dishes in the sink, he washed his hands and went to his room to read the letter.

He opened the envelope carefully, wanting to save the beautiful paper. He slid the pages out and began to read. The first few pages were light and funny, as Maggie recounted the talent show and the silly three-legged races and how she had made friendship bracelets and exchanged them with the other girls in her cabin. Jason smiled, imagining that Maggie's bracelets were probably jewelry that her cabin mates would wear proudly. He turned to the last page.

I need to tell you this before I get home from camp. I will understand if you don't want to talk to me again, but I want you to hear my side of the story. Every year there is a dance with the boys' camp across the lake. Usually it has been a square dance, and we all wear Western costumes and it is a lot of fun. It was terribly different this year. The girls in my cabin were all talking about how they hoped to get their first real kiss this year, and they had picked out boys to be paired up with. They all want to go steady before school starts. I guess the boys had been planning the same thing. I didn't tell the other girls that I didn't want to be kissed because I certainly didn't want it to be something else they could tease me about. The dance was fun until Bryce picked me as his partner. I've known him a long time. His father is a partner in my father's law firm. I guess everybody expects us to be paired up, but I really don't like him very much. We did the square dances, and we all rotated partners until we were back with our original one. Bryce grabbed me, and kissed me in front of everybody. It was awful. Then the dance was over and as we were leaving, he said it wouldn't be the last time, I should learn to like it. He scares me, Jason. I will understand if you don't want to be my friend anymore, but I didn't want you to hear from someone else that I had kissed Bryce. I'm just glad he won't be in school with us this fall. He goes to the private boys' school in the City. I've missed you Jason, and I still really want to be friends with you, always.

Maggie's name was signed in shaky script at the end of the letter.

Jason read the last page again and then crumpled it up and put it in his pocket. He put the rest of the letter back into the envelope and put it back on his desk. He put his head down on the desk and started to cry. He was shaking, and felt sure he was going to throw up. His lips began to pull back, baring his teeth. He wanted to bite Bryce, hard. Could he really think about not being friends with Maggie? He wasn't mad at her, but he was furious with this Bryce guy. Whoever he was, Jason hoped he never got to meet him. He didn't understand why Maggie would think he wouldn't want to be friends with her. It was all so confusing. He wiped his eyes with the back of his hands and dried them on the front of his shirt. He walked quickly out of his room and out the front door.

He unlocked his bike and pedaled as fast as he could down to the dock. After locking his bike, he found a smooth, round rock in the landscaping of the yacht club parking lot. He wrapped the page from the letter around it and slipped a rubber band over it. He always kept a few rubber bands in his pockets to secure the cuffs of his pants when he was riding his bike. He put the paper wrapped rock back into his pocket and untied his boat.

The sun was just about to set. He sailed away from the dock, tears streaming down his face again. Once he got clear of the other boats, he turned the Magic Touch toward the sunset and took the rock out of his pocket. "Nobody is going to keep me from being friends with Maggie!" he yelled as loud as he could as he threw the rock toward the setting sun.

He turned the boat around, tied her up at the dock and rode his bike home to do his chores in the garden on the roof. It was already dark, but he had a flashlight, and knew where everything was, even in the dark. Once he had finished his chores, he went back down to the apartment.

His parents and grandparents were still sitting around the table, talking quietly. He hugged each of them and wished them a good night. He went in to his room and cried himself to sleep after writing in his notebook:

Now I know that I've never really hated anyone before. I want to kill Bryce, and that feels really scary. He robbed me of my chance to kiss Maggie. Even if I do kiss her sometime, she might be afraid, so he's taken something from both of us.
I HATE HIM.

The next day, he went to the library with his grandmother, as he always did. He checked out books on neuromuscular diseases and stretching exercises.

The librarian looked at Jason carefully as he was checking the books out. "It is a little early to be studying for medical school, Jason. I hope you are enjoying your summer."

Jason avoided looking at her directly and mumbled "I'm still planning on going to Engineering School, and no, it hasn't been the best summer like I thought it would be."

She stamped the cards and put them in the pockets in the back of the books. "Okay, Jason, see you next week."

Sophie and Jason walked out to the car. She opened the door for him so he could put all of the books on the back seat. He climbed in. "Don't you want to ride up front with me, Jason? I hope you are not getting too grown up to be seen with your grandmother around town!"

Jason shook his head and went around to the front seat. He was afraid the hate was obvious, like chicken pox. His skin had looked blotchy and mottled in the mirror this morning, and he still felt awful. "Sorry, Grandma. Of course I don't mind being seen with you." He leaned against the door and looked out the window in despair. When they rounded the corner to the apartment, Jason could see the black car pulling up in front. His heart began to race. Maybe Maggie was coming straight from camp to see him! He brightened and sat up a little straighter, and then saw that it was Michael climbing out of the car, with Nikolas helping him to his feet and handing him his crutches. Jason's heart sunk down into the pit of his stomach. He wanted to slam his fists against the windows of the car.

"That's awfully generous of Maggie's father to send a driver around for Michael, isn't it Jason?" Sophie said lightly, not picking up on Jason's black mood. "I hope Michael can get back on a boat soon. He is getting awfully restless."

Jason tried to sound cheerful. "Me, too. Grandma. Thanks for the ride!"

By the time they had parked and Jason got all of his books from the floor behind the front seat, Nikolas was gone. Michael was still standing on the curb.

"Hey Pops, how was your appointment?" Jason tried again to sound upbeat.

Michael looked at the pile of books Jason was carrying and then said slowly, "I feel like I am caught in a riptide, son. I have to just give in and let the current carry me to shore or I will drown."

Jason felt his stomach churn again and clenched his fists under the books. "Yep, I know the feeling, Pops."

Willem came out and held the door for all of them.

Jason waited two days before he called Maggie.

She answered on the first ring. "Oh Jason, I am so glad you called. When can we go sailing again?"

Jason hesitated for just a second, still feeling awful. "Anytime you like, Maggie. How about tomorrow?"

Maggie exhaled loudly, as if she had been holding her breath for a long time under water. "Tomorrow would be the perfect day, Jason. I'll see you down at the dock at 8AM. Thank you so much for calling me."

Jason put the receiver back onto the wall phone. If he had never gotten that letter, it would be just like it had always been, and he would have been really excited to see Maggie tomorrow. Instead, he worried that he might not even recognize her. He shook his head. That was ridiculous. Only a few short months ago, Maggie had been his nemesis. She was the one who had transformed their relationship into something else, and Jason knew she had the power to do that again. As long as she still wanted to be friends, they probably would be. He needed to relax, and just let the current carry him to shore. He felt a dark defiance creep into his brain. He wouldn't relax. He would fight with his last ounce of breath to keep Maggie safe, whether they were in the boat or onshore. He was not going to be passive any longer! He clenched his fists again and looked for something to strike. He left a small, round indentation in the hallway wall.

The sailing lesson didn't go as well this time. Maggie got her arm caught in a rope when they were practicing hoisting the sail and she burst into tears.

"Are you hurt, Maggie?" Jason took her hand.

She began to sob, in big gulping heaves.

Jason was afraid she was going to be sick. He put his arm around her and she leaned against him.

"I'll never get it right, Jason." She pushed the words out toward him between sobs. "I just can't get anything right."

Jason didn't know what to say, so he just sat there, with his arm around her until she started to calm down. "I think you get everything, right, Maggie."

She dried her tears on the sleeve of her shirt. "I'm sorry Jason. It seems like the harder I try, the worse things get."

Jason nodded. "My father says he feels like he is caught in a riptide. He can't make the healing go any faster by struggling against it. He says we just need to relax and let the current carry us to shore. But you know what, Maggie? I don't want to relax. I don't want to be passive and be bullied anymore. I want to fight for us, our friendship!"

Maggie forced a smile, and Jason was afraid he'd said the wrong thing. "That's brave of you, Jason, and it means a lot to me that you still want to be friends. I do need to learn to relax, I guess. I'm too scared to fight. Tell your father thanks from me." She leaned her head on his shoulder and they sat there for a long time, the little boat bobbing gently in the waves.

Jason swallowed his pride and told her all about the clinic, and Maggie held his hand tightly.

"I am so glad you are going to live a long time, and be able to sail, Jason. That really is good news! I am sorry I was so focused on a silly thing that happened at camp. Can you forgive me, Jason?"

He looked her straight in the eyes, his heart pounding in his ears, as he held both of her hands. "No, Maggie, I don't need to forgive you, because you didn't do anything wrong! I don't think it was a silly thing, not at all. It has all been so confusing this summer. I'll be glad when school starts!"

Finally, Jason took them back to the dock and helped Maggie out of the boat after they had put the sail cover on. "I threw the last page of your letter out to sea, Maggie. I was so angry. I wanted to pretend it never happened and we could just go back to being friends like before."

Maggie shook her head. "Thanks, Jason, but I can't pretend. It did happen, even though I didn't want it to. If you are still willing to be my friend, then we will figure out a way to make it work. Thank you for trusting me and telling me all about the neuromuscular disease clinic. Maybe I'll be able to sleep tonight, instead of crying."

They walked to the curb and Jason watched as she got into the car. He walked slowly back to his bike. He didn't feel like punching anything anymore. Maybe he would be able to sleep tonight, too.

CHAPTER THIRTEEN

When the family's blood test results came back a few weeks later, they all went to the clinic together to discuss them with the team. Jason felt nervous and excited, the way he had when he went to see his score on the entrance exam.

Dr. Fishback shook Michael's hand as soon as they walked into the conference room, and put his arm around him. "The good news, Michael, is that we certainly know more about your parents now. The even better news is that it may explain why Jason's symptoms have presented so much earlier than we might have expected." He greeted everyone else and invited them to sit down. "I am going to draw some diagrams for you here on the board, and you are welcome to copy them down in your own notes, please feel free to ask questions along the way."

Jason took a deep breath and exhaled loudly, trying to calm his jittery nerves.

Dr. Fishback drew a tree diagram with circles and boxes. Some of them were simply open shapes, some had dots in the center, and others were filled in completely.

He began to point to each individual shape. "The squares represent males, and the circles are females. The dot indicates a carrier, and a filled in shape is an affected individual. If the shape is just open, the individual is unaffected. When we draw the tree for Michael's family, we see that his father was affected, and married his mother, an unaffected woman.

Their children would all be all unaffected carriers of SMA, having inherited one chromosome 5 with a mutation from their father and one without this mutation from their mother. All of the children of this man had to inherit a chromosome 5 SMA mutation, because they had to get one chromosome 5 from their father and both of his chromosome 5s have this mutation. You couldn't have inherited this kind of mutation from your mother, Michael because she was not a carrier. SMA is shorthand for spinal muscular atrophy. The reports of your father having difficulty walking, Michael, would bear this out. So, Jason, essentially you have won the neuromuscular disease lottery."

Jason copied the tree onto his notepad and said quietly, trying not to show his nervousness, "So I guess we will qualify for the study group, then."

Dr. Fishback erased his notes on the board and nodded. "Yes, Jason. It is very exciting for us to be able to have this information, and more importantly, actual patients to help move the field forward. I know it is a lot of information to process, but do you have any other questions right now? No? Okay, now let's diagram your mother's side of the tree, Jason."

He went back to the board and drew more circles and squares. "In this case, we have Willem, who is an unaffected male, who married Sophie, who is a carrier female. Their child, your mother Paula, is also a carrier female. She married Michael, who is an unaffected male for Kennedy's disease, but is a carrier for SMA. This is you, Jason. You are an affected male and a carrier. It is too early to think about this of course, but if you ever decide to have children of your own, we'll recommend genetic counseling and testing."

Jason filled out the rest of his family tree diagram. "From

what I have been reading since our last appointment doctor, there is nothing that has been developed to stop my muscles and nerves from wasting away, is that correct?"

Dr. Fishback erased the board again and sat down at the head of the table. "Yes, Jason that is true. Aileen and I are working on some promising ideas, and we hope that you will become an integral part of our work. We have colleagues around the world in different labs, all trying to solve this mystery. To be honest, we first have to understand what goes right for the rest of us, Jason. It might be helpful for you to think about the wiring diagram of a car. Any number of things can cause an interruption in the circuitry and blow a fuse for instance. It is pretty easy to figure out which fuse is blown, and replace it. I really hope we can work toward figuring out how to do that in humans. The wiring is so incredibly complex, and we can't just take out different fuses to see whether that cures the problem. We have to work in model systems that mimic the human wiring."

Willem raised his hand. "You make it sound like science fiction, Doctor. Do you really think it is possible to have something like, what was that called on Star Trek, that thing that they waved over your body and it would tell you what was malfunctioning?"

Dr. Fishback smiled. "Actually Willem, that is the perfect analogy in many ways. We really do think those kinds of diagnostics are possible in the future. Right now, the field is making rapid advances in the understanding of which diseases have a genetic basis to them, but it only tells us what we already suspect, the test confirms the symptomology. If Jason never had any symptoms, we wouldn't have any reason to do testing, and we wouldn't have all the information we just drew on the board. Our group has funding to study this kind of genetic inheritance, so we have access to the labs that do this kind of testing, at no cost to the patient."

Dr. Fishback handed each of them a thick packet of materials. "Take your time, but it is important for each of you to read these packets before our next meeting. Feel free to call us with any questions. I want you to have a thorough understanding of what we are trying to accomplish as a team. If the language is too technical, please let us know. We do want this information to make sense to patients, and sometimes we speak in what seems like a foreign language. Any other questions for today?"

Jason looked around the room. He knew his family would stick together through this, and maybe they would help bring a scientific breakthrough to the field. He cleared his throat. "I think we have a lot to digest, Doctor. Thank you for accepting us into your study group." He pushed on the sides of the chair to stand up. "How soon is our next appointment?"

Dr. Fishback smiled again. "From here on out, Jason, the appointments will be up to you, on your schedule. We'd like to see you every six months unless you have new symptoms or something you'd like to talk about." He stood up and shook each family member's hand as they filed out of the room.

He put his hand on Michael's shoulder. "I hope this shed some light on questions you might have had about your father, Michael. It might actually lead to an important advance in our field of study. Thank you for asking the questions and providing the clue about him having difficulty walking."

Michael shook his head. "I need to try and find some of the people who might have known him, back in Wisconsin. Perhaps now while I am laid up with this cast would be a good time to do that. Thanks again."

There wasn't much conversation in the car on the way home from the clinic. Jason was looking forward to getting home and checking the mail. He hoped he'd have a notice from the library about a book he had requested. He wanted to start studying right away. It was a book about sailing. He had decided to take the reference librarian's suggestion to heart and enjoy the rest of his summer. He could think of nothing he'd rather do than study about Sail Power.

CHAPTER FOURTEEN

Jason and Maggie sailed together almost every day for the rest of the summer. They agreed that they wouldn't discuss what had happened to Maggie at camp, but instead focus on what was ahead of them.

Maggie signed up for the basic boating safety courses and passed them with ease. At the diploma ceremony, Jason and his family all applauded when Maggie came up to get her certificates. Jason beamed with pride and pumped his fist in the air.

Paula took pictures of all of the sailors together for the Yacht Club newsletter. Sophie gave Maggie a big hug.

"Where are your parents, Maggie? I'd love to meet them!"

Maggie frowned and looked at the ground. She said very quietly, "They are working, as usual. Thanks for coming to celebrate with me. I made dinner reservations for all of us at the banquet after the ceremony. I hope you will join me."

Once they were all seated inside at the banquet, Maggie asked Paula if she would take some pictures of the two of them at the end of the summer.

"I'll pay for the portraits, Mrs. Visser. I just want to be in the pictures instead of taking them all myself."

Paula laughed. "It is the photographer's dilemma, Maggie. I'd be happy to take some pictures of you and Jason. Would you like to come to the darkroom and see how I develop them?"

Maggie nodded happily. "I think we may have an elective

in photography at the new school. My father is going to have a darkroom put in. Maybe you can help him design it!"

Paula put her arm around Maggie. "I'd love that, dear, but your family has done so much for us already..."

Maggie frowned. "He'll have to pay somebody to do it, Mrs. Visser. I think it will be a happier place to work in if you design it. Will you consider it?"

Paula nodded. "Of course, Maggie."

Jason was amazed at how Maggie managed to command attention at these kinds of events. The waiters hovered over her and the event coordinator came by to make sure everything was to her liking. Maggie was polite, and always treated everyone fairly, but there was something incongruous about the Maggie who had sobbed in his arms about never getting anything right, and the Maggie who made things happen seemingly effortlessly. He knew she had to "Keep up appearances" as she referred to it, but he wondered which Maggie would be attending school with him in the fall.

Jason looked at his father sitting across the table from him.

Michael was walking with a cane now, instead of the crutches and had a smaller cast on his leg. He had spent the last few days making phone calls to Wisconsin, and he seemed far less restless than he had in the first few weeks after the accident.

Michael smiled at Maggie across the table and raised his glass. "To our newest sailor. Welcome to the family, Maggie!" They all raised their glasses and Maggie blushed.

"Thank you Mr. Visser. It means the world to me that you are all here celebrating with me."

Just then, a large centerpiece of flowers was delivered to their table. The event coordinator leaned over to whisper something to Maggie.

"I guess my parents are here now too," she said carefully, reading the card that was tucked into the arrangement, "at least in spirit." The display took up most of the center of the table.

Sophie sighed, "What an incredible arrangement, Maggie. I'd love to paint those gorgeous flowers!"

Maggie twisted her napkin in her lap and smiled at Sophie. "Please take them home with you and paint them to your heart's content. I insist. They'll just get thrown out after we leave otherwise."

Willem stood up and raised his glass. "To our dear, generous, Miss Mary Margaret. Congratulations!"

They all clinked their glasses together around the flowers, and Jason smiled. He felt so fortunate to be here with all of the people he loved.

He wiped his hands on his pants and nervously took a small box out of his pocket and handed it to Maggie. "Here, Maggie. I wanted to get you something to remember our summer of sailing. I hope you like it."

Maggie opened the box very slowly and lifted a small silver bracelet out of the box. There was a charm on one of the links, shaped like an anchor.

Jason helped her secure it around her wrist and she held it up for all of them to admire.

"Oh it's perfect, Jason! Thank you. I'll always wear it to remember this summer, and learning to sail." She reached for his hand under the table and squeezed it tightly. She leaned over and whispered to him, "You are the best friend I could possibly imagine, Jason Visser." Jason felt like the room was awfully warm all of a sudden, and his throat was too dry to speak.

The servers took away the place settings and returned with dessert plates and forks. Each of them had a chocolate cupcake in front of them now, with a plastic sailboat perched on top of the white icing.

Maggie removed the decorative sailboat and put it on the side of her plate. She carefully peeled back the paper around the cupcake and took a small bite off of her fork. She nodded to the server.

"Delicious," she said. "Does anyone want coffee?"

After they were finished, Maggie asked for a box from the server.

"Could you pack up an extra meal for Nikolas? Put it all on my father's tab please." The server bowed, and went back into the kitchen.

Jason was confused. "I didn't know you were members here, Maggie. Does your father have a boat I don't know about?"

Maggie sighed. "No, Jason. We have reciprocal privileges with the golf and tennis country club. My father does business at both places. We used to come here a lot for dinner when my parents weren't as busy as they are now. It is kind of amazing that we didn't run in to each other before this."

Jason shook his head. "My mother worked here as a waitress Maggie, and we've never eaten dinner here as a family before. We live in different worlds."

Maggie reached for his hand. "No, Jason, we don't. We live in the very same world, and we'll be going to the same school together next week. I cannot wait for school to start!"

Jason laughed and relaxed. "Okay, Maggie. Whatever you say. Thank you for dinner. It was really delicious."

Maggie took his other hand and leaned forward, until their foreheads were touching. "The bracelet is beautiful, Jason. I love it." They stood there for a moment, not noticing that Paula was taking pictures from across the room.

Finally, she walked over to them. "Come on, you two, let's go outside and get a few pictures with the sunset and the boats." They followed her outside, still holding hands.

CHAPTER FIFTEEN

Jason turned the pages of the photo album and looked at the pictures from the Yacht Club. It seemed like a lifetime ago.

He had been so excited about the Math and Science school, and they looked so young in the pictures. He looked up at his mother and took a deep breath.

"I guess Maggie graduated from Smith with honors this weekend, Ma. She sent me an invitation, but I emailed our regrets. I wonder if we'll see her this summer."

Paula sat down next to him on the couch. "I don't know, Jason. Are you two still friends?"

Jason half-heartedly turned another page in the album. "I think so. I mean, she said we'd always be friends, no matter what."

There were pages of pictures of Jason with his medals from the Special Olympics in cycling and swimming.

He pointed to one of the pictures in the album. "Remember when we graduated? We flipped a coin to see who would be valedictorian. Maggie won."

Paula laughed. "I didn't know it was a coin toss, Jason. I figured you just let her have the honor."

Jason shook his head and sighed, "Nope, she beat me fair and square, Ma." Jason peeled back the plastic covering on the album page and took one of the pictures out of the album and looked at it closely.

"We all look so happy in this picture, don't we? I think

this is the one that Nikolas took." He handed the photograph to Paula.

She looked at it for a long time and handed it back to him. There weren't any photographs in the rest of the album.

Paula took a deep breath and turned to face Jason. "I'm so proud of you, son. You've worked really hard at college and it would have meant the world to your father to see you graduate. I haven't wanted to bother you with all of the details, but the court case was settled last week. They ruled in our favor, and declared it a wrongful death."

Jason's heart sank, and he started to say something, but Paula held up her hand.

"Please let me finish, Jason. It has been such a long, hard road. I just want to tell you the whole story in one short synopsis."

Jason inhaled sharply, to keep from crying, and held his mother's hand tightly as she continued.

"To make a long story very short, Jason, all of your student loans will be paid in full by the end of the month, and this apartment building will be ours to do as we like with it. One of the tenants on the other side will be moving out, and of course you are welcome to your grandparent's place, but we have a lot of decisions to make. I'm actually thinking about buying a houseboat and renting out all of these units. This building has felt like an obligation for so long, for all of us, but I want to be sure you are okay with it. I cannot manage the live aboard by myself, but I thought you might like to be my partner in it. "

Jason's eyes widened as his mother continued.

"It is a Dutch barge from the 1950s that is in great shape. The engine even sounds like it is in great condition. I'm having it checked out by a diesel mechanic now. Captain

Carter is willing to rent us one of his slips, so we'd be right here in the Harbor. We've had such a run of bad news, Jason that I wanted to wait until she passed all of her tests before I showed her to you. Now that you are graduated, and home again, I feel like a huge weight is off of my shoulders."

Jason was relieved but didn't want to interrupt his mother's story.

It had been a terrible shock when his Pops had been killed, just a week before his high school graduation. He didn't even really remember much about that summer, except that he had pretty much stopped talking to anybody outside of his family, even Maggie. She had called him and left a message after writing him a number of beautiful condolence letters, but he had just not had the heart to reply. They'd had a short phone conversation, and he had probably been rude to her, but he just couldn't seem to get his head above water long enough to think straight. He'd let the garden go, except for a few small flowerpots that Willem and Sophie said they would take care of while he was off at college. He wasn't sure he should go, and leave his family, but they all insisted it was what Michael would have wanted. He applied for and was approved for a sailing scholarship and took out a few loans for the rest of his expenses.

Jason had worked hard in college, finishing at the top of his Engineering class and winning a Regional regatta for the school. He kept to himself, and didn't really have any friends to speak of. The first semester in the dorm, his leg cramps at night got so bad that his roommate moved out, saying that Jason's screams of pain terrified him. Jason requested a single room from the housing committee and ended up with the room to himself for the whole four years. Since he couldn't afford the travel expenses to go home on breaks or during the summers, he worked at a Yacht Club near the college, teaching sailing and first aid courses.

In his sophomore year, Willem passed away from a heart attack. Sophie slipped into a kind of fog, wandering around the apartment, calling Willem's name, sure that he was just about to come back from the grocery store.

Jason took out another student loan and came home from college that summer to help his mother and grandmother. He went to the neuromuscular disease clinic to see Dr. Fishback and his team. They had been able to work with the research hospital where Jason went to college to do the six month checkups, and were pleased that Jason was still active in sailing and doing so well in his studies.

The next semester, Sophie died from complications of pneumonia. Jason withdrew even further after that, but studied hard and finally graduated with honors as an Engineer.

Paula kept in touch with him by email, and they talked once a week, but they were both caught in the riptide, and neither of them was willing to relax and let the tide carry them in to shore.

Now, Jason felt like he had just taken his first real deep breath in years. They weren't going to drown in debt, apparently, and he would have his choice of places to live, with access to the neuromuscular clinic and the chance to help his mother.

Paula continued, "I am so proud of you, Jason. I probably should have included you in some of the details of the court case, but I was so worried that we might not win, and I didn't want to place yet another burden on you. Maggie's father put his whole legal team at my disposal, working for us. They found out that there had been a defective chain plate on the boat, and the mast never should have snapped. The insurance companies tried to say that your father wasn't in good enough shape to sail at that level after breaking his leg in the earlier accident, but all of the doctors testified that he had been medically cleared to race and that he was as fit or maybe even fitter than before. It was awful, Jason. I think Willem and Sophie died from broken hearts over it. I came pretty close to giving up and going under, myself. Your Pops would have wanted us to be strong and continue on, just as he did after losing his parents. Honestly Jason, I feel like we are the luckiest people on earth to have had Michael in our lives, you know?"

Paula started to cry. "Now I think he would want me to realize the dream we always had of retiring and living on the water. There is just so much stuff to deal with though. I want us to decide together how to go forward."

Jason relaxed just a little, and hugged his mother. "That's a lot to process, Ma. Off the top of my head I'd say we should keep our apartment and rent out the other three. That way we won't have to sort through so much stuff. I'd love to live on the water with you, of course, but first, why don't we take the adaptive sculling classes together? I think it would be great to have you in a boat with me. I'm working on some projects, as a continuation of my thesis, to help me with my muscles as they weaken. The devices might actually be best suited to be used in a sculling program before I start to apply them to sailing. Thanks for coming to the physical therapy appointment with me today. I'm so thankful that we signed up for that clinical study with Dr. Fishback."

Paula nodded. "Yes, Jason, we are so lucky, in so many ways. I am so relieved that you are home again. I'll call right now and see if there is still space in the sculling classes." She kissed him on the cheek and got up to make the phone call.

Jason leaned back into the couch cushions and flipped back through the pictures again. He wondered if Maggie would be coming home after college. He needed to at least thank her for persuading her father to take the original case for his Pops. She probably would be going to Medical school in the fall. He guessed she was probably also engaged by now, to one of the Ivy League fraternity boys, but perhaps they could still be friends if he hadn't completely alienated her.

They had talked about going steady in High School, but Jason assumed he'd never be good enough for Maggie's mother's approval, and he had told her that when they'd gone out for a Saturday afternoon sail. It was the only time they'd ever really had a fight.

Maggie had pushed him overboard, and threatened to sail the boat back in without him. "Get over yourself, Jason Visser. I'm tired of you being such a martyr. You are just as good as anybody else."

She'd helped him back on board, of course, and they seemed to be even better friends after that, but Jason wondered now what might have happened if they had gone steady, instead of just being study partners and sailing buddies.

He sighed, and pushed himself up to standing, using the arm of the couch for support. He was always stiff and sore after the physical therapy sessions, but knew he'd feel better by tomorrow morning.

Jason and Paula went down to the sculling center the next day and listened to the presentation about the new program. They were training teams to work together, with an able bodied volunteer partnered with a differently abled athlete.

Jason raised his hand during the question and answer session. "Are any of the participants using assistive devices?"

The presenter nodded. "As long as you have a prescription from a physical or rehabilitative therapist, we're happy to work with your program. We just aren't able to permit them without a prescription, for liability reasons."

Jason leaned over and whispered to his mother "I'm working on a device that may help electrically generate the reflexes in my knees."

Paula nodded. "That sounds kind of scary. I thought electricity and water didn't mix. What do you think, Jason? Should we sign up?"

The presenter was going over the different types of adaptations they had made to the boats for previous participants.

Jason was impressed that they worked with each individual, instead of just having an adaptive boat in a one size fits all configuration. He whispered to Paula, "I think so, Ma. It does sound like fun. We could use some fun."

They listened to the rest of the presentation, signed up for the course, and then walked out onto the dock.

Paula took a deep breath. "I haven't been out on the water since Michael died, and I'm not sure how the first few sessions will go Jason, but I'm willing to try. I think I'm the one who needs you to be my abled assistant."

They laughed together and continued down the walkway to the slip where the Magic Touch was still tied up.

Captain Carter had made sure it was attended to while Jason was away at school.

"Want to go out for a sunset sail, Ma? It is a beautiful evening."

Paula shook her head. "I'm not ready for that yet, Jason. I think starting with the sculling will be a good way to ease back in to being on the water. Thanks for coming to the presentation with me."

Jason put his arm protectively around his mother. He knew that it was because he had grown taller while he was away at college, but she seemed smaller and more fragile than he ever remembered.

He squeezed her shoulders. "It'll be great, Ma. Healing for both of us. Want to have some dinner while we are here? We have lots to celebrate."

Paula stood very still, looking out at the water. She leaned against Jason and took a deep breath. "Sure, son. Let's do that. Let's focus on what we have to celebrate."

They walked back to the club dining room and asked if there was an available table.

The young man at the podium looked around the room doubtfully. "I'm not sure I have anything at the moment. Let me check." He had two menus in his hand, and went toward the back of the dining room.

Paula sighed. "We probably should have made a reservation, Jason."

The young man returned. "You're in luck. Captain Carter would like you to join him at his table by the window. Follow me, please."

Jason and Paula exchanged a look and a smile.

"See Ma, the Magic Touch is still with me."

Jason followed his mother to the large table by the window where Captain Carter was holding court.

Jason extended his hand to his sponsor, who said "Please pardon me for not standing and pulling out your chair Mrs. Visser, these days my arthritis means I'm a captive in this chair." He nodded to Jason. "Congratulations on the degree, young man. What kind of engineering did you study?"

Jason shook his hand firmly. "Biomedical Engineering, sir. Thank you."

They sat down and the servers brought two more place settings.

Jason put his napkin in his lap. "Thank you again for taking such good care of the Magic Touch while I was at school, sir. She looks great! I can't wait to get her out in the water again."

The Captain smiled. "I'm sure she'll be happy to have you back, Jason. Will you be in town for a while? I have a business proposition to discuss with you."

Jason was surprised. "It looks like I'm going to be settling back in here, sir. I'd be happy to meet with you, any time that is convenient for you."

Jason was even more surprised as he listened to his mother, speaking easily and freely. "I need something to look forward to, instead of dwelling in the past," she was saying to Captain Carter "But I don't want to get my hopes up until we get the report back from the diesel mechanic."

Captain Carter smiled and turned to Jason. "Your mother is a very smart woman, and braver than most."

Jason smiled. "Yes, sir. She certainly is. Thank you again for inviting us to dine with you this evening."

The servers came around to see if they wanted dessert or coffee, but they all declined.

Captain Carter said, a little too loudly for Jason's taste, "Put them on my tab. My treat tonight to celebrate my new business associate's graduation!"

Jason turned red with embarrassment as he extended his hand. "Thank you sir, that's very kind. I'll be in touch about meeting with you. I'm awfully tired now, and think we'll head back to the apartment if you don't mind."

Captain Carter shook both of their hands and waved to excuse them from the table. As they were walking out to the car, Paula sighed deeply.

"What a delicious meal that was. It was nice of him to put us on his tab, wasn't it Jason?"

Jason shook his head. "I'm not sure it was all that nice, Ma. I think he wants me to feel obligated to him. I'm curious about what kind of business proposition he has for me, but I'm suspicious as well."

Paula laughed. "Oh Jason, I see so much of your father in you. Keep that stubborn independent streak, son. It becomes you." She slid into the driver's seat of the old rusty station wagon and after a few tries, got it started.

They drove slowly back to the apartment, each lost in their own thoughts.

Jason slept well in his old room, and was looking forward to seeing the Dutch barge his mother had been telling him about, but first he wanted to go up to the roof and see his old garden.

It had been four years since he had climbed those stairs, and he was strangely apprehensive about opening the door at the top of the stairs. He put the key in the lock and pushed open the heavy door. Once it was open, he stood there for a long time, looking at what had once been his business empire.

There was not a single green shoot of anything up here any more. Someone had piled all of the buckets and planters in a corner and covered them with a tarp. It looked like there had been some roof repairs.

Jason closed his eyes and tried to remember what it had looked like with his grandparents out here doing their art projects. Instead, he pictured the first time Maggie had seen the garden.

After a few minutes of reflection, he walked around the perimeter of the roof, leaned on the railing and looked out over the town. It was time to move on from here. It didn't feel like home any more.

He went back down to the apartment to make coffee. While the water was heating up in the coffee machine, he flipped through the mail on the counter.

There was an envelope addressed to the Visser family in Maggie's familiar handwriting. He took the letter opener and carefully slit the envelope open. He unfolded the invitation to her graduation, and a small sheet of paper fell to the floor. He leaned down to pick it up. The coffee machine beeped. He poured himself a cup and put the carafe back on the warming plate. He leaned against the refrigerator and started to read the note.

Dearest Paula,

Thank you for keeping me up to date about Jason. I'm so glad to hear he is doing well and am excited to see you both this summer after I graduate. The news about the barge is so exciting! It has been wonderful to correspond with you during my stay here at Smith. I think I would have been terribly homesick had it not been for your delightful hometown reports. Thank you for the good advice regarding my engagement. I have broken it off. Although it caused a great deal of anguish for all of the parties involved, I know it was the right thing to do. I will be forever grateful for your wise counsel.

Very truly yours,
Maggie

Jason ran his finger sadly over Maggie's signature, trying to conjure her up next to him. He stood there for a long time, reading the letter over and over.

He didn't hear his mother come into the kitchen and nearly spilled what was left of his coffee when she said "Good Morning Jason, thanks for making coffee!"

Paula kissed him on the cheek and turned away from him to get her coffee cup down from the shelf.

Jason reached for the envelope with the invitation and tucked them in his shirt. "You're welcome, Ma. I hope you like your coffee strong. I've gotten used to making it that way in school."

He headed down the hall to his room, his heart pounding in his ears. He opened his desk drawer and put the note and the invitation in there with all of his old notebooks. He wasn't ready to discuss it with his mother yet, and he wanted to read the note again later, when his brain was fully awake.

After taking a shower and getting dressed, Jason read the letter again and wept for a full five minutes with his head on his desk. He pulled himself together as best he could, and went to find his mother.

She was scrambling eggs in the kitchen. "Do you want toast, Jason? I'm just about finished with these eggs."

Jason put his arm around her, trying to keep from crying, and gave her a quick hug. "Sure, Ma. I'll get the toast and the butter. Thanks for making breakfast!"

They stood in the kitchen and ate quickly, just as they had always done.

Jason looked anxiously over at the refrigerator, half expecting Michael to materialize in his usual spot. He thought it might be good for both of them to start a new pattern on the barge. Maybe they shouldn't go slowly after all. It was feeling awfully claustrophobic in the apartment to Jason at the moment. He ran his hand over the clenched muscles in the back of his neck and tried to keep his stomach from churning and gurgling out loud. "Delicious, Ma. Thank you."

Paula smiled wearily. "You're welcome Jason. It is nice to have someone here. I feel like I have just been rattling around here in the apartment, trying to keep myself going. I don't know what I would have done without Maggie and her family, Jason. They have been such a huge help to me through all of this."

Jason felt a wave of guilt wash over him, and his neck muscles spasmed "I'm sorry I couldn't have done more, Ma."

Paula shook her head. "You did the most important thing, Jason. It was such a dream for all of us that you would get to go to Engineering School and..."

The phone rang. Paula picked up the receiver. "Hello, Visser residence, Paula speaking. In an hour? Yes, that would be fine. Thank you for calling."

She hung the phone back up on the wall. "I'd better go take a shower and get dressed. We're getting a tour of the barge in an hour." She gave Jason a quick hug and headed down the hall.

Jason did the breakfast dishes and wiped down the counters. Then he went back into his room and read Maggie's letter to his mother one more time.

He tried to hold back the tears, but they just overcame him. He sobbed at his desk again until he heard his mother coming down the hall. He put the letter back in the desk drawer, and made his bed. He wiped his eyes with the sleeve of his shirt and rubbed his neck again.

He took a small camera out of his backpack and slid it into his pocket. He wanted to document this day.

Paula and Jason drove to the Yacht Club and parked in the visitors' section. Jason was amazed that the old station wagon was still chugging along. It was probably held together with rust and good intentions. He made a mental note to ask his mother when the last time the oil was changed. He wondered what had happened to the old van they had driven to the sailing races.

They walked down to the end of the dock and Paula pointed to the barge at the end of the row.

"There she is, Jason. She's called the Renewal. Apparently a librarian who then lived on her for 20 years originally brought her over here from Amsterdam. I thought it was a clever name. What do you think?"

Jason couldn't think of a reply. The hair on his arms and on the back of his neck was standing up. It was a feeling he could not quite identify, but he thought it was an odd sort of recognition, like meeting an old friend, or a distant relative.

The broker came up the stairs from the boat and welcomed them aboard. "It is nice to meet you, Jason. I've heard so much about you from your mother that I feel like I know you already. Watch your head as you come aboard."

Jason was not prepared for what was below the deck. The entire interior was still the original wood, lovingly polished over the years. It smelled faintly of lemon oil and fish. He remembered the feeling of elegance he had experienced in Captain Carter's yacht salon, all of those years ago. This was different, though. More of a cozy, welcoming elegance.

There was a small functional galley, with a brass sink and hardware. Over the sink was a window that looked out just over the water level. Next to the kitchen was a dinette, with a wooden table and two bench seats. A small hallway was created with closets on either side. The doors slid open effortlessly. Jason was amazed at the craftsmanship of every small detail. At the end of the hallway was a large bed, built into a cabinet. There were porthole windows and reading lamps built into the walls. Jason turned to look at his mother. She was grinning.

"Wait until you see the best part, Jason. Your quarters are at the other end of the barge, under the pilot house."

The broker nodded, and turned around to lead the way.

Jason tried to take it all in. He remembered the camera in his pocket. "Do you mind if I take a few pictures, Ma? This is a lot to process."

Paula laughed. "I took a whole roll of pictures the first time I saw her, Jason. I'll be curious to compare them to your point of view.

Jason took pictures of the galley and the wood-burning stove, with its traditional Dutch tiles. He tried to capture the details of the wood and the brass door pulls and the couch with the bookshelves above it. He slid open the door opposite the galley. It was a fully functioning bathroom with a tub. The hand held showerhead and the sink hardware were all brass as well. Jason slid the door closed and followed the broker on the tour. He laughed out loud when he saw the brass plaque above his quarters. It said "VISSER".

The broker smiled. "It is an amazing coincidence, isn't it? The story goes that the librarian fell in love with the Captain who came over with the boat, he was a fisherman, and I gather that's a Visser in Dutch. She had the plaque made for his quarters and he never returned to the old country. Do you want to go up and see the pilothouse Jason? The mechanic should be here in a few minutes to give you two the run down on the engine and all of the mechanicals. Watch your head as we go up."

Jason climbed the ladder behind the broker.

Paula was already up on the deck. She was leaning on the railing, looking out at the water.

Jason listened as the broker described the original wooden wheel and the brass bell and all of the instruments. Jason took the wheel, felt his neck muscles relax and looked out of the pilothouse windows. This was an amazing opportunity. He swallowed hard. "It's fantastic," he said to the broker. "How long has it been on the market?"

Before he could answer, the mechanic came down the dock. "AHOY there," he yelled, "permission to come aboard?"

The broker went to meet him and Paula came back to join them.

Jason could see that she had been crying.

"Isn't it amazing, Jason? I feel like your father would have loved this boat. It is almost as if he is here with us." She grabbed his hand and squeezed it tightly. "I don't want to make an emotional decision, Jason. Do you think we could really pull this off and live on this boat?"

Jason nodded slowly and whispered to his mother, "Let's see what the mechanic has to say, Ma. Right now I'm thinking we should definitely go for it."

He extended his hand to the mechanic, who wiped his hand on his grease stained coveralls before shaking hands with Jason.

"Nice to meet you, Mr. Visser. I'm Jan DeVries. She's a real beauty, isn't she?"

Jason nodded and followed the mechanic to the engine room.

The engine started with a few puffs of diesel smoke, but it sounded strong, and the mechanic shouted over the engine.

"These motors run forever if they are properly maintained. I've only seen a few over here in this country, but my people spent their whole lives building and working on these barges in Amsterdam. I feel like she's an old friend."

Jason's arms began to prickle again.

The mechanic went through all of the systems with them and gave Jason his card. "I'd be honored to maintain her for you, sir. She's a real treasure. We have a boat yard about 45 minutes from here where we can do whatever she needs. We'll haul her out there and paint the hull for you. It hasn't been done in a few years, but I don't expect any surprises. She's been well maintained."

The mechanic shut down the motor and continued to shout as if it was still running as he stepped back out onto the dock. "Let me know, won't you? I've got to get back to work, now." He was gone before Jason could thank him or ask any more questions.

He put the card in his shirt pocket and turned to the broker. "I think we are very interested in the Renewal. What are the next steps?"

Paula took Jason's hand and squeezed it tightly. "I've already had the offer to purchase papers drawn up, Jason. I just wanted to be sure you were on board."

Jason laughed. "That's a good one, Ma. I'm totally on board."

He reached out to shake hands with the broker again. "Thanks. I think we're ready to proceed."

They closed up the barge's doors and stepped back onto the dock.

The broker walked ahead of them and headed to the Yacht Club's dining room. "Let's go have a celebratory brunch, shall we? I'll explain all of the next steps while we eat."

Jason looked at his mother. She looked relaxed and happy, but he was taken aback by how much she had aged in the last four years while he had been away at school.

The hair on her temples was beginning to gray, and there were lines around her eyes and mouth that made her look so much like Sophie that Jason choked back a sob.

He put his arm around her. "You okay with the Club, two days in a row, Ma?"

She nodded and leaned her head onto his shoulder. "Yes, Jason. I've been sort of a regular here. Maggie and I ate lunch here almost every day when she was home on school breaks. She has been a tremendous help to me, Jason. She is going to be a fine psychiatrist some day."

Jason stopped suddenly, his heart pounding in his ears again. "I'm sorry I wasn't here for you, Ma. I really am."

Paula gently but firmly pushed him forward. "Don't be so hard on yourself, son. We all had our jobs to do, and yours was to get through college. I knew you were here with me in spirit."

They sat down at the table by the window, with a view of the harbor. Jason sighed with nostalgia. It really was such a lovely place to have grown up.

The broker opened his suitcase and pulled out the paperwork. "You'll both have to sign, in the places I've highlighted. That way you will be tenants in common."

Jason looked at his mother, who was starting to sign the paperwork.

She did not meet his gaze, but kept signing. "It will be easier this way Jason, if anything happens to me. The Renewal will simply become yours, isn't that correct?"

The broker nodded.

Jason shifted uneasily in his chair and took a deep breath

when Paula passed the documents over to him.

Once he had signed them, he leaned back in his chair and tried to breathe normally. "How long does the process take?"

The broker slid the documents into his briefcase. "I'll step outside and call the seller. I'm sure she will be amenable to these terms. The barge has been on the market quite awhile, without much interest. Go ahead and order me a bacon cheeseburger, medium well, if I am not back by the time the waiter comes around. I won't be long."

Paula took Jason's hand. "Isn't it exciting?" she said breathlessly, "We'll finally get to realize the dream that Michael and I had. He'd be so proud of you, Jason. He was always so proud of you."

Jason caught his breath, leaned over and kissed her on the cheek. "Thanks, Ma. That means the world to me."

The broker came back. "We're all set! The seller wants to close as soon as possible, so I'll get the papers drawn up. Has the waiter been around yet? I'm starving."

As if on cue, the waiter appeared at their table. He took their order and asked if there would be separate checks.

"Nope, it's all on me today, pal," the broker said cheerfully, "We're celebrating!"

The waiter nodded and sent another server around to fill their water glasses.

They clinked their glasses together and the broker exclaimed "To the Renewal!"

Paula looked at Jason and smiled. "Your grandparents told me stories about the canal boats in Amsterdam when I was growing up, Jason. It always seemed like such freedom, to be able to take your house anywhere you wanted. I think they'd be very proud, too."

Their food arrived, and they chatted about the lovely

weather and the coincidences of the Renewal with the broker.

"I don't believe in coincidences," Jason said firmly. "Sometimes everything just lines up in the right order and you get the opportunity to appreciate it."

The broker shrugged. "Well, whatever you want to call it sure seems like the Renewal has found the right owners. Congratulations!" He raised his water glass again and Jason could almost hear Michael and Willem and Sophie saying "Aye, Aye."

When they were back in the apartment, Jason went to his room and got the envelope out of his desk and sheepishly showed the note to his mother. "I'm sorry I opened it without asking you, Ma. It was addressed to the whole family and I..."

Paula gave him a quick hug. "Don't worry Jason. I'm sure Maggie will fill you in on everything that has been going on when you see her. She told me many things in confidence, and I'm not at liberty to discus them with you, but I feel sure that she still wants to be friends, and she'll tell you all about it when she's ready. I think she is coming home next week, if I am not mistaken." He watched her go down the hall to the bathroom.

Jason repeated his earlier statement, but this time to himself, firmly.

"I don't believe in coincidences, I really don't. Sometimes everything just lines up in the right order and you get the opportunity to appreciate it. Oh, please let it be true for Maggie and me."

CHAPTER SIXTEEN

The closing for the Renewal went off without a hitch and the broker gave each of them a key ring for the boat.

"Here are all of the keys, folks. The owner had two sets already made, so you are all set to go. Don't forget to tell your friends who might be looking to buy or sell a boat about me. Here are a few of my cards, just in case." He shook hands with each of them and closed his briefcase. "A pleasure doing business with you!"

Paula and Jason watched him walk back to the parking lot from the dock. They spent the rest of the afternoon aboard the Renewal. Jason drew a floor plan and Paula took pictures.

"Did you finish that roll of film, Jason? I am going to drop mine off at the camera shop this afternoon."

Jason shook his head. "I've still got a few pictures left to take, Ma. I'll make sure to finish the roll today."

There was a knock at the top of the stairs and someone called out "Permission to come aboard, Vissers?"

Jason stood up too fast and hit his head on the edge of the bookshelf above the couch. "Is that you, Maggie?" He raced to the ladder, filled with hope.

"It is indeed, Jason. Help me with these flowers before I drop everything down the ladder, would you please?"

Jason climbed up and held out his arms. The scent of the flowers almost overpowered him, but he steadied himself and held back his tears.

Maggie handed him the vase of flowers and he caught a glimpse of her silver bracelet. She was still wearing it, just as she had promised. His heart seemed to be doing back flips in his chest.

It seemed like a lifetime ago when he had given it to her. He handed the vase to his mother and reached for Maggie's hand to help her aboard.

She climbed down as gracefully as he could imagine anyone possibly could, and handed Paula a bottle of champagne.

"To christen the Renewal with!"

Paula took the bottle, set it down on the counter and gave Maggie a big hug. "Oh, it is so lovely to see you, Maggie, dear. Welcome to our new place. Make yourself at home. We're just making plans for what to bring and what to leave at the apartment. I'm sorry we don't have anything to offer you yet in the way of a snack or a drink."

Maggie turned and gave Jason a big hug as well. "Welcome back, my friend. I want to hear all about your adventures at engineering school!"

Jason blushed and stammered his reply. "Can you forgive me, Maggie? I'm so sorry I haven't answered any of your letters or calls, I just didn't know what to say."

Maggie waved her hands in the air. "Nope, nothing to forgive, Jason. Your mother has kept me up to date on all of your accomplishments. Grief takes time, a different amount for everybody, and you had a lot of grieving to do. I figured you'd talk to me when you were ready. Now, give me the grand tour of the Renewal. It is absolutely beautiful in here with all of this wood."

She took Jason's arm in hers, and he showed her all of the details that fascinated him about how the barge was constructed. When they were finally up in the pilothouse, and

Paula was below measuring the cabinets in the galley, Maggie leaned her head on Jason's shoulder.

He desperately wanted to kiss her.

"I think this is the most wonderful place in the world, Jason. Standing here, right next to you. I've missed you terribly."

Jason put his arm around her and tried to think of something to say. He felt lightheaded and dizzy, but stronger than he had in years. The confusion was maddening. "Yes" was all he could manage.

That summer, Maggie and Jason were nearly inseparable. They took the Magic Touch out for sunset sails, worked on building a garden on the Renewal's deck and helped Paula clean out Willem and Sophie's apartment to get it ready for renting.

Maggie was studying for her MCAT test, and planned to take it in August. "I'm going to take a year off before I dive into med school," she told them as they hauled yet another box to the local thrift store. "I've been conditionally accepted at a couple of schools back East, but I'm thinking I'd like to stay close to home."

She and Jason were sitting on the curb in front of the apartment, taking a break from the cleaning process.

"Why psychiatry, Maggie? Don't you want to explore the other specialty options before you decide?"

Jason was stretching his hands and wrists, which were becoming progressively weaker.

Maggie shook her head firmly. "I want to make a difference where I can, Jason. Just like you take things apart to figure out how they work and then come up with some brilliant new invention, I want to figure out how our brains drive our behavior and figure out... actually it is all your fault that I got interested in this in the first place!"

Jason pretended to be hurt "My fault? How could I have…"

Maggie laughed. "Don't you remember? You went on and on and ON about Dr. Charcot and his contributions to science, and so I had to read about him and got totally hooked. Honestly Jason, give yourself some credit once in awhile." She punched him lightly on the arm. "Are you ready to go back in? Has the feeling come back in your hands yet?"

Jason shook his head. "Not quite yet, Maggie, a few more minutes of stretching will probably do it. Maybe a kiss will bring the feeling back." As soon as he said it, he regretted it, but she took his hands and kissed them lightly.

"Is that better?"

"Oh, yes, Maggie. Thank you."

She stood up. "Remember when Nikolas brought me here the first time, Jason? It seems like forever ago, and yesterday, all at the same time. I'm kind of fascinated by our perception of time at the moment. How some days just seem to fly by, and others drag on for an eternity. My mother says time will move so much more quickly when I am older, but I just can't fathom that. Time is a constant, isn't it Jason?"

He stretched his hands one more time and shook them out, getting slowly to his feet. "It is a mystery, Maggie. Sometimes it is best to just wonder, and not try to take it all apart. The most important thing I learned in engineering school is how much we don't understand, about everything."

Maggie held out her hand and helped him into the apartment. "Well, one thing I do understand. We've done enough for today. Let's find Paula and make sure she has a nice dinner and takes a break."

They stood in the front entryway, so close to each other

that Jason was sure he could hear both of their hearts racing.

"I want to give you something, Jason." Maggie stepped even closer to him, and kissed him fully on the lips.

He moaned, involuntarily, and pulled her close to him. "Thank you. Everything I've always wanted, Maggie. Thank you for not giving up on me."

"Never, Jason. We'll always be friends, no matter what."

They'd gotten into the habit of eating at the Club on Thursday nights, sitting by the window and watching the sunset, and then walking down the dock to the Renewal. Maggie would visit with them for an hour or so, and then her father would come and pick her up and drive her home on his way back from the office.

"He really doesn't like the fact that I can drive myself wherever I want, you know," she said to Jason, "he refused to buy me a car until I started looking at cheap used models, and then he freaked out about the safety, and got the Volvo for me. I would have been happy with an old VW bug, but he was not having it." She sighed and put her hands behind her head, leaning back to look at the stars from the deck of the Renewal. "I guess I should be very grateful, but I just want to make a choice for myself for once in my life." She sat up straight and took Jason's hand. "What would you think if I went to medical school here in town Jason? They have a great psychiatry department and I'd be close to home. Is that a crazy idea?"

Jason shook his head. "I think you should do what feels right to you, Maggie. We'll be friends no matter what, remember?" He was still reeling from the kiss, and wanted to reinforce the concept in case it had been a daydream.

She grinned at him. "Yes, I do remember. I just don't

want to lose touch with you or Paula ever again and I want to stay close to help... oh here's Papa, I'd better run, Jason!" She jumped up and ran to the dock and hugged her father. "How was your day, Papa?"

He waved to Jason and said, "Give my very best regards to your mother Jason."

Paula came up the stairs. "Thank you, Carl. You've made all of this possible for us and I am forever in your debt. Maggie has been such a big help this week. I don't think I could have managed it without her."

Maggie blew her a kiss. "It is a joy to help, Paula. I'll see you tomorrow, bright and early. Bye, Jason!"

Jason waved from the deck.

It seemed like the perfect summer. Jason made an appointment to meet with Captain Carter the following Monday. All of the pieces seemed to be falling into place. Especially the most important one. Maggie had kissed him!

They were working on the last boxes from Willem and Sophie's apartment a week later when there was a knock on the door.

Paula went to answer it and then came running to find Maggie. "Your father is here. I think you'd better come quickly." She hugged Maggie tightly and then went to find Jason.

He was organizing some of Willem's photography equipment when he heard Maggie scream.

He and Paula ran to the front steps and saw her weeping in her father's arms. "What happened?" Jason started to run toward her.

Mr. Carlson held out his hand. "Give her some time Jason. Bryce has been killed in a plane crash. We're just now trying to get all of the details from the Air Force. We'll keep you informed." He picked up Maggie as if she were a small child and carried her to the car.

Paula put her arm around Jason and they stood on the curb watching the car speed away.

Jason walked slowly, helplessly, back into the apartment and went back to sorting the photographic equipment. He moved mechanically, as if his brain was no longer connected to his arms or legs. He carried the box to their apartment and put it in his bedroom closet.

Paula followed him and sat down on his bed. "Has Maggie talked to you about Bryce, Jason?"

He shook his head, clenching his jaw and grinding his teeth. "I guess I haven't wanted to know, Ma. We've talked about lots of other things, but it just hasn't come up. I guess we'll talk about it now, when she is ready."

Paula patted the bed next to her. "Come sit down, Jason. I think we need to take a break from cleaning and just, I don't know, mourn with Maggie. Regardless of what happened, they've known each other since they were small. It is a tragic loss."

Jason nodded. "Yes, I know it is, Ma. I just don't seem to have much mourning left in me. I'm kind of numb. What do you mean by regardless of what happened?"

Paula took his hand. "I will have to let Maggie tell you about that, when she is ready, Jason. It is not my story to tell."

Over the rest of that week, Jason and Paula finished cleaning out the apartment and arranged to have it painted. They settled themselves on the Renewal, spending more and more time there each day.

That weekend they slept onboard for the first time.

Jason climbed awkwardly into his bunk underneath the

pilothouse, pulled his sleeping bag up over his neck and realized that he was cocooned in the most comforting space he'd ever been in. It smelled faintly of old books and ancient pipe tobacco. He listened to the boats in the marina, creaking and gently rocking on the water, and he fell asleep almost immediately.

The next morning Paula was up making coffee in the tiny galley. "I think that was the best sleep of my life, Jason. I hope you slept well."

Jason stretched and smiled, his neck free from tension for the first time in awhile. "It's amazing, Ma. The world just seems to disappear when we are here. This boat has your magic touch on it."

They stood quietly together in the galley, watching the coffee maker and then took their mugs up on deck. There were four canvas folding chairs arranged in a semicircle in the garden.

Jason had improved on his rooftop garden prototypes so that the boat garden nearly took care of itself. All they had to do was enjoy it. They'd have fresh lettuce and herbs and a few vegetables. He'd put in cheerful marigolds and bright red spicy scented geraniums at Maggie's request.

"She says the fish will be happier with the flowers to look at, Ma."

Paula sipped her coffee. "I think it looks lovely, Jason. Thanks for all of your help this week. I'm glad the painters can get started today. I'm going to head up to the apartment to let them in. Do you want to come?"

Jason held his coffee mug to warm his hands and looked out at the water. "No thanks, Ma. I'm going to enjoy the peace and quiet out here for a little bit."

Paula kissed him on the top of the head. "I'll be back

soon, Jason."

Jason finished his coffee, rinsed out the cup and the coffee maker and thought again about the kiss Maggie had given him. He could do anything, now; it had given him new life. He walked purposefully down to Captain Carter's slip. He rang the small bell and heard a gruff voice inviting him aboard. He went down to the yacht's salon and took a deep breath. It was still as beautiful as he remembered.

Captain Carter was sitting at the head of the table reading the newspaper and drinking a cup of coffee. He looked at Jason over his reading glasses. "How can I help you, Jason?"

Jason fidgeted a bit and said quietly, "I'd like to hear your proposal today, Captain. No time like the present to seize an opportunity, sir."

The Captain put down his paper and took another sip of coffee. "Well put, Jason. I do like your initiative. I'll give you the fifty-cent version and you can think about it until Monday. If it is agreeable to you then we'll sign the papers at the time of our regularly scheduled meeting." He waved to the chairs around the salon table. "Have a seat anywhere you'd like, Jason. You'll excuse me if I don't get up. My arthritis is getting the best of me these days."

Jason slid around on the salon's bench seating and took the seat next to Captain Carter, on his right hand side. Captain Carter laughed. "That's exactly what I was hoping, Jason. I am looking for a new right hand man."

Jason grinned, and felt the hair on the back of his neck stand up. "We're off to a good start then."

Captain Carter leaned back into his chair. "We are, Jason. I am starting a new venture with some partners I have in the pharmaceutical industry. I want to speed up the development of some effective arthritis drugs. It isn't entirely selfish; there is a huge market worldwide for these drugs. I need someone to run the quality control and I think you are just the man for the job. You have a great mind for problem solving Jason, and I think your degree in Bio whatever it is Engineering will look good to the other investors. I need someone to be my eyes and ears around the place."

Jason exhaled slowly. "That's a lot of responsibility, right out of college, sir. I am honored that you thought of me. Where is the company located?"

The Captain smiled. "Right here in town, Jason. We've taken over a warehouse down the street from the University research facilities. If all goes well we'll be partnering with them to do the clinical trials. I understand from your mother that you know a thing or two about clinical trials as well. Don't sell yourself short, young man. I made a boatload of money from your fish poop tomato production ideas. You could have done this job back then and run circles around all of these business school bean counter types."

Jason smiled, warily. It seemed too good to be true. "It sounds like a great opportunity, sir. I'll discuss it with my mother today and meet you back here at our previously scheduled appointment on Monday." He fidgeted, rubbed his knees for a moment, then stood up and shook hands with the Captain and walked back down the dock to the Renewal. Was this an opportunity, or a trap?

Paula arrived a few minutes later.

"Sorry it took me so long, Jason. The station wagon wouldn't start again and I ended up walking. I think we may have to think about retiring the old girl and getting something more reliable. She's had a good long, useful life."

Jason told his mother about the meeting with Captain Carter. She smiled. "Good for you, Jason. I don't imagine he'll be easy to work for, but what a great opportunity. If you have to go into town everyday for work, we will really need to find a dependable car."

"But, Ma. I don't have the strength to drive a car. I tried again at college to take a Driver's Ed class, but I couldn't pass the driving test. I hate being dependent on other people to drive me around." He covered his face with his hands and slumped forward.

She grabbed his wrists and held them tightly. "Don't be so hard on yourself, Jason. We'll figure something out. I can ride a bike around here and so can you. I've been thinking of getting one of those beach cruisers. Oh, I almost forgot. Maggie left a message. She's coming down today around lunchtime, said she's bringing a picnic to share with us here on the Renewal. I took a shower at the apartment and changed clothes. Do you want to have the first shower in the fancy bathroom here on the boat?"

Jason shrugged. "I guess so, Ma. I hope Maggie is doing okay." He got up and hugged his mother. "I'll be ready in a few minutes." As he stood under the shower, Jason felt his neck muscles unclench, and he let himself believe that it might all turn out okay. He could ride his bike to his job on the pirate ship and save the planet.

CHAPTER SEVENTEEN

Maggie set the picnic basket down on the dinette table inside the salon of the Renewal. She hugged Paula and then Jason. "I love this little nook," she said, "it is so cozy."

Jason watched her carefully, trying to get a bearing on her feelings, but she was outwardly calm and organized, as always.

She took out sandwiches and paper plates and napkins with anchors printed on them. There were small plastic containers with sweet pickles and potato salad and a larger container with a green salad.

"I hope this is okay," she said quietly, "I just wanted a chance to talk with both of you. It has been such a crazy week."

Paula hugged her again and sat down on one of the dinette benches. "We brought a large bottle of spring water from the apartment. Jason, would you get it?"

Jason reached under the sink to get the bottle of water and brought three of the pottery mugs from the galley as well.

"Are those the mugs that Sophie made?" Maggie asked, "They are wonderful."

Paula nodded. "She's always with us, Maggie."

Maggie took a bite of her sandwich and set it down on the paper plate. "I haven't been very hungry, but I know I need to eat. What has been going on around here?"

Jason slid in to the booth next to her and told her about his meeting with Captain Carter.

"Oh, that sounds wonderful, Jason. Are you going to accept it?"

Jason shook his head and finished his sandwich. "We'll see Maggie. It does sound too good to be true, actually, but I don't have any other job offers on the table."

Maggie tilted her head thoughtfully and took another small bite of her sandwich. "Could you pass me the water, Jason?" She took a drink and then closed her eyes. "It is so peaceful here on the Renewal. I just love it."

Paula dished out salad for each of them. "It really is, Maggie. We slept better here than I can ever remember. There is just something magical about being rocked to sleep by the water in a good, sound boat."

Maggie took a deep breath. "I guess I should fill you in on what is going on. It has been such an awful time for my family, and I need to get back home for dinner, but I want you both to know how much you mean to me. Paula, I've told you some of the story, but I guess I'll just start from the beginning so Jason can know too." She reached for Jason's hand under the table. "I guess I should have told you from the start, when we first became friends, but there just never seemed to be a good time to bring it up."

Jason squeezed her hand. "We'll be friends, no matter what, Maggie. That's what you've always said."

Maggie nodded and reached out her other hand for Paula. "That's what I believe, Jason. I really hope it is true."

Maggie settled in to her story telling voice. "I have told you that Bryce and I have known each other since we were small. He was Peter's best friend in kindergarten, and I was a year younger."

Jason looked confused, and repeated what she had

just said. "He was Peter's best friend and you were a year younger?

Maggie looked out the window before she continued. "Peter is my older brother, Jason. You'll meet him at the Memorial service if you choose to attend. We were at the park on a Saturday, and the boys were all playing soccer. We were having a picnic with Bryce's family and we were waiting for his father to get there. He had just joined my father's firm and was working on something at the office. It was a lovely spring day, and we had a blanket spread out on the grass. Bryce kicked the ball and Peter ran after it. He ran out into the street and was hit by Bryce's father's car. It was the worst day of my life, Jason. My mother tried to keep me from seeing what had happened, but it is forever etched in my mind. Peter was lying there in the street, there was blood everywhere and Bryce was screaming. The fire department came immediately, and the police, and they took Peter away in an ambulance, and it was awful. Bryce would not stop screaming. He kept insisting that it was his fault, that he had killed his best friend." Maggie took another drink of water and Jason took her hand again.

"He killed his best friend? I don't understand. I mean, I am so sorry, Maggie but this is such a shock. I can't imagine how you get over something like that."

Maggie shook her head. "Thank you, Jason. You don't actually get over it, as it turns out. Peter spent the rest of that year in the hospital. He had a traumatic brain injury and many broken bones. My mother never left the hospital. She worked her shift and then slept in his room. My father went back to work. It was all he knew how to do. Every Sunday after church, I went to visit Peter in the hospital. At the end of that year, we brought Peter home for Christmas. His room was turned into a hospital, essentially, so we could have him at home. He had nurses around the clock. I am ashamed to admit this, but I was really jealous of all of the attention everyone was paying to Peter. I worked harder and harder at my schoolwork, trying to get my parents to at least notice me. My father hired Nikolas to drive me everywhere. His work was getting busier and he couldn't even take me to school or pick me up anymore.

Bryce's parents sent him to a private school and he came to see Peter every weekend and on holidays. He was sure Peter was going to wake up and be his best friend again. He was always kind of mean to me, and I never liked him. It seems so obvious now, looking back, but our families insisted that we try to be good friends, that we'd need to stick together to take care of Peter when we got older. I didn't really believe that Peter was going to get better, not the way that Bryce did."

Maggie took another drink of water. "He seemed to have this weird idea, Bryce did. I know now that it was what they call Magical Thinking, that it would all be all right and he'd be able to fix it. He talked about how they'd become professional soccer players together and be champions of the world. He didn't seem to be able to accept that if Peter were able to breathe on his own again it would be a miracle. Anyway, Peter did get a little bit better, and was able to breathe on his own and get around in a wheelchair.

"He has a kind of calm about him, Jason, I think of him as a saint. Through all of that, he would just smile at us from his bed. He is still that way. He lives in a group home now, and has a device that he can communicate with. He has a very good sense of humor and is always trying to play practical jokes on his staff."

Maggie was quiet for a few moments before she continued. "Over the years, Bryce tried to kill himself a number of times. He said his life wasn't worth anything and he should be sacrificed so that Peter wouldn't have to look at him anymore. He was in therapy and was hospitalized almost every year around the time of the accident. His parents pushed to have the records closed when he was old enough; they claimed he'd been hospitalized for exhaustion.

She looked out of the window again, and Jason almost couldn't hear her, she was speaking so softly.

"He got into the Air Force Academy, and had a really hard time there. Once he came to visit me at Smith and he was just absolutely distraught. He had been drinking and asked me to marry him. He said we were bound together to take care of Peter once our parents couldn't anymore and that we might as well be married to do that. He said he'd kill himself if I refused." Maggie twisted her napkin and looked down at the table.

"I didn't know what else to do, so I accepted. I didn't tell my parents about the circumstances and so they were delighted for us. It was just awful. It felt like a continuation of the camp episode. I wanted to talk with you about it, Jason. I tried, but you had your own grief to deal with. I guess I thought, I don't know what I thought."

Jason felt his face grow hot with shame. He'd let her down so many times.

"So, to make a long story short, I started talking to Paula when I was home on breaks, and it helped me so much. Thank you dear Paula, for all of your wise counsel." She squeezed Paula's hand. "Would you excuse me to the bathroom for a minute?"

Jason stood up and stretched as Maggie made her way

to the bathroom.

He stood there, waiting for Maggie to come back, and thought about what he could have, or should have done. He remembered what his mother had said, that his one job was to get through school and get the Engineering degree. He'd done that, but at the moment it didn't feel like enough. Not nearly enough. He hung his head.

He hugged Maggie when she came back to the table. "I'm sorry I let you down, Maggie. I should have been there for you."

Maggie shook her head firmly. "No, Jason. You didn't let me down. In fact, it actually worked out for the best that you were not involved."

She sat down again at the table and continued. "I took a psychology class in school and we had a section about co-dependency, and Paula and I talked about it a lot over the Christmas break. I felt like I was enabling Bryce's bad behavior, and sacrificing myself in the process. I told him I was going to break off the engagement if he did not stop drinking. He promised to go to Alcoholics Anonymous and get counseling, but he just couldn't do it. He was self-medicating with the alcohol, Jason, and he just couldn't get out of the downward spiral. I know now that AA is not right for everybody, and perhaps if he had counseling where he could be honest about his suicidal thoughts, he could have gotten help. He asked if I was breaking up with him because I loved you. I was able to tell him honestly that I hadn't heard from you at all in years."

Maggie took a deep breath and closed her eyes. She spoke very softly. Jason could hardly hear what she was saying. "He crashed the plane on purpose. He sent me an email that morning, saying he couldn't go on, and that I should take care of Peter." She started to cry. "I'm so angry at him. It was such a selfish thing to do. I'm not sure I can be a psychiatrist, Jason. I feel like I did all the wrong things, and Bryce is gone." She stood up and moved toward Jason.

Jason looked at his mother as he put his arms around Maggie. "I'm so sorry, Maggie. I really am. What can I do to help?" He felt like his legs were going to buckle underneath him. He braced himself against the table and stood there unsteadily for a few minutes while Maggie dried her eyes on the edges of her sweater.

"Just don't stop talking to me, Jason. That's the best thing you can do for me. Always be my friend, no matter what, and don't ever stop talking to me again." She tried to stop crying, but couldn't.

Jason hugged her as tightly as he could.

She looked at Paula once he let her go. "You, either, Paula. Don't ever stop talking to me, promise?"

Paula stood up and hugged Maggie. "We promise, Maggie. We'll always be here for you. When is the service? We'd certainly like to pay our respects, and meet Peter."

Maggie smiled and wiped her eyes. "Thank you, dear Vissers. Peter says he is looking forward to meeting you, too. He insists he needs to look out for his little sister. He's very stubborn that way. Doesn't ever want to be treated as the little brother. I know he will love both of you. I think they are going to have the service next Saturday. They can't have it in the church because of the circumstances, so I'll let you know where it will be. You'll finally get to meet my mother as well as Peter, Jason.

"I should probably get back to the house now, but I feel so much better. It is a huge weight off of my shoulders to be able to tell you all of this and have you still want to be my

197

friend, Jason. Thank you."

She kissed him quickly on the cheek and climbed the ladder out on to the deck. "It's a glorious day out here. I had hardly noticed." She leaned back into the opening. "Things are going to be crazy busy around our house this week. I may be spending a lot of time here on the Renewal, if it is okay with you two, trying to keep myself afloat. See you soon!" She blew kisses to them and was gone.

Jason sat down heavily at the dinette. "Wow. Thanks for being such a good support person for Maggie, Ma. I had no idea any of this was going on while I was away at school. I guess even when you think somebody has the perfect life; you never know what they are dealing with behind the scenes. I think I am going to take the Magic Touch out for a sail and try to begin to sort it out. I hope you don't mind."

Paula shook her head. "She's a remarkable young woman, our Miss Mary Margaret. I am really proud of both of you, and so glad you are going to stay friends. I'm going to go into town and see if I can find a bicycle, Jason. I can keep it right here on the dock, and I won't have to worry about whether the old station wagon will start or not. See you around dinner time?"

Jason took his little boat out to the spot where he remembered throwing the note wrapped around the rock out toward the setting sun. He tried to imagine what Maggie must have felt like when her brother was hit by the car, how strong she was to just keep going through all of that pain and never let on to anybody. He felt terribly selfish now, remembering how angry he had been when he had thrown that rock.

He had been angry because he had wanted to be the first one to kiss her, afraid that their friendship would be ruined by Bryce coming between them. He was ashamed of his inability to respond to her calls and emails when she had needed him most.

She had forgiven him every time, without question or rebuke. The only time she had been angry with him was when he had felt sorry for himself and thought that her mother would not accept him with his limitations.

His mother was right. She was a remarkable young woman and he was lucky to have her as a friend. He rubbed the spot on his cheek where she had kissed him.

The wind picked up, and Jason flew across the water in the Magic Touch. The tears were streaming down his face now, but they were tears of joy. He was determined to make the most of his life going forward. He had an opportunity to work for Captain Carter and help his mother and make things right with Maggie.

By the time he brought the little boat back into the slip he felt like he had been transformed. Somehow, he had left most of his grief out in the waves, where it would sink to the bottom of the ocean and join the remains of the rock and the page from Maggie's letter.

CHAPTER EIGHTEEN

The memorial service for Bryce was held in the auditorium at the private school he had attended on the other side of town.

Paula and Jason had rented a car for the day, as the rusty old station wagon had finally given up the ghost and been towed away to the salvage yard. When they pulled in to the parking lot, Jason took a deep breath.

"I'm really nervous about meeting Maggie's mother, especially under these circumstances. Thanks for helping me pick out this suit, Ma." He fidgeted with his tie. It seemed like it was going to choke him.

Paula put the parking brake on and took the keys out of the ignition. "You look so grown up, Jason. It is hard for me to believe. I wouldn't worry about Maggie's mother. She's actually a really lovely woman. I've only met her a couple of times, but I can certainly see where Maggie gets her strength and character." She gave Jason a quick hug and straightened his tie when they got out of the car.

Jason tried to process this new information. His mother had met Maggie's mother and he never knew anything about it. He must have really been out of touch. He shook his head and started to walk toward the building.

He thought there would have been a big crowd, but when they got inside there were only a few dozen people. He took a program from the usher and sat down with his mother in the second row.

Maggie and her family were seated in the row in front of them. Jason closed his eyes as the music started. It was a short service, with several of Bryce's classmates getting up to give speeches about their memories of Bryce. They read from pieces of paper in front of them, behind dark glasses to hide their red, tear filled eyes.

Jason didn't learn anything more about Bryce than he already knew. He thought perhaps the speakers had a future in politics, and that this was good practice for the many speeches they might give in their future careers. Bryce's father came to the podium and thanked everyone for coming to the service. He invited them to come forward and greet the family, and to join them for a reception after the service at their home.

As Jason and Paula joined the line to pay their respects, he thought about the lack of closure he had experienced after his father and grandparents died. They hadn't had these kinds of gatherings. He guessed that would have been hard for his mother to pull off on her own. He felt another wave of regret wash over him. He shook hands with Bryce's parents, and then with Maggie's father, who patted him on the shoulder.

"Thanks for coming today, Jason. It really means a lot to us. Please do come to the reception. You can follow us to the house."

Jason nodded. "Thank you sir. We'll be there."

He watched as his mother hugged Mr. Carlson and wiped a few tears away. Maggie's father leaned over to whisper something to her that Jason could not hear and she nodded.

She took Jason's hand and they went back to the front row where Maggie and Peter and their mother were sitting. Paula hugged Maggie and shook Peter's hand. She put her arm around Maggie's mother and turned to face Jason. "Grace, this is my son, Jason."

Jason extended his hand and she shook it firmly. He smiled "Very nice to meet you Mrs. Carlson."

She pulled him close to her and gave him a hug. "You are just as handsome as Mary Margaret keeps telling us, Jason. I'm glad to finally meet you. This is my son, Peter."

Jason turned to shake hands with Peter.

Peter's hand trembled as he reached toward Jason. Their eyes met and Jason was suddenly overcome with an idea.

This was not the time or the place for it, but he could not wait to tell Maggie about it. She was holding the back of Peter's wheelchair and smiling at him.

Jason nodded to her. "Good to see you, Maggie."

Peter clapped his hands and Maggie leaned over to whisper in his ear. When she stood up again, Jason could see that tears were running down her cheeks.

He reached into his jacket pocket and pulled out a handkerchief. As he handed it to her, she started to whimper. He wanted to hold her, to protect her from the pain.

Maggie tried to compose herself. "We wanted to let you speak, Peter, but there wasn't a ramp to the stage. I'm so sorry."

Her mother put her arm around her and with the other hand started to push Peter's wheelchair forward. He was typing into his communication device. "All is forgiven! All is forgiven!" Peter's amplified words echoed in the large space. Grace pushed him firmly toward the exit.

Jason jumped out of the way, but caught Peter's eye as he rolled past. He winked at Jason and flashed him the "I Love You" sign. Maggie had showed it to him once, it seemed like a long time ago.

"We'll see you at the reception, Jason. Thanks for coming

to the service." Mrs. Carlson said, as if it were a command, and then a dismissal.

Jason stood with Paula for a few moments and watched the three of them make their way to the exit. He wished he had signed back to Peter. It seemed like a missed opportunity.

Mr. Carlson joined them and they all went out into the sunshine, silently separating to go to their individual cars.

Jason took his mother's hand. "I'd guess we'd better go if we are going to follow them, Ma." He tried to sound brave.

Paula nodded and squeezed his hand. "I'm so glad we have the rental car for today, Jason. It is a real luxury."

They followed the Carlsons' van through the city streets and then up into the foothills. Jason had never been to this neighborhood before, and he gawked out the window at the houses. The properties got larger and more palatial as they climbed. When they finally pulled up in front of the house and got out of the car, Jason turned to look back down.

"It's a whole different world up here, Ma. I had no idea."

Paula joined him on the curb. "I know, Jason. The first time I came up here I thought the same thing. Come on, let's go in and see what we can do to help." She put her arm around Jason and they walked up to the front entrance together. Jason felt like his legs were going to betray him and turn to rubber at any moment.

After chatting with Bryce's parents for a few moments, Jason spent the rest of the evening with Peter. The communication device strapped across the arms of his wheelchair fascinated him. Peter showed him how he used it, and Jason asked lots of questions.

Peter explained that it was very slow, although he could program in things ahead of time. "In person, only a few words."

When Paula came over to tell him it was time to go, Jason straightened up and asked Peter if he could come visit him at the group home sometime.

Peter smiled and tapped on the keyboard. "Yes, anytime." The answer was delivered in a kind of electronic voice synthesizer, different from the amplified voice Jason had heard in the hall at the service. Jason and Peter shook hands. Before he turned to leave, Jason awkwardly signed to Peter. He hoped he got the "I Love You" sign right, and followed it with two fingers, hoping it meant "I Love You, Too." Peter grinned and tapped on his keyboard again. "Nice try!" He winked.

Jason flushed in embarrassment. He vowed to get it right the next time he saw Peter.

On the drive back down the hill, Jason started talking excitedly about his idea. "Ma, how great would it be if we could have a four person team? You and Maggie and me and Peter all rowing in a boat?"

Paula kept her eyes on the road and her hands firmly on the wheel. "Let's talk about it with Maggie once she's had a chance to see us row, Jason. Right now I just want to get this car safely back to the rental agency."

Jason nodded and looked out the window. His mind was racing with ideas. He could test out his knee reflex device on himself, but eventually, he felt sure that he could build a support system that would allow Peter to stand, and maybe even walk to the boat. Once strapped into the boat, Peter and Jason would be like the bionic man on TV, stronger and faster than anyone else on the water. He stopped and took a deep breath. "I think I need to talk to Maggie about the Magical Thinking idea, Ma. I'm letting my imagination run away with me."

Paula pulled in to the rental car agency lot at the Marina.

A young woman came out and recorded the mileage on the car and checked it back in to the fleet. "Do you folks need a ride home?" The agent said cheerfully, writing out a receipt for Paula.

"No thanks," said Jason quickly, "it is a beautiful evening. I think we'll walk. It isn't far to the Renewal."

The rental car agent looked confused. "Do you need to renew the contract? I can extend the..."

Jason and Paula were already outside, walking down toward the dock.

CHAPTER NINETEEN

That fall, Jason and Maggie drove to town together everyday.

Jason would walk to the parking lot of the yacht club after breakfast and coffee with Paula to meet Maggie. He bought the gas for their commute and worked on the Volvo whenever it needed anything.

She had a University parking pass, having secured an internship in one of the research labs on campus.

Jason's office was just a block away from the parking garage, and he could see the building where Maggie worked from the conference room windows.

Maggie had passed the MCAT at the end of the summer and once Jason started telling her about his ideas for a support system that would allow Peter more mobility, she dedicated herself to the idea. She applied for a job with the mobility lab in the rehab department, and they offered her an internship keeping all of the patient data up to date.

After his workday was done, Jason would walk over to Maggie's office. They would eat a quick dinner in the cafeteria and then they often worked late into the night on Jason's prototype of his bionic knee.

On Thursday nights they had dinner with Paula in the yacht club dining room. They would get her caught up on what was going on during the week, and she fretted over how hard they worked.

"I really wish you two would slow down, just a little."

Jason laughed. "We do slow down, Ma. It isn't all work and no play. We have dinner with you every Thursday, and we go to the sculling center with you and Peter on Saturdays, and we take the Magic Touch out on Sunday afternoons after church with the Carlsons. It is a perfectly reasonable schedule for two young professionals."

The sculling center became the real world test facility for their ideas. Maggie picked up Peter from the group home in the family's van, and Jason walked with Paula from the Renewal. Every week they tried something new, and Maggie kept the records in a special notebook that had water resistant paper.

Peter loved being out on the water, but wasn't as interested in rowing as he was in just being in the boat. "You row, I will ride!" He tapped out the message on his new smaller assistive device and grinned.

Maggie shook her head. "You are part of the team, Peter, we need you to row."

Paula was becoming an excellent rower, and often went out two or three days a week in a single scull.

"Paula can do it," Peter typed mischievously on his device, "I will ride."

Maggie rolled her eyes. "Peter, please try to be a good team player." She fastened the straps over Peter's knees and adjusted his feet in the supports. "We thought this might help to strengthen your leg muscles, Peter. The electric motor will do most of the work. All you have to do is ride, today."

Peter smiled and gave her a confident thumbs up.

Maggie made some notes in her notebook, tucked it into her jacket's zippered pocket and got in to her own seat.

Once they settled into a comfortable rhythm, the boat seemed to fly across the water. They passed under the finishing line flags and Jason tapped the stopwatch he had rigged to his wrist. "Fastest time yet, team! I think we've got a winner, here."

They often had a picnic after the sculling sessions were over, and one afternoon late in the season, Peter insisted on seeing the Magic Touch before they went back to the van. Jason had been telling him about his boat on his visits to Peter's home.

Paula and Maggie stood with him on the dock as they watched Jason take the small wooden skiff out.

Peter typed into his device. "Peter will ride."

Maggie patted him on the shoulder. "We're working on that, Peter. Soon you may be able to ride with Jason." She waved to Jason out on the water and turned to give Paula a hug. "I've got to get Peter back to his house now. It's getting awfully windy out here. Tell Jason I'll see him tomorrow."

Paula watched them as they went out to the van, and then turned back to see Jason flying over the waves. She sighed and whispered, "You are so much like your father, Jason. He always loved it when the wind came up like this."

Jason's biggest concern with his new inventions was weight. He fretted about it out loud to his mother when he got back to the Renewal. "I just have to figure out how to make them lighter, Ma. I can't add weight to someone out on the water, especially if they go overboard. It isn't as much of a concern with the sculls, the added pontoons make it extremely difficult to capsize them, but a sailboat is an entirely different proposition." He scribbled in his notebook and looked up at Paula from the dinette. "I wish Pops was here. I know it is silly, but I really need to ask him some questions about racing and boatbuilding."

Paula was stirring soup on the stove. "I know, Jason. I

wish he were here everyday. There are so many things I would love to talk to him about."

Jason got up from the dinette and came over to put his arm around his mother. "I'm sorry, Ma. I know you must miss him. That wasn't very sensitive of me."

Paula shook her head. "We need to talk about how we are feeling, Jason. It doesn't help anybody or change the situation to bury our feelings about him. When I was watching you out there on the Magic Touch, I was just thinking how much you are growing to be like him. He loved days like this."

The wind was howling outside now, and Jason heard something crash onto the deck.

"I think I'd better go secure the garden, Ma. I'll be right back for dinner." Jason went out onto the deck and saw the pot of geraniums that had toppled in the wind. Everything else seemed to be stable and secure the way he had designed it with Maggie. He picked up the pot and lashed it securely to the rest of the garden set up. The rain was just beginning to move in to the harbor, and Jason stood up to watch the line of black clouds rolling in.

The hair on his arms stood up and then the thunder and lightening arrived nearly simultaneously. The flash of light and loud cracking sound made him jump. He hurried back down below to have dinner with his mother.

"That sounded awfully close, Jason. Has the rain started yet?" Paula put the crocks of soup and loaf of bread on the table. Just then the sound of rain pounded the deck above them.

Jason grinned. "I think so, Ma. This looks delicious."

They laughed together and ate their dinner. Jason couldn't imagine a better place to be than on the Renewal in a storm.

Jason dreamt that night of being tossed in the waves by a storm and trying to climb back aboard the Magic Touch, but the bionic knees kept dragging him down under the water and he woke up in a cold sweat, gasping for air.

"I've got it!" he shouted, and hit his head on the low part of the ceiling above his bunk while he was reaching for his notebook. He spent an hour drawing his new prototype and then went up on deck to watch the sunrise.

Paula emerged a few minutes later, with two cups of coffee. "I'm headed out for an early morning row, Jason. It is the most peaceful hour of the day, especially after a storm. How did you sleep?" She handed Jason his mug of coffee.

"Nightmares. Ma. I think I finally figured out how to deal with the quick release system I've been stumped by, though. So all in all it was a productive night. How about you?"

Paula took a long drink of her coffee. "I had another one of those dreams where it seems like Michael is right here, trying to tell me something. I need to get out on the water. That's where I feel like I am closest to him." She went back below the deck and Jason looked out on the water. He couldn't have said it better himself.

Jason went back to his drawings. He was trying to develop a quick release system that would free him from the bionic knee devices as soon as a capsizing was imminent. He had sketched a red line that could be pulled easily by the sailor, but he also wanted to build in a feature that would release automatically and it was proving to be a harder challenge than he had anticipated. Perhaps it was time to go to the library and do some research. He hadn't been to the local library since high school and wondered if his card was still good.

He jumped when Maggie tapped him on the shoulder.

"You scared me, Maggie! Don't sneak up on me like that!"

She just grinned and looked over his shoulder at the drawings. "It looks good, Jason. Want to go for a ride with me? I have something I want to show you."

Jason stretched and finished the last of his coffee. "I haven't even had a shower yet, Maggie. Give me a few minutes to get ready, okay?"

Maggie nodded and went back up the ladder to the deck. She sat in one of the canvas folding chairs and looked out over the water. Jason kissed the back of her neck when he came up on deck and pulled her up out of the chair. She kissed him long and hard and then gasped a little as she stepped back and blushed. She looked around and adjusted her blouse, tucking it in to her skirt. "Well, that was certainly worth waiting for."

"Couldn't have said it better myself, Maggie. Now what is it you want to show me?" Jason was hoping for more kissing, but Maggie took his hand and explained that they needed to go for a drive.

They drove up into the neighborhood where Bryce's family lived. Jason could not help himself and gawked at the houses again. "These places are huge, Maggie. I can't imagine living up here."

She laughed out loud. "Why not, Jason? I have lived here most of my life and I'm not such a terrible person, am I?"

He frowned and kept looking out the window. "No, of course not, I just feel like it is a whole different world up here."

She said quietly, "You are part of this world, too, Jason. I need your help this morning. My mother's garden took an awful beating in that storm last night and she is off at work. My father was going to call in a crew to redo the whole thing, but I want you to look at it and help me figure something out before he has it all redone." Maggie pulled the car into a circular driveway.

Jason saw the van and several other cars on a parking pad off to the side of the main driveway. He stepped out of the car and looked back down the hill.

Maggie's house had an incredible view, and as they walked up to the front door, Jason tried to imagine what Maggie's life had been like up here.

The large front doors opened and Mr. Carlson greeted them warmly. "Thanks for coming, Jason. Maggie tells me you have some great ideas for saving and recycling water in garden systems. We're about to start a major remodeling project, and I'd certainly welcome your input."

Jason shook his hand and followed him through the large entryway. The garden was already visible, and Jason could see that there had been extensive damage. Two large trees were down, one of them on top of a gazebo, and the other across what looked like a lap pool. There were smaller limbs and leaves scattered everywhere in the area.

Maggie took his hand as they followed her father out to the garden. She leaned over and whispered, "That gazebo is where I'm supposed to get married someday." Jason squeezed her hand. His scalp was tingling.

Mr. Carlson opened one of the French doors and stepped out onto a crushed gravel path. "Be careful out here, it is a real mess. The insurance adjusters are due here any minute. We aren't supposed to move anything. I've already taken pictures, but what do you think, Jason?"

Jason shook his head. "It will be an entirely different garden without the big trees for shade, sir. Perhaps we can run some automatic drip irrigation systems and use a fish pond for nutrients."

Maggie clapped her hands. "Exactly what I was thinking. A koi pond would be so beautiful out here."

Jason was stepping carefully over the downed limbs and looking back toward the house from the farthest corner of the garden. It was clear that the layout had been very formal, with the hedges clipped and trimmed into neat shapes. All of the blooming plants that he could see under the storm damage were white. It all seemed very controlled and sterile to him, even with the mess. A pond with brightly colored fish would certainly liven the place up. He shaded his eyes with his hand and looked at the windows on the upper floor of the house and wondered what it looked like from Maggie's room.

The insurance adjusters had arrived, and Mr. Carlson was speaking to them authoritatively. "I have before and after pictures, as well as the formal plans and drawings from when the garden was first installed." They took pictures and wrote on their clipboards.

Maggie took Jason's hand and led him back into the house. "Come on, Jason, I'll show you my little world."

Jason started to take off his shoes, but thought better of it and followed Maggie up the winding staircase. There was a huge chandelier in the center of the space, and it glittered as they made their way to the second story. The hallway had three doors and Maggie opened the middle one.

"Come on in, Jason. It isn't as cozy as the Renewal, but it…"

Jason looked around the immaculately decorated room. It looked like something straight out of *Architectural Digest.* Maggie was opening the French doors out on to a small balcony.

"I have the best view of the garden from here, come on out, Jason." She leaned on the railing and waved her arm across the back yard.

Jason held his breath and then stepped out on the balcony to join her. "Wow, Maggie. This is amazing." He could see Mr. Carlson and the insurance adjusters making their way through the piles of debris. "The damage looks much worse from up here. It is going to be a big job to redo all of that."

Maggie leaned against him and pointed to the biggest tree that was sprawled across the pool. "I saw the lightning hit it, Jason. Can you see the burnt part? There was a really loud noise, and then it fell, almost in slow motion. I saw the whole thing from up here."

They went back down the stairs and Maggie showed Jason the rest of the house, and they finished the tour in the kitchen. It was a starkly modern space, all white and stainless steel. It felt like an operating room to Jason, and he wondered if anybody actually cooked or made coffee in there. It made his skin crawl.

Maggie pointed out of the window over the kitchen sink. "See, Jason, the gazebo is exactly in the center of the line of sight from this window. What do you think of it?"

Jason was a little confused by the question. ""I think the design is very precise, Maggie," he said slowly, "but it is a little too stark for my taste. I'd like to see more color out there if it were my view."

Maggie laughed and hugged him. "Exactly, Jason. This is our chance to get a little more life and color out there!"

Jason shook his head. "It's not my place to say, Maggie. Isn't it what your mother wants in her garden that is the most important?"

Maggie punched him on the arm and stomped her foot.

"Honestly, Jason Visser, you drive me crazy. Aren't you the one who is always telling me I should ask for what I want? Well, I want to bring a lot more color and a lot more life to this place and marry you out in the gazebo and live happily ever after. So THERE!" She stomped out into the back yard, slamming the French door behind her.

Jason looked out of the window and grinned. His arms went up over his head, triumphantly and he did an awkward jig in the sterile kitchen to the beat of his jubilantly pounding heart. "Well, all right then, Miss Mary Margaret," he said softly under his breath, "that sounds like a fine plan to me."

CHAPTER TWENTY

Jason's work was going well, and Captain Carter was pleased. They had their weekly meetings in the yacht's salon where Jason went over the spreadsheets and the data with him.

"We are getting ready to narrow down the compounds for the pipeline, but I want to consider expanding the research to include genomics testing for early stage patients who aren't showing symptoms yet."

Captain Carter shook his head. "You've lost me there, Jason. What are you talking about?"

Jason took out another set of data. "What I am really interested in, sir, is how can we identify who will respond best to these compounds before the disease becomes full blown. If we can identify a marker that will indicate who will not benefit from treatment, we can stratify our trials and..."

Captain Carter put his hand over Jason's. The joints in his fingers were swollen and deformed. "Are you telling me it might be possible to tell if a new medication will work for me or not, before I take it, based on genetic tests? Am I understanding that correctly?"

Jason nodded. "Yes, sir. That is the hope. Not only would it get the most effective treatment to the right patients, but also it would save so much money and suffering in not prescribing medications that we can predict will not be effective. Not to mention the adverse effects, which are a huge cost."

Captain Carter leaned closer to Jason and smiled. "Sign me up. I want to have the tests. How much does it cost?"

Jason shuffled the papers in front of him, not looking directly at the Captain. "What I am proposing is that we set up a new preclinical study, so that we can stratify patients. We can bring the cost of testing down and..."

Captain Carter pounded his fist on the table. "I knew you were the right man for the job, Jason. My own children are very good at spending money, but they haven't proven themselves to be very good at making any. I'm giving you a raise, effective immediately. I'll call a meeting of our Executive Committee and I want you to present this proposal. Give my best to your mother."

Jason knew that this was the signal that their meeting was over. He gathered up his papers and reached out to shake the Captain's hand. "Thank you sir, I will. She's doing well."

As he walked down the dock to the Renewal, he looked out at the water. He thought about the conversation he might have with Michael, and all of the things he wanted to tell him. "Thanks, Pops. Wish you were here." He wasn't sure if he had said it out loud, but he hurried to the Renewal to put the papers away in his new briefcase. Maggie had given it to him for his birthday.

They had settled into a steady rhythm of spending Sunday afternoons working in the Carlson garden and having dinner with her parents. Sometimes Peter joined them as well. Jason had arranged for his old boss at the nursery to oversee the installation of the koi pond, and today was the day they were going to pick out the fish.

Maggie knocked on the side of the ladder of the Renewal. "Afternoon, Vissers! Permission to come aboard?"

Jason was just getting ready to brush his hair in front of

the mirror in the bathroom. He took a deep breath, ran the brush through quickly and slid the door open. "Come on down, Maggie. I'm just about ready."

He saw Paula drying her hands at the sink and then turning to hug Maggie. He blinked back tears, so happy at seeing them together. "Okay, you two, ready to go live up to our name, Ma? Let's go catch some fish!"

Paula giggled and put her arm around Maggie. "He's a clever one, isn't he dear?"

Maggie grinned. "Very clever, Paula. He comes by it honestly. I cannot wait to go pick out these fish, come on let's hit the road!" She climbed up the ladder and Jason winked at his mother.

"After you, ladies."

Paula gave him a quick hug and patted the large camera bag she had over her shoulder.

Maggie drove the trusty Volvo, following Jason's directions to the fish hatchery. At the end of a long gravel road, they pulled up in front of a nondescript warehouse with a rollup door.

A small sign above a doorbell said "Exotic Pond supply. Ring for service." Jason pushed the button firmly and waited. After a long wait, the door began to slowly roll up. Jason stepped back and waited for Maggie's response. He had been here several times before with his boss, but he knew she would, well he thought she would be impressed. He turned to see her reaction. It wasn't what he had expected. His normally chatty, excited Maggie was standing perfectly still, her mouth open.

"Take a picture, Ma," Jason said quietly, "I think we've rendered her speechless."

As the door rolled all the way to the top, the young man

pulling the rope called out "Step inside please, we try to maintain the humidity in here, so I need to lower the door again." He started reversing the rope's direction. The three of them stepped inside.

Maggie still hadn't said anything.

Jason grinned at his mother. "Isn't it amazing?" he said cheerfully, "I just love this place."

Paula was taking pictures of the hundreds of tanks lined up in neat rows, with palm trees in pots between them. It was almost constantly misting from a system of tubes running along the walls and ceiling of the warehouse. The door was completely closed now, and the young man handed each of them a clipboard.

"Take your time making your selections," he said "I'll help you catch them when you are ready."

They walked slowly through the numbered tanks, reading the corresponding descriptions on the clipboards. Jason was watching Maggie carefully. She still hadn't said much, and he tried to catch his mother's eye.

"Aren't they beautiful, Ma? Which ones do you like the best?"

Paula shook her head and reached for her camera. "Honestly, Jason, they are all so beautiful. I'd never be able to choose. How about you, Maggie?"

Maggie was looking at the list and trying to find a tank with a specific number on it. "Oh, Jason, here they are! The fish I showed you in the picture of the catalog. Come look, Paula!" Maggie was leaning over the edge of the tank, and Jason knelt down beside her.

"Are you sure those are the ones you want, Maggie?"

She didn't turn around. "Yes, Jason, I want two of those incredible golden fish. The others can be any of the multi colored, but these two golden fish, Jason, what are you doing?" She turned around to face him and gasped.

He was holding a small ring box and said quietly, "Will you do us the honor of joining our family and becoming a Visser, Maggie? Will you marry me?" His hand shook a little.

Paula was snapping pictures.

Maggie looked at her, and then back at Jason. "Of course, I will, Jason. I thought you'd never ask!"

Jason stood up and slid the ring onto her finger.

Maggie threw her arms around him and kissed him. His heart was winning the Olympic gymnastics competition and he was having a little trouble breathing.

The whole staff of the fish hatchery began to applaud and whistle. The young man who had operated the door came over with a large net.

"I assume these are going to be the first of your fish, then?"

Maggie nodded, and he quickly scooped two of the golden fish out of the tank and into a large plastic bag in a cooler. He shook Jason's hand.

"That was the coolest thing ever to happen here at work, man. Congratulations!"

Jason had his arm around Maggie as he shook hands.

Paula took another picture and then wiped the tears from her eyes. She hugged Maggie and said, "Welcome to the family, Maggie. Hold up the ring for one more quick picture."

Maggie leaned her head on Jason's shoulder and put her hand on his chest. Jason finally exhaled and smiled for the camera.

Once they had made their final selections and the fish

were loaded into the back of the Volvo, Maggie drove carefully home.

"This is making me so nervous, Jason. I can hear the water sloshing around back there."

Paula leaned over the back seat to take a look. "They look fine, Maggie. I'll keep an eye on them for you."

Jason grinned. "The tricky part is going to be releasing them into the new pond. We'll let the plastic bags sit open in the water for a few hours and then you'll get to introduce them to their new home. I'm so glad you liked the place, Maggie."

She smiled, and put on her turn signal, watching her ring catch the light from the dashboard. "Best day I've had since our first date, Jason. Thank you."

When they got to the Carlson's house there were already cars in the driveway. Maggie frowned.

"What is going on, here? I want to park as close to the garden gate as I can." She pulled around the cars and backed up to the gate.

Jason hopped out and opened the gate, waving her through. After she parked the car and got out, Jason opened the back of the Volvo.

"We'll just leave them here for a few minutes, come on Maggie."

When they stepped around the corner, Peter was there with golden balloons tied to the handles of his wheelchair. He reached out to shake Jason's hand and then typed into his device.

"She said YES?" his electronic voice asked.

Jason nodded happily, trying to catch his breath, and Peter clapped his hands.

Maggie showed Peter the ring and hugged him, and then

looked at the group of people on the terrace. They were all holding champagne glasses up toward them. There was a large cake in the center of the table. It said "Congratulations J&M." Maggie and Jason pushed Peter's wheelchair towards the group and she whispered "Best day, ever, Jason Visser. I had no idea."

Jason grinned. "Well, I had a lot of co-conspirators. Your parents and Peter and I discussed it last weekend after dinner, and they gave me permission to ask you. Peter actually took the most convincing. He made me promise to take good care of you and not let you worry too much about him. I'm so happy you said yes, Maggie. Let's go say hello to Nikolas. I'm glad he could make it out here to celebrate with us! I even got your favorite cake. Yellow cake with raspberry filling and chocolate icing!"

After they cut the cake and served the guests, Maggie and Jason ran back to the car and carried the cooler to the edge of the pond. They lifted the plastic bags gently into the pond and untied the tops of the bags. The fish were bumping against the edges of the bags, and Jason made sure they were close together so they wouldn't release themselves too soon. He put the bag with the two golden fish right in the center.

"I hope they will be happy here," said Maggie "They certainly are beautiful Jason. Thanks for making my dream come true."

Jason felt like fireworks were going off in his brain.

Once the guests had departed, Maggie and Jason went out to release the fish into their new home. Peter rolled out to the edge of the pond and clapped his hands as each fish swam free of the plastic bag. He named them, using his electronic voice, as if he were the play-by-play announcer. "Here comes Aegaeon, god of violent sea storms. Next we have Achelous, the Greek river god. This one is Poseidon, and that one is Amphitrite, his sea goddess companion. Oh look, here is Anapos, an up and coming Italian water god. On his way into the pond is the shark sea spirit of Akheilos. Coming in fast is Alpheus, another river god. Last but not least is Brizos. Patron goddess of sailors!" Peter winked at Jason.

Maggie laughed out loud. "That's brilliant Peter. I'll never be able to remember all of their names."

Jason's boss from the nursery helped him pull layers of netting over the pond and secure it to the edges. They tested the motion sensing high velocity sprinklers that would switch on if a large bird or a raccoon tried to raid the pond.

Maggie's parents came over to admire the pond. "We have an engagement gift for the two of you," said Mr. Carlson. "I hope you like it."

Four men carried a huge crate into the back yard and set it next to the pond. They slid a large arched bridge out of one end and placed it over the water, securing it to a foundation that had been put in place earlier.

"It's a wishing bridge," said Mrs. Carlson. "We had your names and the date carved into it to commemorate the occasion. Make the first wish, you two."

Maggie hugged her parents and took Jason's hand. They walked out onto the center of the bridge and looked out over the brightly colored koi swimming around beneath them.

Paula took pictures and they made their wish. "Please let me live long enough to take care of Maggie." Jason couldn't help himself. He probably shouldn't have made such a selfish wish.

"Happily ever after, Jason" whispered Maggie.

CHAPTER TWENTY-ONE

Maggie was accepted to Medical School and took the general curriculum for the first two years. She and Jason still carpooled together to town and worked on his inventions whenever she wasn't studying.

One evening on their way home, Maggie announced that she had decided not to pursue the idea of being a psychiatrist.

"I think I'd like to become a physiatrist, Jason, and work in rehabilitation medicine. The subspecialty of neuromuscular medicine would allow me to have a lab like the one I've been working in. What do you think?"

Jason grinned. "I think you've made up your mind, Maggie, and it sounds terrific. Maybe we can form a company once the exoskeleton and the bionic knees are fully tested and developed, and you can be the Medical Director. Let's see what Ma thinks of it when we take her to dinner tonight."

Paula was waiting for them at their regular table when they arrived at the Club. She stood up to hug each of them and then sat down quickly with a grimace.

"Are you okay, Paula?" Maggie asked, "Did you hurt yourself?"

Paula grimaced. "I slipped on the dock this afternoon and took a tumble. I'm sure I'll be fine. What have you two been up to?"

Maggie started to tell Paula all about her decision to specialize in rehabilitative medicine, but before she could get very far into the story, they heard a loud crash a few tables away.

Captain Carter was lying on the carpet, moaning in pain. The table had toppled over when he had tried to get up, and there was broken china and glass all around him.

"Someone call 911," said Maggie, who was already kneeling next to the Captain, "I think he's broken his hip."

Moments later, the local Fire department and paramedics arrived on the scene. They wheeled Captain Carter out on a stretcher as he waved to the applause of the other diners.

Maggie came back to the table. "He was able to give them the name and phone number of his oldest son, so he'll have family at the hospital."

Paula reached over and squeezed her hand. "You are going to be a great doctor, Maggie. I am so proud of you!"

Jason looked worried. "I think I'd better head over to the hospital after we finish dinner, Ma. I have a bad feeling about this."

Maggie drove Jason to the hospital after calling her parents to let them know what had happened. They parked in the visitor's lot and walked hand in hand to the reception desk.

"Is Captain Carter in a room yet?" Maggie asked the receptionist, "We'd like to wait with his son, if that would be possible."

The receptionist checked her screen. "He's just gone into pre-op. Here is a map to the waiting area for orthopedic surgery."

When they got to the waiting room, they sat down and looked around.

"I don't see Sam, do you?" Maggie whispered to Jason.

"I've never met him Maggie, only talked to him on the phone a couple of times after board meetings. Maybe he is in pre-op with his father." Jason was fidgeting in the waiting room chair, rubbing the back of his neck. "He doesn't seem to appreciate my input at the company. He just wants to know what his shares are valued at..." Jason didn't have a chance to finish his sentence.

Samuel Carter burst into the waiting room and sat down heavily next to Maggie. "Thanks for coming Mary Margaret. I understand you were first on the scene. Dad is pitching quite a fit in there. He is insisting they do some sort of genetic testing as long as they are taking his blood. I don't know what all he is ranting on about, but I am sure they will be glad to get him sedated and into surgery."

Maggie nodded and introduced Samuel to Jason who extended his hand, but Sam didn't shake it.

He nodded curtly and said "Ah, the wunderkind. Dad is convinced that you and your science fiction ideas are going to cure his arthritis. I notice the shares have fallen off a bit this week. What is going on?"

Jason rubbed his neck again. "The whole biotech sector is down this week, especially the pharmaceuticals. We're still ahead of our milestones, and on track with our research, Sam."

Maggie stood up. "We just wanted to lend our support, Samuel. Call the house if there are any updates, won't you?" She pulled Jason to his feet and practically dragged him out of the waiting room and into the elevator. After the doors had closed she threw her arms around him.

"I love you so much, Jason Visser. Sam Carter is the worst. He's got a gambling problem from what I understand, and the Captain has cut him off a couple of times. I just wanted to punch him, he was so rude to you."

Jason hugged her and laughed. "Thanks Maggie. I'm used to it. He's a total jerk on the conference calls, and not just to me. The other investors seem to understand that he is not interested in anything but his own short term gain, but I worry if something happens to the Captain that he will try to take over."

Maggie pulled into the Yacht Club parking lot and turned off the ignition. "Perhaps we need a Plan B, Jason. Let's draw up a business plan for the exoskeleton lab and pitch it to my parents. They'd be glad for you not to be associated with Captain Carter anymore, and seeing Sam's behavior tonight, I have a really bad feeling about where this might be going. I'd better get home and study. See you in the morning!"

Jason climbed out of the car and waited until he saw her pull out of the parking lot and head up the hill for home. He turned and walked slowly to the Renewal, deep in thought. The lights were on in the barge, and Jason knocked lightly before climbing down the ladder. He called out for his mother, so as not to surprise her, but didn't get an immediate answer. He heard the toilet flush in the bathroom, and then the water running in the sink and waited for the door to slide open.

"Hi, Ma. Are you feeling any better after your tumble today?"

Paula hugged him tightly. "I just took some Aleve, Jason. I am sure I will feel better in the morning. How is Captain Carter?"

Jason leaned back against the galley sink. "He's probably in surgery right about now, Ma. His oldest son Sam was there at the hospital and was a complete jerk as usual. He didn't even mention his father's condition, only wanted to know about his stock price. Maggie and I discussed it on the way home; we are going to come up with a Plan B to start the exoskeleton lab before she graduates instead of waiting until after she is a doctor. What would you think, Ma?"

Paula sat down with a pained expression at the dinette. "I think it is a great idea, Jason. Captain Carter has been very generous to us, but if he is out of the picture even for a short while it might get messy with Sam and the Board of Directors. From what you've told me, he could really throw a monkey wrench in the works, couldn't he?"

Jason sat down across from his mother. "It could be a real mess, Ma. We are in early stage, preclinical research and although we are ahead of schedule in terms of our milestones, Sam is pushing for some shortcuts already that some of the research folks feel could be downright dangerous. The board is pretty well divided about Sam, but the Captain just overrules him and gets everybody back on track. I am not sure what the succession plan looks like for Captain Carter's businesses, but if Sam takes over he'll just suck out all of the cash as quickly as he possibly can. He isn't really interested in what the business does, just what it does for him."

Paula laughed. "That seems to be a family trait, Jason. There are many people around the Club who say that Sam is the heir apparent to Captain Carter's slippery behavior, not just his businesses. The other kids seem to have done well for themselves and live back East somewhere. I guess I do need to tell you Jason that our slip rental for the Renewal reverts back to the Harbor if anything happens to the Captain or if he doesn't pay his bills, so we are protected in that regard. Carl made sure to include that in the lease when it was drawn up." She shifted her weight and winced again. "I hope this Aleve kicks in soon, Jason. I could really use a good night's sleep."

Jason smiled. "Yeah, I know the feeling, Ma. If it isn't better by Saturday, maybe Maggie can take a look. She's getting really good at the diagnostic stuff. It is the last weekend for the sculling group practice, and then we'll be back inside the training space on the simulators, so I hope you'll be able to make it. I think I'd better get to bed. Tomorrow is sure to be a busy day at work."

Paula blew him a kiss. "Sweet dreams, son. I think I'll stay up and read for awhile and then turn in."

CHAPTER TWENTY-TWO

Jason waited in the parking lot for Maggie to pick him up the next morning.

"Friday the 13th, let's be careful on the way." He said it under his breath, but Maggie giggled.

"I thought 13 was a lucky number, or you Dutch people didn't believe in the superstition or something. How is Paula this morning?"

Jason shook his head. "She was still sleeping when I left, Maggie. I hope it is just a sprain or something. Maybe you can look at it when we are at sculling practice tomorrow."

She nodded and steered the Volvo out of the parking lot. "Sam called late last night and spoke to my father. I was still up studying. The surgery went well, but the Captain will be in the hospital for a few more days and then in the rehab facility for at least ten days. Sam seems to think he's in charge while his father is recuperating."

Jason didn't respond immediately. He looked out the window and then cleared his throat several times. "We'll see how it goes today. There is a conference call with all of the investors and Board members this morning."

Maggie kissed him quickly before she ran off to class.

Jason sighed and began to walk despondently toward his office. On the one hand, he felt like the luckiest guy in the world. He and Maggie were planning to get married after she graduated from Med School, and they were well on their way to forming their own start up company with his exoskeleton ideas. He had hoped he would be able to stay in his current job until the company went public, or was acquired by a larger pharmaceutical company, but he felt like the sword of Damocles was hanging over his head. He wished he could ignore the feeling that it was all about to come crashing down around him. He took a deep breath and walked into the building.

The first part of the morning went entirely as scheduled. Jason read through the reports in his email and assembled his presentation for the conference call. He looked out of the window and hoped Maggie and his mother would not be disappointed in what he was about to do. He pushed himself up from his desk and walked slowly down to the rest room at the end of the hall. As he was washing his hands, he looked at himself in the mirror. He wished Michael could give him some fatherly advice. He splashed some water on his face and dried himself off.

"Wish me luck, Pops!" he said in a whisper.

When it was time for the conference call, Jason dialed in to the number and pressed the button to enable the "speaker" mode and set the handset back in to the cradle. He logged in to the presentation screen and waited for the call to begin.

There were the usual announcements by the Board members and it was determined that everyone was present and accounted for.

Sam announced his presence and called the meeting to order.

Jason looked at the pictures on his desk of the Magic Touch, and the engagement picture with Maggie, and the family photos that Paula had put into a frame for him. He started to doodle in his notebook. He muted his phone and began to take long deep breaths. He squared his shoulders and sat up straight in his chair.

Sam was going off on a tangent about stock prices and Jason smiled. Just as he had thought, the Board members began to heatedly debate the timeline that Sam was bringing in to question. Then something happened that Jason had not foreseen.

Sam announced that he had brought a special guest to the meeting, and introduced one of his fraternity brothers who had a PhD in Chemistry and was interested in joining their team.

"As you are all well aware, Jason has an engineering degree, but is not well versed in Medicinal Chemistry. Joe is well respected by the regulatory agencies we will be dealing with as we move forward and I'd like to ask the Board for a vote of confidence in this new hire. I discussed it with my father last night in the hospital and he has put his full confidence in me and my decision to move in this direction. Any comments before we take a vote?"

Jason pushed the button to unmute his phone. "I'd like to comment, Sam. I have nothing but the highest regard for Joe, and think he would be terrific addition to the team. At this time I would like to tender my resignation and ask the Board to accept it, effective immediately. I have loaded all of the documents associated with this week's presentation to the shared drive, and will of course be available to discuss any of the details with Joe during the transition. I have prepared a statement for the press release, and am moving on to focus on my own research. It has been a pleasure and an honor to work with you. Thank you." Jason's hand shook violently as he pressed the mute button again. He loosened his tie and wiped his forehead with it. He was breathing so fast he was afraid he might hyperventilate.

A heated argument ensued among the Board members as Jason began to clear out his desk. He waited until he heard the Board members vote on his resignation, which passed by only the narrowest of margins, and then he hung up the phone. He was gasping for air and reached for the inhaler in his pocket.

After removing the keys to the building from his key ring and leaving them in the middle of the desk, he carried his briefcase and his box of pictures and walked slowly out into the real world. He felt like he was floating, and that he might not be able to see clearly through the tears in his eyes, but he walked purposefully toward the Medical School building. He put the box of momentos from his desk in the trunk of the Volvo and waited for Maggie to get out of class.

She threw her arms around him. "Jason! How did it go?"

Jason grinned. "Better than we could have imagined, Maggie. Sam brought in his fraternity brother to try and force me out because I didn't have a PhD in Chemistry, and I tendered my resignation. The Board accepted it. I'm sure Sam feels like he's won, but I am so relieved to be out of there. I'm not a quitter Maggie, but..."

Maggie hugged him tightly. "Oh, Jason, I am so proud of you. It couldn't have worked out any better, could it? I mean, I guess it would have been better if you could have discussed it with the Captain ahead of time, but this way it looks like Sam forced you out and now we can move forward with the new venture. I am so happy to have it all out in the open now. Let's go have lunch to celebrate!"

Jason smiled. "Actually Maggie, I have had several conversations over the last few months with the Captain about bringing in a PhD with regulatory experience to lead the team. Joe was on my short list of candidates to recommend.

Sam actually picked the best man for the job without even knowing it. If Joe is willing to work with the Captain and Sam and get this all pushed through for a fast track acceptance, all power to him. I hope he can make it work, Maggie. It would be the highest possible outcome for all involved. I am starving, let's go get some lunch!"

As they ate their sandwiches in the cafeteria, Jason felt himself returning to a more normal state. His hands stopped shaking so violently, his breathing slowed back to its usual rate. He looked at Maggie. How had he gotten so lucky?

The next day was the last sculling session for the season. Once they had returned the boat to the storage shed, Maggie and Jason joined the rest of the group for a picnic.

Paula was pushing Peter toward the tables in the shade, and Jason saw that they were talking to a tall, thin man in a shirt and tie. Paula shaded her eyes and pointed to Jason. As they got closer, the tall man came forward to meet them and extended his hand to Jason.

"Good afternoon Mr. Visser. I am very interested to meet you. My name is Ewan Fletcher."

Jason shook his hand and laughed. "Pleased to meet you as well, sir. Please call me Jason. My father, Mr. Visser, is no longer with us."

The tall man looked stricken. "Oh, my deepest apologies and condolences, Jason. I guess I haven't gotten off to a very good start. I'm not good at these social gatherings. You could call me Ewan, if you like." He twisted his tie in his hands and then untwisted it again. "I came here to talk to the Director of the sculling program about my assistive devices, and she recommended that I speak to you. Could I join your group for the picnic and talk to you about them?" This time he rolled his tie all the way up to the top and then back down again as he was waiting for Jason's reply.

"Of course Ewan, you are welcome to join us. I am very interested to hear about your devices."

Ewan walked quickly back to Paula and Peter and sat down at the picnic table with them.

Jason and Maggie joined them a few minutes later after carrying the cooler from the back of the van to the table. They unloaded a large bowl of fruit salad and set the table with brightly colored dishes and cups.

Maggie attached a tray to Peter's wheelchair and poured him a glass of lemonade from the large thermos.

Paula stood up and rubbed her leg, trying to massage some feeling of normalcy back into it. "I think being out in the boat was just what my leg needed. I am feeling so much better today. Jason, How about if you and I go and get the grilled items for the table. Ewan, would you like a cheeseburger or some grilled chicken?"

Ewan rolled his tie up and down several more times. "A cheeseburger please. Just the meat patty, cooked well, with cheese and mayonnaise and nothing else on the bun. Thank you."

Paula nodded and took everybody else's order.

As they were walking toward the grill, Paula said quietly, "How did it go yesterday, Jason? You haven't said anything about the Board meeting."

Jason took her hand. "I'm sorry Ma, I got in late and you were already asleep. It actually went better than expected. Sam made a play to force me out and I resigned and the Board accepted my resignation. Captain Carter and I had already talked about the need for someone with a PhD in Chemistry to lead the team forward, so it's all good. Maggie and I stayed up late writing our business plan for the startup and we're going to start looking for office space this week. I've been saving most of my salary in order to have a cushion, so I think we'll be okay. We can talk more about it tonight, okay?"

Paula squeezed his hand. "Whenever you want to talk about it, Jason. I just want you to know how proud I am of you."

They had arrived at the end of the line for the grilled items provided by the Club. Paula took a serving tray and assembled Ewan's cheeseburger the way he had specified. Then she added three grilled chicken pieces and another cheeseburger with everything on it for Peter.

As they ate their food, they listened to Ewan talk about his devices. He had eaten his cheeseburger in several large bites and washed it down with a bottle of water before anyone else had even started eating.

"I've always been fascinated by radio controlled trains and planes. I built a lot of them growing up. I figured out ways to make the motors smaller and lighter and then when I went off to University, I studied electrical engineering. I got a Master's degree and then a PhD and came over here to the States to work for a group here at the University who has funding from the Defense department. We have some exoskeleton prototypes and now we are looking for pilots. I have my own assistive devices that I am working on, outside of the group and Mary Margaret said I should come to this adaptive sculling event today, so that's how I ended up here." He stopped abruptly. "Am I talking too much, or going too fast? I never know how to manage that." He rolled his tie up and down a few times.

Jason swallowed his mouthful of fruit salad and said, "That's fascinating, Ewan. We are just about to start work on an exoskeleton project ourselves. Tell us more about the assistive devices, though."

Ewan nodded. "When Mary Margaret's class came in to view our lab, she was very interested in my work with decoding the neural network signals. Essentially what we are trying to do is to program an exoskeleton to recognize computer commands as if they were coming from the pilot's brain. Once we get the basic movements programmed in, it is a matter of learning the individual pilot's mannerisms. Their preferred gait, for instance. At this point, it is a huge puzzle to work out how we can help the physiatrists program in a patient's rehab needs. Each neuromuscular disease patient has a different level of processing dysfunction and unless we know what isn't working, we can't assist them very well."

Ewan pointed to Peter's communication device. "I've been working on something like that, for a long time now. I sometimes get very overwhelmed in social situations, and I wanted to have a device that would help with auditory overstimulation. I thought I might be able to make a device that combines the best parts of noise cancelling headphones and speech translators, so that I would be able to have a small screen that would display what someone is saying and filter out all of the other noise. It works great on the telephone, and now I am testing it out in the field." He pulled a device out of his pocket that looked like a calculator. He extended two small feet out of one side of it and propped it up in front of him on the table. "Go ahead and say something, Jason."

Jason began to describe his own bionic knee project, and Ewan showed him the small screen on the device.

"This helps me pinpoint the range of frequency of your voice, Jason. Then I can cancel out some of the competing signals, and hopefully hear you more clearly. Does that make sense to you?" Ewan put in some ear buds that were attached to the small device and nodded at Jason again. "Tell me more about these knees, Jason. I think we could work together and help the knees get the signals from your brain and give productive feedback. The data could be downloaded and shared with a physiatrist to speed rehab. Do you mind if I record what you are saying, Jason? Sometimes I have to play it back later to fully process it."

Jason shook his head. "That's amazing, Ewan. It is as if we have been working on the same problems in parallel, from different points of view. I am so glad you came out here today. It is fine to record the conversation. I'd be very curious to discuss our work further with you and see what you think."

Ewan grinned. "That's it exactly, Jason. I am trying to see what someone else is thinking! It gets all jumbled up in the auditory channel and I have to sort it out visually. Thank you for clarifying that for me."

Paula and Maggie started to collect the remains of the picnic and clean up.

Peter typed into his device "Cake for dessert?" and Maggie sighed, annoyed with herself for not being well organized enough to remember dessert.

"Thank you, Peter, I almost forgot. I think my brain is broken lately. The cake is in the refrigerator inside the sculling center. Let's go get it!" She took the tray off of Peter's wheelchair and laid it on the table. "We'll be right back!" she called over her shoulder as she pushed Peter toward the building.

Paula waved and continued to clean up around Ewan and Jason as they huddled together to discuss their ideas.

Jason described his attempts to make his knees respond to

stimuli and Ewan nodded thoughtfully.

"It seems to me that I ought to be able to retrain the nerve pathways to produce the response that the nerves would have done without the damage from the neuromuscular disease. I am trying to create the same reflex the nerves were designed to produce. I guess I think of the nervous system as having its own intelligence and an ability to learn, separate from the brain."

Ewan was quiet for a moment. Jason thought he could almost hear the processing wheels turning in his brain. "Yes, Jason. I believe that, too. In fact, there are some neuroscientists in our group who have demonstrated that the spinal cord has its own learning curve. They are working on the understanding of nerve regeneration after spinal cord injury by using functional electrical stimulation. Your work is very similar. I wonder if you would like to meet some of them."

Jason thought Ewan's manner of speech was rather odd. It was almost as if he was talking to himself, rather than asking Jason a question. Before Jason could respond that he would very much be interested in meeting the members of Ewan's group, Peter and Maggie returned with the cake.

Ewan declined the offer of cake and packed up his listening device, as he called it, and stood awkwardly on one foot for a moment before saying "Well, I'll be off then, see you again soon, I hope." He walked off across the grass in long, purposeful strides.

Jason shook his head. "That was amazing, listening to Ewan. How did you ever connect with him Maggie?"

Maggie finished her cake and helped Peter get cleaned up and then said quietly, "I'm always curious, Jason. Our professor takes us on tours of the research groups to try and help us understand the difference between working as a clinician and a researcher, and I found Ewan's group to be particularly interesting. We can talk more about it tonight. I think we'd better get Peter back home now, it is almost time for his meds." She was wiping Peter's hands with a warm washcloth as she was speaking. She handed him a towel to dry his hands and replaced the washcloth in a Ziploc bag. "Did he tell you the story about his parents, Jason? How he got interested in speech and language in the first place?"

Jason shook his head. "I'm afraid we were discussing wiring diagrams and the process of generating nerve impulses, Maggie. Maybe you can share the story with me later. You have the magical storytelling gift."

Paula and Jason waved to Peter and Maggie as they pulled away in the van, and then walked to the Renewal.

Jason stopped several times to rest his knees and then said quietly, "I think meeting Ewan is some kind of turning point, Ma. What do you think?"

Paula looked out at the water and then turned toward Jason. "To be honest, it feels the same way it did when I first saw the Renewal. Some things just seem like they fall in to place at exactly the right time. Ewan told me he is going to need a place to rent, and I can't think of a better tenant for Willem and Sophie's apartment, can you?"

CHAPTER TWENTY-THREE

Maggie pulled in to the parking lot of the Club and started to walk down the dock to the Renewal. She noticed some activity on Captain Carter's boat and slowed her pace to get a closer look.

There were three or four men with clipboards, and one of them had a camera. Just as she was about to pass the boat, she heard Sam's voice from below deck, "Let's get this over with, I need to get back to the hospital."

She ran the rest of the way to the Renewal, not wanting to hear any more. After knocking and asking for permission to board, as she always did, Maggie quickly climbed down the ladder and joined Paula and Jason at the dinette table.

"Hello, dear Vissers, how are you this fine evening? I am sorry it took me so long. After I got Peter back home, I stopped in at the rehab facility to see Captain Carter. He is not doing as well as they had hoped and is pretty heavily medicated. I didn't get a chance to talk with him, just the nursing staff. Wasn't that a lovely picnic today?"

Paula got up from the table and offered Maggie and Jason some tea. "I'm going to make myself some and go up and sit on the deck. Do you want to join me?"

Maggie looked at Jason and shook her head. "Why don't we just stay down here and I'll tell you both the back story of Ewan. We can go up a little later, if that is alright with you two."

Paula shrugged and turned away from them to make the tea.

Maggie squeezed Jason's hand under the table and leaned her head on his shoulder.

He kissed the top of her head. "Whatever you'd like, Maggie. I am interested in hearing the story about Ewan. He seems like a really interesting guy."

Once they had their tea and Paula had joined them at the dinette table, Maggie started her story.

"I first met Ewan on one of our lab tours with class, I think I told you that part already. Our professor is very keen on the neural prosthesis group and I wanted to ask some questions about Peter's augmentative communication device. It doesn't seem like it is working very well for him, and I wondered whether there was anything new available that we could test. The Director of the lab told me that Ewan was really the expert in the field and perhaps we could all have lunch together after the class tour was over. I thought it was kind of odd that the Director seemed so protective of Ewan and didn't seem to want me to talk with him one to one. When we went to lunch though, the Director explained to me that Ewan needed some time to get used to the frequency of my voice and did I mind if the conversation was recorded."

Maggie took a sip of her tea and continued, "This is delicious, Paula. Thank you so much. Anyway, all of this mystery made me even more curious about Ewan. I agreed to have the conversation recorded and the Director explained that in a crowded situation like the cafeteria it was very difficult for Ewan to process what I was saying, but that he had been working on a device to help with that. I think that is what he brought to the picnic today. He probably thought it was going to be a similar situation to the med school cafeteria. Once he was able to focus in on the frequency of my voice and tune out some of the other ambient noise, he told me that his mother became deaf in a workplace accident when he was just a year old. His father left shortly after that, and Ewan had to learn to communicate with his mother visually. She still tried to speak with him, but the quality of her voice deteriorated without the feedback loop of hearing herself and they developed their own sort of sign language. He says it is particularly difficult for him to process female voices and so he came up with the idea of his device."

Paula shook her head. "It really makes me so grateful, when I hear these stories of people trying to learn to communicate, that we can just have this conversation so easily. I've always sort of taken it for granted, I guess. Even though I was very shy, it was hearing Michael's stories of the adventures we'd have at sea that first made me fall in love with him. It must be so difficult to suddenly lose your hearing and be left alone with a small child." She took another sip of her tea.

Maggie stood up and took her mug over to the sink and rinsed it out. "Let's go up on deck and enjoy the sunset while I finish the story, shall we?" She climbed the ladder first and looked down the dock before Jason and Paula came up. She saw Sam and the group of men walking quickly away from Captain Carter's boat. She sighed with relief and noted the time on her watch. "Come on up, Vissers, it is a beautiful evening!"

The three of them sat in the deck chairs and watched the sun go down while Maggie's story unfolded. The water was lapping at the boat and the seagulls were diving and chattering in the light breeze.

"Ewan has been staying with the Director of the lab he is

working in, I believe there is an apartment above his garage or some such arrangement, but he will have to go back to England at the end of the month to renew his visa. He very much wants to rent his own place, and stay here in America. I think the neural prosthesis lab has funding to keep him on as a part time consultant, but in order to renew his visa he has to have more work than that. I don't know all of the details, but we could certainly contact an immigration lawyer to get that all sorted out for him. He has some kind of income from patents he holds in Europe, but I don't know the details of that, either. Anyway, I move to write Ewan into our business plan for the exoskeleton start up. All in favor?"

Jason and Paula raised their mugs toward the sunset. "Aye, Aye."

Maggie looked at her watch. "I'd better go home and get to my studies. Would you mind walking me to the car?"

Paula and Jason walked with Maggie to her car and waved as she drove away. As they made their way back to the Renewal, Jason slipped his arm through his mother's.

"We really are so lucky, aren't we, Ma? Ewan's story has me thinking of all of the ways that people manage to cope with whatever their situation is. We haven't had to be nearly as flexible as someone like Ewan. I mean, I guess some people would not want to be in my position, what with the neuromuscular disease and all, but I think it has made me a better, stronger person. Does that make sense?"

Paula nodded. "It does, Jason. I think the way a person responds to challenges, however big or small, really is the measure of their character." She stopped as they passed Captain Carter's boat. "I do hope the Captain is going to be all right. Do you think we should go and visit him at the rehab hospital? From what Maggie said it might be a few days before he is comfortable enough to have visitors. Maybe we could at least drop in for a short visit."

Jason sighed. "I think that is a great idea, Ma. I don't know how I feel about the Captain anymore. I am grateful for all of the sponsorship and the opportunity to work for him, but I know the biggest lesson is that I don't want to put profit over people. If we do start this company, I don't want the people I work with to worry everyday that they are about to lose their job or not be able to pay their rent. Especially not if I am pulling all of the cash out of the company at any moment. I guess having a mentor who inadvertently teaches you what you don't want to do and how you won't behave is really valuable. It is confusing, though. There is a part of me that thinks he really does care about people, he just doesn't know how to express it."

Paula laughed. "You get the wishful thinking from your parents, Jason. We always wanted to see the best in everybody, even when it was hard to find. I'm grateful for Captain Carter and the lessons we've all learned from him." She stopped to look at the Renewal before they climbed aboard. "I hope we have the chance to tell him that when we go see him tomorrow. I'm going to read for awhile and then call it a night."

As it turned out, they didn't get the chance to tell the Captain anything.

Maggie broke the news to them the next morning. "He threw a blood clot and died late last night. Sam called the house with the news. I imagine there will be some changes here in the Renewal's neighborhood once the estate is settled. It is hard to believe he is gone." Maggie shook her head and hugged Jason tightly. "It sounds like a strange thing to say, but I am so glad you got out of the arthritis drug discovery company before he died, Jason. It is going to be a real mess once Sam starts getting some actual power." She turned and threw her arms around Paula. "How is your leg doing? Is the bruising better?"

Paula nodded and patted her hip. "I'm very fortunate that I did not break my hip. I'll have to be more careful. You two have a good day, and I'll see you around dinnertime. Please let me know when the services have been scheduled for Captain Carter."

Paula waved to them as they headed down the dock toward the parking lot. As soon as they were out of sight she walked quickly to the sculling center and took her boat out for a long workout. By the time she got back to the dock she thought she had cried all of her tears for the Captain, but walking back to the Renewal she saw a group of people boarding his boat, and the tears began to flow again. She patted the dinette table once she was below the deck and whispered, "We may have to try out that diesel motor and find a new neighborhood, dear little boat, and at least the Captain was always a quiet neighbor."

While Maggie was in class, Jason spent every day in the University library. He searched for commercial real estate listings in the local paper and read as much as he could about business plans and start-ups and who was doing what in the bioengineering world. He made lists of all of the projects he could find involving exoskeletons and where their funding was coming from. Then he started reading about Ewan and his list of patents and publications. When they had dinner with Paula that Thursday night, Jason presented his findings. "You really found the perfect person for us to work with Maggie. I am absolutely convinced that Ewan is the key to our success as a team."

Maggie nodded absently. "I'm sorry Jason. I'm not very focused tonight. What did you say about Ewan? I was just thinking about Sam deciding not to have services for his father. It seems so odd, doesn't it?"

Jason repeated himself, slowly, and Maggie laughed. "Oh Jason, you are so patient with me. I couldn't possibly love anybody more than I love you!" She took his hand and squeezed it tightly, drawing him in close to her for a kiss. "Do you have a plan for recruiting Ewan?"

Paula listened as Maggie and Jason brainstormed about how to get Ewan to join them in the exoskeleton startup.

When dessert was offered and coffee was served, she said quietly, "Have you asked Ewan what he wants to do? From what I understand, he has certain requirements for his visa to be granted and he seems to have a very clear vision of how to get his ideas patented and into production. He doesn't seem like the kind of guy who would respond to a recruitment campaign." She put her coffee cup down carefully and reached out for Jason and Maggie's hands. "You may be overthinking this."

Maggie laughed. "Well of course we are overthinking it, that is what we do, isn't it Jason? I'm sure you are right Paula. Perhaps we should invite Ewan to see the apartment and ask him if he would be comfortable living there before we assume it will be what he wants. Then we can show him our plans and ask him if he'd like to join us. That's brilliant, actually. Thanks for the wise advice." She got up and went around the table to hug Paula. "I'd better get back to my studies, Vissers. Big day tomorrow with lots of exams." She kissed Paula on the cheek as Jason got up slowly from his chair.

*   *   *

They arranged to meet Ewan on Saturday morning at the apartment. He was already there when they arrived, pacing back and forth in front of the building.

He jumped, startled, when Maggie called his name.

They all went up the steps together and Paula unlocked the front door. Ewan followed them around the apartment as Paula described the various rooms.

He kept his hands in his pockets and when they had finished the tour, he took a notebook out of one and a mechanical pencil out of the other. He quickly sketched the rooms and their dimensions.

"Would you like to see the roof, Ewan? Access to the roof is part of the rental of this apartment." Paula took the keys off of the top of the refrigerator.

Ewan looked nervous. "Why would I want access to the roof, Mrs. Visser? Would I be expected to keep it in good repair?"

Paula shook her head. "No, Ewan, we always had a garden up there, and my parents used it as sort of an outdoor art studio. It has a great view of the neighborhood."

Ewan nodded and said quietly, "Lead on, then. To the roof!"

As they stepped out onto the roof, Ewan began writing quickly in his notebook. He paced off the area and drew the dimensions.

"What do you think, Ewan?" said Jason slowly, "Isn't it fantastic up here?"

Ewan hesitated for a moment. He took a deep breath. "I'll finally have a place to set up my telescope. I haven't brought it over from England yet, but this would be ideal. Who else has access to the roof?"

Jason frowned. "Just us, Ewan. We haven't had any issues up here. What do you think of the apartment? Would it suit you?"

Ewan paced back and forth on the roof. Jason thought maybe he was checking his measurements to calculate the square footage of the space.

He wished he could stride that effortlessly. "Ewan, would you like to go back down to the apartment to discuss it?"

Ewan kept pacing, seeming not to hear Jason's question. Suddenly he stopped at the railing and looked out over the neighborhood. He stood there for a long time. Jason looked nervously at Paula and Maggie.

When Ewan turned around, he had a big grin on his face. "Yes, let's go and discuss. Lead the way, Jason!"

Paula had decided to leave the kitchen table in the apartment and they all sat down around it.

Jason stroked the edge of the table as if he could conjure up his grandparents and Michael's ghost by doing so. "We have had many a family meeting around this table, Ewan. We're pleased to have you join us here."

Ewan nodded and began to describe the drawings he had made. "This apartment is way too big for me, just one person. What would you think of making this the headquarters for the startup? I would only need the bedroom and master bathroom for myself. The rest of the space could be set up as our working…" he quickly sketched in conference tables and computer workstations.

Jason was amazed at the accuracy of the scale and the perspective.

Maggie leaned in closely to admire the sketches. "I do

believe you've captured what I've imagined, Ewan. What fantastic drawings!" She turned to Paula. "Do you know if there are any restrictions in terms of live/work situations in this neighborhood?"

Paula shook her head. "I don't think so, my parents always worked out of this apartment. I think they would be honored to have the tradition continued. We'll check with the code enforcement people to see if there are any changes we'd need to make. What a fantastic idea, Ewan!"

Ewan blushed and lowered his eyes to his drawings. He said very slowly and quietly, "Thank you, Mrs. Visser. I don't show my drawings to many people. I don't want..." he trailed off and didn't look up from his drawings.

Maggie looked anxiously at Jason and Paula. She reached for their hands under the table.

Paula finally spoke. "Why don't you take the rest of the weekend to think about it, Ewan? If you are interested in the place we can draw up a lease on Monday. Would that suit you?"

Ewan looked up. He appeared to be focused on the refrigerator rather than looking at any of them directly. "I think I'd like to decide now, Mrs. Visser. It would make me too anxious to think of all of the possibilities for the whole weekend. I have a representative in England who handles all of my financial affairs. He and I usually communicate by email, as it is easier for me than the telephone. I will give you his email address, and explain to him the situation." He stood up and extended his hand across the table. "Thank you. I am so relieved to know I will have a place to live when I return to the States." He shook Paula's hand, then Jason's, and then Maggie's without looking directly at any of them. There was an awkward pause. Ewan closed up his notebook and put it back in his pocket. He retracted the tip of his mechanical pencil and put it back in the other pocket. He patted his hands against the front of his trousers and turned toward the front door. "I'll be off, then." He stopped, halfway to the door and turned back again. He reached into his back pocket and pulled out his wallet. He took a business card out and handed it to Paula with a slight bow. "Here is the contact information. I'll email him as soon as I get back to the lab on Monday morning. Thanks again."

Paula took the card and smiled at Ewan. She started to say something, but he had already slipped out of the front door and closed it behind him.

The three of them sat down at the table again. "I feel like Willem and Sophie would approve," Paula said quietly. "Michael, too." They all sat quietly for a few moments. Jason tried desperately to catch his breath, which seemed to have escaped him.

Maggie took their hands in hers again. "This is such a wonderful place, with so many good memories. I can't imagine a lovelier way to launch our startup, can you, Jason?"

He squeezed her hand as tightly as he could. "All in favor say Aye."

They bowed their heads and said "Aye, Aye."

Paula was sure she could hear three more voices added to the affirmation.

CHAPTER TWENTY-FOUR

Paula found an orange notice in the mailbox at the apartment. It required a trip to the post office and a signature before a large envelope was handed across the counter. The return address was from a law firm, and it made her a little nervous. Since it was addressed to Paula Visser and family, she decided to wait until Jason came home from the City to open it.

They were enjoying a cup of tea on the deck and watching the sunset. "It never gets old, Jason. I feel like we have the privilege of witnessing a new artwork being created every day. Sophie always tried to capture it, in her paintings."

Jason nodded, "Did you say there was a package? Let's open it now so I can get on with my stretching exercises. My legs have been really stiff and sore today."

They waited until the sun slipped beneath the horizon and went below deck to the galley and sat at the dinette.

Paula slid the edge of a scissors blade along the fold at the top of the envelope. She took out the thick sheaf of paper. "Oh my goodness, Jason. It is Captain Carter's will and trust documents. I wonder why they would be sending us a copy?"

Jason leaned over to take a look. "Maybe we should take that over to the Carlson's and have Maggie's father go over it with us, Ma."

Paula nodded. "That's a great idea, Jason. I think I'll read it tonight and see what I can learn. Do you want a chance to read it before we meet with Mr. Carlson?"

Jason yawned and shook his head. He was mildly curious, but his desire was pinned on stretching and sleep. "My brain is full of research and business plans at the moment, Ma. Maybe after we get the translation from legalese I might try to read through it. Right now I think I am going to stretch and then call it a night. I'm exhausted."

Jason had a rough night. His leg cramps woke him up every few hours, just as they had when he was a teenager. He took the anti inflammatory medicine and tried to stretch his legs, but the effort left him exhausted and shaking. When he finally was able to fall asleep, he had nightmares about trying to save his father from a huge wave that was about to over-take their boat. He woke up with a start, dripping with sweat. He went out to the galley to get a glass of water and another ice pack for his legs. The sun was just coming up, but he noticed that the light was on in his mother's bedroom. He thought she had probably fallen asleep with it on, bored by the legal documents. Instead, he heard her calling his name.

"Jason, are you alright? I hope my reading light didn't keep you awake."

He called back to her, "No, Ma. Just my legs cramping up. I'm going to try and get one more round of sleep." He struggled back to his bunk and got the ice packs situated. When he woke up, it was full daylight.

Paula was sitting at the dinette table with her reading glasses on, paging through the trust documents. She glanced up when Jason made his way into the galley. "Maggie came by early this morning and said she was on her way to study for exams. You were snoring so loudly that we decided to just let you keep sleeping. How are the legs this morning?"

Jason grimaced. "The worst they've been for awhile, Ma. I think I'll try to see Dr. Fishback this afternoon, or Monday at the latest. Now that I'm unemployed, it is probably a good time to get a full workup." He tried to smile, but Paula could see that he was really struggling.

She patted the seat next to her. "Come and sit down, Jason. I'll make you some breakfast."

Jason sat down heavily. "Thanks, Ma. Anything interesting in the trust documents?"

Paula didn't answer right away. She got up and made coffee and scrambled eggs, then sliced off a few thick pieces of bread for toast. Jason rubbed the sides of his knees. When Paula brought the plates to the table, she said quietly "Yes, Jason. They are quite fascinating. Captain Carter has been very generous to us. Eat your eggs before they get cold. There is plenty of time to discuss it."

Jason shook his head. "It has always been a mystery to me, Ma. How did he make his money?"

Paula had her mouth full of breakfast and held up her finger. When she was finished she said slowly, "It is all in the trust documents, Jason. I think you will find them a very compelling read." She got up again and poured them each a large mug of strong black coffee.

Paula took a deep breath. "I guess I should explain a few things, Jason. When your father died and you were away at school, I spent a lot of time with Captain Carter. We had dinner together a couple of times a week at the club and had a lot of long conversations about losing the great loves of our lives. His wife died when his three boys were still quite young, and he never got over it. He threw himself into his work and bought every status symbol he could think of but it never made him any happier. He made his money as a vulture, is the way he put it. Picking over the bones of the dead. He started out as a garbage collector in the City and realized that a lot of what went out for trash was actually worth something. He bought landfills and salvage yards and handled divorce and estate sales. He sent his kids to boarding schools with the profits and bought businesses when they were on the verge of bankruptcy. He had a knack for turning things from trash into treasure, that's what he always said, Jason." She took a long sip of her coffee and looked into the cup as if it were a crystal ball. "He thought the world of your father, and of you." They sat quietly, drinking their coffee.

Jason was trying to process all of this new information. "So, were you dating him, Ma?"

Paula laughed. "Oh goodness, no. I was just trying to figure out how I was going to survive losing Michael. I couldn't really talk to Willem and Sophie about it, they were grieving too. I just needed somebody to talk to who had been through it and figured out how to keep on going. I never had many close friends, Jason. Michael was my whole world. We had so many plans... but Captain Carter encouraged me to live them in Michael's honor. He was the one who said the Renewal might be just what I needed. He was very smart about a lot of things, Jason. I think when he first lost his wife he was out for revenge against the world. He did a lot of things that he regretted later. Some of what is in the trust documents is his attempt to make things right. I hope his children see it that way."

Jason reached for the thick stack of paper. "Ok, Ma. You've piqued my curiosity. Now I have to read all about my first investor. That's how I'll always think of him."

Jason was astonished to find that the legacy left behind by his business mentor was mostly philanthropic. He had set up a generous endowment for the boarding school the boys had attended in each of their names. Nearly half of his estate was divided between the American Cancer society in honor of his late wife, and the Arthritis Foundation. Sam was to inherit the pharmaceutical venture stock, and the other two boys were gifted the salvage and landfill stocks.

Jason kept reading. The house, cars and material possessions named in the documents were to be split equitably and fairly between the three boys. Captain Carter had named a mediator to take care of those negotiations with the stipulation that if the three boys could not agree, all of the proceeds would go to the charities previously mentioned. Jason laughed out loud. That certainly sounded like the Captain Carter he knew! Near the end of the document, Jason was surprised to find that Captain Carter had set up a sailing scholarship in Michael's name. He wiped the tears from his eyes.

Then came the biggest surprise of all. Apparently, right about the time that Jason had come up with his science project, things were pretty dire for Captain Carter's financial situation. The forty-five dollar investment that he had made in Jason's hydroponics system turned into a multi million dollar business, with a steady cash flow. The yacht was just days from being repossessed when Jason and Captain Carter had drawn up their agreement. He had mortgaged it and everything else to try and keep the boys in college, and as he put it in the trust documents "The lifestyles they had grown accustomed to."

Jason's hair on the back of his neck stood up as he turned the page. "Therefore, the assets of the Carter Hydroponics Company, including the yacht that is the primary place of business for the company, I hereby bequeath to Jason Visser."

Jason read the paragraph over again and then the rest of

the documents to try and figure out if there was some clause that might negate the bequest. He stood up slowly and went up the ladder to find his mother on the deck. As he did, he looked over at the yacht docked next to them. Surely this was a dream that he would wake up from at any moment now. He walked slowly toward Paula, tears streaming down his cheeks.

She stood up and wrapped her arms around him as he cried.

CHAPTER TWENTY-FIVE

The yacht was a Nautor Swan 51. German Frers had designed it, and only 36 of them had been built in the 1980s.

Jason remembered all of the drawings he had made of the boat and the salon where he and Captain Carter had signed their agreement. He also remembered the races that Michael had won for Captain Carter, and the pictures his mother had taken. It seemed impossible that his dreams to own a yacht like this were actually going to come true.

As he stood on the deck of the Renewal, staring at the yacht, he was overcome with a feeling of resolve. He'd keep the wood gleaming and the brass polished and make sure the boat was well loved. Whatever it took to keep the boat afloat. He smiled and said firmly, "Okay, Pops, I'm counting on you to help me through this!"

Somebody waved to him from the dock. It was Sam Carter.

Jason felt his stomach turn over, and he took a deep breath before he waved back. He climbed over the lifeline on the Renewal and stepped onto the dock. He was a full foot shorter than Sam, but he extended his hand and stood as tall as he could.

"Sorry to meet again under these circumstances, Sam. I'm very sorry for your loss. It must have been quite a shock."

Sam did not shake Jason's hand. He was wearing dark sunglasses and it was impossible to tell whether it had been a shock to him or not. He reached into his pocket and pulled out a ring of keys. He tossed them to Jason.

"I had every intention of selling this boat and using the proceeds to fund the pharma business, Jason, but when we did a title search it became clear that my Dad had set it up in a trust for you years ago. Once I read the documents, I realized I owed you an apology. I had no idea Dad was that close to bankruptcy. Your science project saved us all."

Jason closed his hand tightly around the keys.

"Apology accepted, Sam. I think with Joe on board you won't have any trouble raising the capital."

Sam shook his head and looked up at the yacht. He sighed and turned away from Jason. As he was walking down the dock, he stopped and turned back.

"I'm going to get my life back on track, Jason. My Dad will haunt me forever if I don't. This is totally uncharted territory for me, but would you be willing to walk me through some of the documents you put on the shared drive? I actually don't even know how to access them."

Jason walked toward Sam, slowly and purposefully. He extended his hand once again, and this time Sam shook it.

"I'd be happy to, Sam. I really do hope you can move forward with the applications to the FDA."

Sam sighed and his shoulders slumped. "I honestly have no idea where to begin. I've always been a disappointment to my Dad, Jason. I hope this time I can make up for all of that. Thanks for being so gracious. Would you mind stopping by the offices on Monday morning? I'll have a contract drawn up to pay you for your consulting services."

Jason started to decline the offer, but changed his mind. "Sure thing, Sam. See you then."

Sam turned and walked away slowly, as if he was carrying

a very large load on his back.

Jason looked down at the keys in his hand. He realized he had been holding his breath, and let out a long exhale. Squaring his shoulders, he walked purposefully back to the Renewal.

"Thanks, Pops. I tried to be gracious." Jason whispered as he climbed back aboard the Renewal and went to write in his journal.

Dear Pops,

Thanks for being with me today, and reminding me to be the gracious one. I try, but sometimes I get really angry and want to control things.

We miss you every day. I have so many questions that I never got to ask you about, and I wish there was a way I could be sure that you are proud of me.

I know you were there at my graduation, I felt it so strongly, I could even smell that wool sweater you wore in the winter out on the boat, and the diesel that got splashed on it.

I'm trying to be strong for Ma, like you always told me. She is doing really well, and is living the dream the two of you had to be on the water. I'm sure you know all of that.

I need you to stand up with me at my wedding, Pops. Maggie and I are going to try and live happily ever after.

Jason closed the book and his eyes. He was suddenly very tired.

CHAPTER TWENTY-SIX

E wan turned out to be a remarkably skilled sailor as well as a startup partner. He never told the whole story, but mumbled something about having "some experience messing about in boats, growing up."

Jason looked around at his crew as they motored out of the slip at the Yacht Club. From his position at the helm, he felt a deep sense of responsibility and gratitude for everyone on board.

Ewan managed the duties on the foredeck. He was agile, strong, and exact in his movements, seemingly calculating the most efficient way to do each task as it was presented to him. Without any wasted motion at all, he scrambled across the deck barefooted and hoisted the sails, keeping a close eye on the sail trim as they headed out of the harbor. He and Jason had developed a system of hand signals for communicating on board. When Ewan was facing forward, Jason would tap out a series of simple signals on the deck and Ewan would hold up a number of fingers in response. Unlike many of the boats out on the water, there was very little yelling onboard.

Michael had once told Jason that his competitors seemed to think they could beat him by yelling louder at each other. "It never worked, son. Better to be a man of few words. Mean what you say and say what you mean. On the water and off." He had winked at Jason and smiled.

Paula was in the Pit position. It suited her personality to

265

multitask and communicate between the front and the back of the boat. She picked up the hand signals quickly and fell back into the position she had enjoyed with Michael when they had sailed together. She also kept meticulous records and took photographs whenever possible.

Maggie was the tactician and secondary sail trimmer of the group. She had become quite proficient at reading the charts and learning about various wind conditions and Jason felt confident in her abilities to guide them safely on their journeys.

Jason loved the responsive feel of the Nautor. He couldn't quite explain it, but he always felt like Michael was there with him, whispering confidently in his ear as they picked up speed across the water. This was a boat that Michael had loved to sail, and Jason treasured the connection to his father.

On this particular day, they had Peter on board with them. After several months of planning and preparation, Jason was thrilled to be able to grant his wish of "Peter will ride."

Ewan and Jason had spent many hours over the winter coming up with a system for securing Peter's wheelchair on board, and all of them had practiced the safety drills that Maggie had drawn up. They were all wearing the new life vests that Paula had ordered and Jason hoped they would never have to use the feature that inflated the vest and activated an emergency beacon if any of them were thrown overboard.

The day was glorious for sailing, with a good steady breeze and warm spring temperatures. Jason could not have been happier as he guided the yacht back into her slip at the end of the afternoon.

Once the sail covers had been secured and Maggie had rolled Peter back onto the dock, Paula came up from below with glasses of champagne for each of them. They toasted their successful voyage and Jason said a silent thank you to Michael for his guidance. Ewan dumped his champagne in the water after the toast and busied himself with washing down the boat.

Peter handed his glass back to Maggie without drinking, and typed into his new communication device. "Best day, ever! Peter will ride again." The electronic voice was clearer and easier to understand with this new version.

Jason shook Peter's hand and grinned. "You bet, Peter. We'll get you out on the water as often as we can."

Maggie was standing behind Peter's wheelchair. She winked at Jason. "Can you guess who is coming to pick Peter up today?"

Peter typed quickly into his device. "Nikolas!" He raised his hand for a high-five from Jason.

"Oh that's wonderful, it will be great to see him. How is he doing these days?" Jason took the glasses from Maggie and carried them back down to the galley where Paula was washing up and stowing the gear.

Maggie shaded her eyes with her hand and looked off toward the parking lot. "He says he's pretty bored, so my parents asked if he wanted to drive Peter's van. He was so thrilled, won't even let them pay him. I think I see him pulling in now."

The van was backing in to the accessible parking place right at the end of the dock. Nikolas jumped out of the drivers' side and came jogging towards them, waving. "I hope I am not late, Miss Mary Margaret. Hello Master Peter, good day sailing?"

Peter nodded happily and typed "Best day ever. Next time you ride with us."

Nikolas laughed. "Oh that would be a treat. I haven't been sailing since my school days. Come on now Master Peter, we need to get you in out of this wind." He waved to Jason as he pushed the wheelchair to the van.

Jason started back to the boat to help Ewan with the cleanup, but he was suddenly seized with cramping in his legs and fell heavily to the ground in excruciating pain. Maggie and Paula came running as soon as they heard his cries.

Paula dialed 911 as Maggie held Jason's hand and felt for his pulse to take his vital signs. The last thing Jason remembered was looking into Maggie's eyes as she said, "Try to breathe, Jason. You aren't—"

CHAPTER TWENTY-SEVEN

Jason couldn't remember anything about the day of sailing, or the ride in the ambulance. When he woke up in the ER, he had a nebulizer mask on and for a few minutes, he seemed to be looking up at everyone from under water, in a slow motion replay.

Dr. Fishback had been called right after 911 and was there by Jason's bedside. "You've suffered a mild concussion, Jason. We'd like to keep you over night for observation here in the hospital and we'll run some additional tests."

Jason nodded weakly and tried to focus on Dr. Fishback's voice. He closed his eyes and concentrated on letting the nebulizer help him breathe. He just wanted to go to sleep. He tried to open his eyes again when he heard Maggie's voice, but his eyelids seemed impossibly heavy and breathing was his primary objective.

"I think he hit his head when he fell, Doctor. I am not sure if he tripped on the concrete or if the leg cramps just knocked him off balance. Thank you for joining us here in the ER." Maggie sounded strong and confident, and Jason smiled.

When he woke up again, he was in a hospital room and the phlebotomist was patting him on the arm.

"I just need to get a few more tubes of blood, Mr. Visser. Then you can go right back to sleep if you want to. This should only pinch a little."

Jason tried to smile. He was just so incredibly tired, and had an excruciating headache. There wasn't a place on his body that didn't ache.

Over the next few days, Jason slept in between tests. He thought he remembered a conversation with Dr. Fishback about trying a new medication, but he couldn't be sure.

Maggie was sitting on the edge of his bed, holding his hand. "Jason, we need you to wake up now."

Her voice sounded like it was coming from a long way away. Jason struggled to move toward it, but his body felt like it weighed a ton. He tried to say something, but nothing happened. Slowly, he forced himself to focus on her hand in his. He willed his eyelids to open. Everything was blurry and throbbing at first, but eventually he was able to focus on her face. He tried again to speak, but nothing happened. He started to panic.

Maggie smiled. "It is okay, Jason. I just wanted you to know that we are here, and that I love you. Dr. Fishback is coming by in a few minutes to talk about next steps." She leaned forward and kissed him on the forehead. "Do you want some ice chips?"

Jason thought ice chips sounded delicious at the moment. He squeezed Maggie's hand.

She rubbed the ice on his lips and put a few on his tongue.

Jason felt like his tongue was swollen and heavy, but the cold ice chips were wonderful. He started to choke as the melting ice slid down his throat.

Maggie quickly propped him up with some pillows and pressed the button by the side of the bed.

A nurse came into the room and turned off the call button. "What is going on here, Mr. Visser?" She winked at Maggie. "It is great to see you awake, but the choking not so much."

Maggie moved out of the way to allow the nurse to take Jason's vitals and tried to explain what had just happened. "I only gave him a couple of ice chips, but he seems to be having trouble swallowing."

The nurse frowned as she wrote on Jason's chart. "Dr. Fishback is on his way. Jason, can you take a deep breath for me?"

Jason tried his best, but starting coughing again.

The nurse slipped the nebulizer mask over Jason's face and held him up in a sitting position.

Slowly, his breathing became almost regular again, but he was only able to take shallow breaths.

"That's great, keep breathing Jason." Maggie held his hand on the other side of the bed from the nurse who was taking his blood pressure again.

Dr. Fishback came sprinting into the room. He sat down on the edge of the bed and looked at Jason's chart notes. After the nurse had finished and had moved on to the next patient, he stood up and closed the door.

"I think it is time to consider the hormone suppressing treatments, Jason. The two of you will have to discuss the possibility that it will make it even more difficult for you to consider having a family, but I don't want to see you having these kinds of flares at such a young age."

Jason squeezed Maggie's hand and tried to say something, but only a weak squeak came out.

Dr. Fishback looked alarmed. "We need to get you started with a speech therapist, Jason. As we have discussed, your voice may weaken as part of the disease process, but I believe this episode is related to a hormone spike. We'll know when we get the rest of the blood work back. Have you two thought about the treatments we've looked at?"

Maggie squared her shoulders and squeezed Jason's hand

tightly again. "We have, Dr. Fishback. I don't want to speak for Jason, but I had decided long ago to remain childless by choice. I'm devoted to my work, and the care of my brother and I don't think I can do any of that well if I add the responsibilities of parenthood to the mix. I am very encouraged by some of the results of the hormone suppressing treatments. I'm not the one who would have to endure the monthly shots and the side effects, though, so it is ultimately up to Jason."

Dr. Fishback wrote a few more notes in Jason's chart. He stood up and patted Jason's arm. "Try to get some rest. We'll have the blood work results back tomorrow morning and then we can discuss some treatment options."

After he left the room, Maggie kissed Jason on the forehead. "I'm going to drive Paula back to the Renewal and go home and get a shower. I'll bring my books back and study here. Love you."

Jason tried to rise up through the heavy, swirling fog of his confusion to answer her. He couldn't manage it though, and closed his eyes and slipped immediately into a deep sleep.

CHAPTER TWENTY-EIGHT

Jason was released from the hospital after three days. He didn't really remember much about it, but Maggie told him that it was common to sleep for days after a concussion, that it was the brain's way of protecting itself from further injury.

"We need to protect that wonderful brain of yours. Do you want to come to dinner tonight with the family, or just go home and rest?"

Jason tried to figure out what he wanted to do. He still felt like he was moving in a very dense fog, and that everything was speeding by him in fast-forward. After taking a deep breath he said quietly, "I think I'd like to try and come for dinner. I want to get back to my regular routine."

Maggie dropped him off at the apartment so he could shower and change clothes. "I'll pick you up at six, Jason. Are you sure you are okay with this by yourself?"

Jason tried to smile reassuringly. "Yes, Maggie. I don't think they would have let me come home from the hospital if they didn't think I could take care of myself."

Maggie waved as he opened the apartment door with his key and he watched her drive away.

He closed the door behind him and leaned heavily on it. The tears just started to pour down his cheeks and he gasped for several minutes before he could begin to take deep breaths again. He jumped, startled, as Paula walked out of the hallway.

She put her arm around him and helped him to the bathroom. The water was already warming up in the shower and there were towels laid out on the counter. A change of clothes was hanging on the back of the door.

"Thanks, Ma. I really hope I can manage the shower."

"Leave the door open to the bathroom Jason, I'll come back and check on you in a few minutes. Dr. Fishback says it will take a few days to get your strength back, so don't be afraid to ask for help if you need it."

Jason got undressed slowly, leaning on the counter to be able to take off his socks. He stepped into the shower and felt the warm water pour over him. He couldn't remember a time when a shower had felt this luxurious. Washing his hair seemed like something he hadn't done in a very long time. It felt like a very complicated task. He rinsed the shampoo out of his hair and let the warm water loosen up his neck. When he turned off the water, he tried to push the shower door open, but couldn't remember how it worked. The panic began to rise in his throat. He took a couple of deep breaths and tried again. The door slid to the side, and suddenly it made sense to him. He shook his head as he stepped out to dry himself off. That small movement made him incredibly dizzy, and he grabbed on to the counter and leaned forward so he wouldn't fall over.

Paula stepped into the bathroom. "Are you okay, Jason?"

"I feel sick, Ma. The room is spinning around."

She quickly wrapped a towel around him, closed the toilet seat lid and sat him down. Drying his hair gently with another towel, she said quietly, "Is that better?"

Jason formed the three fingers sign for "clear of obstacles ahead".

Paula laughed. "Perfect, Jason. I'm so glad you and Ewan

clued me in on the hand signals. What else can I do for you?"

"I think I'd better lean on you while I get dressed, Ma. I'm still feeling a little wobbly."

Paula helped him get dressed and carried the laundry to the hamper in the bedroom. "I'm so glad we have the luxury of keeping this apartment. It is awfully nice to be able to come and take a shower and do laundry. Don't get me wrong, I love the Renewal, but somehow this place is-" she stopped and looked at Jason lurching down the hallway unsteadily. "Are you sure you want to go to the Carlsons' tonight for dinner?"

Jason gave the thumbs up sign and sat down heavily at the kitchen table. "I need to get back to my regular routine, Ma. I just have to remember not to shake my head." He tried to smile reassuringly, but he was terrified. "I'm really thirsty, though. Would you mind bringing me a glass of water?"

"Of course not Jason. Do you want ice?"

Jason grinned and gave the thumbs down sign. "No ice, Ma."

Paula watched nervously as Jason gulped down the water. He choked on the last swallow and began to gasp for air. She pounded him on the back and massaged his neck until he could breathe regularly again. Just as she had done when he was a baby. She slid open one of the kitchen drawers and handed him a rescue inhaler. After a few puffs, his breathing returned to normal. She pretended to be busy washing something in the sink so Jason would not see her tears.

"Thanks, Ma. I guess it is going to take longer than I thought to get back on track. I'll take the inhaler with me to the Carlsons' house tonight." Jason slipped the inhaler into his shirt pocket and tried to stand up. He sat back down quickly, gripping the edge of the table. "Maybe I'll just sit for a few minutes until Maggie gets here."

Paula wiped her eyes with the back of her hands and dried them on the dishtowel. "Take it easy, son. You don't have to rush. Remember what Dr. Fishback said about the next few days."

Jason tried to smile. "Yes, Ma. I'll try to remember, but I've had a head injury, so you might have to remind me."

Paula was really alarmed now. "Jason, I've never heard you make an excuse like that. Are you sure you are okay?"

Jason smiled weakly. "It was supposed to be a joke, Ma. I'm doing okay. Just really tired and off balance. I'm sure it will pass in a few days. Dr. Fishback says the first few shots of the hormone blocking treatment will determine if I can take the oral course of the medicine. Let's hope for that."

Paula put her arm around her son's shoulders and hugged him gently. "We'll get through this together, Jason."

Maggie knocked on the door of the apartment and Paula ran to let her in. They hugged briefly and Paula motioned to the kitchen table where Jason was sitting.

"He's been really dizzy and had to use the inhaler once already, but insists he wants to go to dinner."

"Thanks Paula, would you like to join us for dinner this evening?"

"Maybe another time, dear. I am going to go to the sculling center and work out on the simulator. It really helps to release tension, and I missed a few days while we were all at the hospital. Give my regards to your parents, though."

Jason was still sitting at the kitchen table, trying to keep the room from spinning.

Maggie walked over and kissed him on the forehead. She slipped her hands under his armpits and helped him to a stand.

"All that practice over the years helping Peter up out of his wheelchair is going to come in handy." Jason said with a wink.

"Indeed it is, Jason. Do you have everything you need?" Maggie squeezed his hand.

Jason patted his pockets. "Wallet, keys, phone, inhaler. Yep, I think I'm all set. See you later, Ma."

There wasn't any answer. Paula had already left to ride her bicycle to the sculling center.

Jason locked the apartment behind them and leaned on Maggie unsteadily as they made their way to the car.

"Are you still dizzy, Jason? One finger for yes, two for no."

Jason held up one finger and grinned.

Maggie rolled her eyes. "Honestly Jason, I'm so glad you are out of the hospital. Let's not do that again for awhile, shall we?"

Jason held up two fingers.

They started laughing and could not stop. The tears rolled down their cheeks and they held on to each other, standing on the curb next to the trusty Volvo.

Finally, Maggie wiped the tears from her cheeks and managed to get the door open and Jason seated on the passenger side. He got his seat belt fastened and she went around to open her door. As she slid into the driver's seat she turned to him and whispered, "Happily ever after, no matter what happens Jason."

Jason held up one finger and blew her a kiss.

Maggie giggled most of the way to her parents' house. Jason felt better by the time they arrived and wanted to get out of the car by himself.

He pushed himself to a stand using the doorframe and the

top of the seat. He turned to give Maggie two thumbs up and wobbled unsteadily. She quickly put her arm around him and braced her feet to hold them both up.

"Steady there, Jason. Let's take this slowly."

Jason held up two fingers and made a dramatic grimace, miming the word "NO." He was terrified he would miss his chance to marry Maggie if he moved too slowly. Just like when he had wanted to kiss her when they were younger. He might run out of time. Sweat began to pour down the back of his neck and he wiped his now damp forehead.

Maggie closed the car door behind him and they walked together to the front door of her parents' house.

"It's like the three-legged sack race from camp. I've always been terrible at it." Maggie started to giggle again.

Jason stood very still and refused to go another step forward. "No, Maggie." he whispered quietly, "It is nothing like camp, and it isn't a race. This may be a big part of our life going forward Maggie. Are you sure this is what you want?"

Maggie punched him on the arm. "Yes. I am sure. Happily ever after, no matter WHAT. Get over yourself."

They took the last few steps together to the door.

CHAPTER TWENTY-NINE

Jason responded well to the hormone blocking treatments, and after a few months of injections was able to transition to a daily oral dose. He was fatigued and foggy in the mornings, but managed to keep his daily schedule of work and sailing.

Maggie was in her last few weeks of medical school and planning the wedding with Paula and Grace.

Unbeknownst to any of them, Peter, Gisele and Ewan were hatching a plan to surprise them at the wedding. Nikolas was in on the plot as well, driving Peter to the apartment to meet with Ewan when he knew that Maggie and Jason were otherwise occupied. Peter was driving the exoskeleton project in large part these days and insisted he was going to show everybody they had underestimated him. He and Ewan worked tirelessly on the new communication device as well, which would be hands free and allow him to fully express himself while standing or walking in the exoskeleton. It operated from a heads up display on some glasses that looked very much like Clark Kent might have worn them to the office. Peter could control the keyboard with his eye movements, and was getting used to standing upright in a suit as well as the exoskeleton, when he burst out with "I feel like a PENGUIN on land, this is awful!"

Ewan rushed over to steady him, and said wryly, "Oh, you mean the whole upright bipedal thing isn't giving you the feeling of immense superpowers the way the brochure indicated?"

They laughed easily, and Gisele interrupted their gaiety. "Why do the doctors always think the most important thing for us is to WALK like they do? I get it, but I worry far more about falling down the stairs in my chair trying to get in to an inaccessible building when I need to use the bathroom and having people just walk by and not bother to help me."

Peter nodded and said, "It isn't all that efficient to be honest, but it will make Maggie happy on her big day, and that will be worth it." His words came out almost effortlessly now, and his only issue with the heads up display had come when he had some rapid eye movements preceding a small seizure.

Ewan had programmed in a sensitivity feature that would alert Peter's caregivers by text message if the eye movements repeated the pre seizure patterns.

Paula was now sculling long distances every day, either on the water or in the simulator, and sometimes showed up at the very last minute for the wedding planning meetings still dressed in her rowing clothes.

On this particular day, Maggie was having her wedding dress hemmed. She stood on the dressmaker's platform, a notebook in her hands. She and her mother were quizzing each other on exam questions when Paula arrived.

"Sorry I am late Grace, I had to go back for my camera… oh Maggie you look so bea…utiful in that dress!"

She began taking pictures of Maggie and Grace, thinking of all the wedding photography tips Willem had given her over the years. Paula remembered the simple white dress she had worn when she married Michael, and how she had felt like Princess Grace of Monaco that day. Her eyes filled with tears, and she turned the auto focus feature of the camera on.

As Grace continued to quiz Maggie on her test questions, the seamstress moved rapidly around the base of the platform, expertly marking and pinning the hem of the heavily beaded skirt of the gown.

Maggie closed the notebook and handed it to Grace. She looked at the reflection in the mirror as the seamstress stepped away from the hem of the skirt.

"I can hardly believe the wedding is almost here. I just hope I don't trip over the dress. It really is beautiful, don't you think?" She turned slightly to look at the back of the dress and caught Paula's eye. She blew her a kiss and turned to face her mother.

"You look lovely in the dress, Maggie. Maybe you can practice walking in it when we have the final fitting. Are the shoes comfortable?" Grace handed the seamstress a tip and helped Maggie out of the dress.

Paula took one last picture of the dress hanging in the afternoon sun streaming in through the clerestory windows in the seamstress' studio. She wiped her eyes with the back of her hand.

Jason was sitting in the local coffee shop, interviewing a potential new project manager for the European operations of the hydroponics business.

She fidgeted nervously in her chair. "I brought my CV and some examples of my work." She slid a presentation folder across the table to Jason who opened it and smiled.

"Thank you Gisele, this is excellent. I hope we can conduct most of our meetings over email and Skype, if that works for you. This next month is going to be busy for me. I have the wedding and…"

"You can count on me to keep things running smoothly, Jason. Thank you for considering me for the position. It really is a good fit for my skill set."

Jason laughed. "Don't under estimate yourself, Gisele. You are by far the most qualified candidate, and I feel sure that I can make you a job offer in the next few days. I just have to consult with my fiancé, and she is at the moment having her wedding dress fitted while she crams for her med school final exams."

Gisele replied calmly but firmly. "I am not usually the one who underestimates my potential, Jason. I will appreciate hearing from you at your earliest convenience." She extended her hand to shake Jason's, packed up her laptop and purse, and wheeled herself away from the table. She waved over her shoulder as she went out the door.

Jason looked over Gisele's portfolio one more time and smiled. This would take a huge load off of his shoulders, and he was glad Maggie had made the suggestion to hire a project manager.

The other candidates were mediocre at best, and Jason had tried to keep from yawning during many of those interviews. Gisele had actually responded to their ad about test pilots for the new exoskeleton prototype and during those conversations over Skype, Jason had learned about her experience managing complex international projects and asked her to apply. She spoke at least five languages, having been born and raised in Switzerland, and was an avid gardener.

Jason reflected on how things were falling into place as he walked to the park to meet Maggie. He had texted her when the interview was over and she replied that it was perfect timing and she would meet him in a few minutes.

He was about to marry his best friend and their new life together looked to be filled with promise.

Maggie pulled into the parking lot and jumped out to greet

him. She threw her arms around him in a hug and started chatting about the dress fitting. "I'm glad I only have to wear the dress for a few hours, it is so heavy I felt like I was going to topple over!"

Jason laughed. "I am sure you will carry it off perfectly, just like you do everything else, my love. How is the studying going?"

Maggie rolled her eyes. "Oh, I think I'm over prepared as usual, Jason. I just want to get these exams out of the way and have the wedding and get on with our life!"

As they drove to the Marina, they discussed the interview with Gisele. "It almost seems too good to be true, Maggie, but she will take so much pressure off of my shoulders and I think she will give excellent feedback as a test pilot and get along fine with Ewan." Jason read some of Gisele's resume to Maggie as they drove.

Maggie nodded. "It does seem pretty perfect, Jason. We are so lucky!"

Jason turned to look out the window and stretch his neck a little. "Yes, we really are, Maggie. I am so glad you think of it that way. I just can't quite wrap my mind around all of the things that are happening right now. Life seems to be speeding up, doesn't it?"

Maggie smiled and winked. "Or maybe all the stars are aligned right now and we just have to accept our good fortune and roll with it instead of questioning whether or not we can keep up."

CHAPTER THIRTY

The day of the wedding began with a spectacular sunrise. Jason was pacing on the deck of the Nautor Swan, trying to calm himself down. As he turned to look up toward the top of the hill where he was about to be married, the candy colored sky made him gasp.

He had spent his last night as a bachelor on the Swan in the Captain's Cabin. It had been a long night of anxiety-fueled dreams and not much sleep. He was glad that Maggie had vetoed the idea of having their honeymoon on the yacht. She had argued that their first days and nights together as a married couple should be completely away from either of their workplaces. They were scheduled to fly to Bermuda and stay in a hotel overlooking the pink sandy beaches for five days.

Jason took a deep breath and turned to look out to sea. It was choppy and grey. He tried not to think about how much they would miss Michael at the ceremony.

Paula waved to him from the deck of the Renewal. "Ahoy there, neighbor! Beautiful day for a wedding, isn't it? Coffee is ready if you would like to join me."

Jason grinned and waved back. He climbed off of the yacht and headed down the dock to have coffee with his mother.

She wrapped him in a hug as he stepped aboard the Renewal. "That sunrise was amazing, wasn't it Jason? I'm guessing this whole day will be a series of miracles."

Jason leaned on his mother for support in so many ways, but it was her unfailing sense of the bright side of life that helped him the most. He took a deep breath and held her close. "Thanks Ma."

They talked quietly as they sipped their coffee on the deck and watched the day begin to unfold.

Once they had buttoned up the Renewal, they rode their bikes to the apartment to get ready for the wedding. Everything was carefully laid out, with a clipboard to check off each individual task.

As Paula straightened Jason's tie and took a few quick pictures, she began to tear up. "We are so lucky, Jason. I am so proud of you and Maggie and the life you are building."

Jason cleared his throat and tried to speak, but only managed a small squeak. He held up the "OK" sign and grinned.

Paula giggled and got the rest of her camera equipment ready. "I'm going to head up to the Carlsons' house and take pictures of Maggie and her parents getting ready. See you at the wedding!" She kissed Jason on the cheek and scurried out the door.

Once she was gone, Jason grabbed the rescue inhaler from the kitchen drawer and took a few small puffs. He slid it into his pants pocket and patted it. "Just in case," he whispered, "I need to be able to say I do, at the very least."

He leaned against the refrigerator and willed his breathing to become somewhat regular again. He caught a whiff of diesel fuel mixed with wet wool, and his skin was covered with goose bumps. "Pops? Thanks for coming..." he walked slowly around the apartment, trying to conjure up his grandparents as well.

Before he knew it, there was a knock on the door and Nikolas was there to take him to his wedding day with Maggie.

Everything went precisely to plan. Paula walked with Jason down the aisle and waited with him for the music to begin that signaled the bride's processional. The garden had been transformed into an even more magical place than it normally was, and the rows of guests seated in the white folding chairs stood and turned to witness Maggie's entrance.

The French doors opened as the organist started the next selection and Jason gasped with the rest of the crowd as the family stepped out onto the terrace with Maggie. Her parents flanked her, but holding her hand and walking her down the aisle was Peter!

The original plan, and the way they had practiced it at the rehearsal only a few nights before, was that Maggie would walk with her father after Peter and Grace went before them to stand opposite Jason and Paula. In the rehearsal, Grace had pushed Peter's wheelchair and he had waved in time to the music.

Now, Peter was walking next to his sister, albeit slowly and mechanically, with the aid of the exoskeleton that they had all worked on together. Grace and Carl walked arm in arm behind them.

Jason's senses were on high alert. His scalp tingled, and the feeling ran all the way down his spine. He wondered when in the world the team had the time to fine-tune all of the gait issues they had been working on. Ewan and Gisele must have been working around the clock practicing with Peter to get ready on time. Apparently the whole Carlson family was in on the plan.

Maggie was grinning from ear to ear and there wasn't a dry eye in the place. Peter waved to the guests and when the priest asked, "Who gives this woman to be married?" Peter joined his parents in saying, "We do!" and pumped his fist in the air to spontaneous applause from the gathered guests.

Jason watched Ewan help Peter get to his wheelchair parked in the front row next to Gisele, who squeezed his hand and wiped tears from her eyes. He turned to face Maggie, overwhelmed by astonishment. His whole body was tingling with electric excitement and he was shaking, but only a little, with nervousness.

"Best day ever, Jason Visser!" she said softly.

The rest of the ceremony was a total blur to Jason, who was trying to breathe and stand up and not pass out, all at the same time. The circuits in his nervous system felt like they had overloaded their capacity and were arcing dangerously.

Somehow they said their vows and kissed as the priest pronounced them "Husband and Wife, Mr. and Mrs. Jason Visser!"

As they walked through the rose petals being tossed by their guests, Jason leaned over and whispered to her, "Happily ever after, no matter what."

ABOUT THE AUTHOR

Usually these are written in the third person. I'd like to change that convention. I am a spinner of stories, a writer with more than thirty years of experience as an advocate for people who are differently abled. The conventional storyline begins with a diagnostic-centered statement such as; "John is autistic. He has social anxiety and a fear of loud noises. Despite the overwhelming odds against him, he has managed to find useful, meaningful work as a website content editor." This creates an image of someone engaged in a constant battle to overcome disability. I try, whenever possible, to use person-centered language. For example, "John likes banjo music, doing crossword puzzles and playing video games. He has a photographic memory and a passion for baseball statistics. He works in the IT department of the local University. John has an autism spectrum disorder." This wording creates an image of a person with abilities. We all have different strengths and weaknesses. As the parent of two amazing and talented adults who happen to have autism spectrum disorders, I would like to encourage you to think about the ways we have been conditioned to speak about others and ourselves.

Several years ago, I decided to write a series of books featuring characters who are differently abled, using person-centered language. This is the second of the books to be published. I have several other books in the pipeline.

I enjoy spinning yarn as well as narratives, and am a life-long knitter. I have a Bachelor's Degree in Art from Guilford College with a minor in Social Justice. Growing up in the San Francisco Bay Area, I defied convention early on, racing quarter midgets at age four. My early career goals included being an outfielder for the San Francisco Giants.